ROBERT DOHERTY

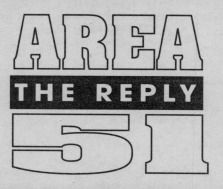

AREA
THE REPLY
51

D0124320

A DELL BOOK

Published by
Dell Publishing
a division of
Bantam Doubleday Dell Publishing Group, Inc.
1540 Broadway
New York, New York 10036

ISBN: 0-440-22378-4

Printed in the United States of America

Published simultaneously in Canada

March 1998

10 9 8 7 6 5 4 3 2 1

OPM

To Margaret Rose (Doherty) Mayer

Prologue

RAPA NUI (Easter Island)

It felt the power come in like a shot of adrenaline. For the first time in over five thousand years it was able to bring all systems on-line. Immediately it put into effect the last program it had been loaded with in case of full power-up.

It reached out and linked with sensors pointed outward from the planet. Then it began transmitting, back in the direction it had come from over ten millennia ago, calling out. "Come. Come and get us."

And there were other machines out there and they were listening.

Chapter 1

He watched the seven spacecraft lift out of the top of the palace, the rays of the rising sun absorbed by the black metal of their lean shapes. He looked down, trying to orient his sudden awareness. His hands were gripping the wooden railing of a three-masted ship. All the sails were set but there was little wind. In the belly of the ship he could hear the beat of drums as rowers pulled in unison, straining against long oars.

He felt out of place, out of himself. The contrast between the seven spacecraft that were now nothing more than rapidly fading dots high above and the technology of the sailing ship only added to the strange feeling.

The hairs on the back of his neck rose and a shiver ran down his spine. He looked over his shoulder and his eyes widened at what he saw. Even the rowers paused as they saw it. He felt the displacement of the air as the massive mothership passed by overhead. The rowers went back to work, pulling even more furiously on their oars. He watched as the *mothership stopped and hovered over the island the ship had left from, blocking out the sun.*

It was all laid out before him in perfect detail. He was amazed how he could see the entire island, yet also focus on individuals who were many miles distant. Concentric rings of land and water surrounded the capital city in the center of the island. Rising up, on the central hill, was the palace where the rulers had governed from. A golden palace, over a mile wide at the base and stretching over three thousand feet into the sky, it was a magnificent spectacle, but one that was all too easily overshadowed by the dark craft that was now centered above it.

Outside the palace, the streets in the city of the humans were choked with people fleeing toward the sea, to their sailing ships. He could look to the ocean around him and see other sails here and there on the blue water, some already going over the horizon.

Gazing back at the city, he saw that there were those who had fallen to their knees in the shadow of the ship, heads bowed, hands raised in supplication, praying that new rulers might replace the old. His gaze knew no bounds, going through walls and seeing inside houses, where others huddled in fear, mothers clutching their children close, men holding useless metal swords and spears, knowing that there was nothing they could do against the power from the sky.

He looked up at the ship. The air crackled. Those others who also dared to look saw a bright golden light race along the black skin of the mothership in long lines from one end to the other. The light pulsed off the ship downward into the palace in a thick beam, a half mile thick.

He flinched, even though he was many miles away. But nothing happened. Those on their knees prayed harder. Those fleeing ran faster. Every muscle in his body tensed as he waited.

Again the light pulsed. And again. Ten times the golden light hit the center of the island and passed through.

He staggered back as the Earth itself exploded. Tens of thousands died in an instant as the core of the island blew upward, the very essence of the planet beneath blasting through. Hot molten magma sprayed miles into the sky, mixed in with rock and dirt and remains of the palace. The scale of the explosion stunned him.

But it was the people that drew his attention. On the main jetty a mother covered her daughter as the magma came down, searing the skin from their bones in a flash. A warrior turned his shield upward in a futile gesture and disappeared under tons of rock. Docked ships burst into flame, the roofs of outlying buildings collapsed under the impact, crushing those hidden inside.

The entire island buckled, then imploded inward and downward. The surrounding sea had spasmed from the power of the blast, rushing outward in a massive wave that enveloped those who had not left soon enough. He felt the wave lift his ship up, teetering it precariously, then pass by. He fell against the railing, his knuckles white from clutching the wood.

Then the sea surged back, racing in where the island had been. Water met magma, and steam roared into the air, but the water won as the island disappeared into the depths. A boiling cauldron of water was all that was left of the mighty kingdom.

Again, he looked up. The mothership was slowly

moving. Toward his location. Golden light began racing along the length of the ship.

Nabinger staggered back, as if hit in the chest by a powerful blow. He felt hands grab him and prevent him from hitting the rock floor of the cavern. He shook his head, trying to clear it of the images that the guardian had just shown him. He opened his eyes and returned to his time and the place he had fought so hard to find, deep under an extinct volcano on Easter Island.

The guardian, a golden pyramid twenty feet high, lay before him, the surface rippling with the strange effect he had been under the spell of. Nabinger shook off the helping hands of the scientists and stared at the machine. His mind could still see the faces of the mother and the daughter as they were burned alive on the quay.

"What happened?" a UN representative asked, but Nabinger ignored them. He stepped forward, hands open, palms forward, and placed them on the skin of the guardian, waiting for the mental contact. Nothing.

He did it again.

Nothing.

After the third attempt he knew that there would be no more contact. Beyond the images of the people who had died, though, another vision was very clear in his mind's eye: the sails that had been over the horizon; the ones who had escaped.

■ ■ ■

Mike Turcotte stared out the window of the BOQ room. Through the gates of Fort Meyers he could make out the very top of the Marine Corps Memorial and beyond that the Capitol dome.

He didn't turn when there was a knock on the door to his room. "Come in," he called out.

The door opened and Lisa Duncan walked in. With a deep sigh she dropped down into one of the hard chairs the military had furnished the room with. Turcotte half turned toward her and smiled. "Long day on the Hill?"

Duncan barely topped five feet in height and Turcotte very much doubted her weight made three digits. She had dark hair cut short and a slender face that was now drawn with exhaustion.

"I hate telling the same story five times," Duncan said, "and answering stupid questions."

"The American public is not happy it was deceived by its own government for decades," Turcotte said, assuming a southern drawl. "At least that's what the senator who questioned me this morning said. Add in some kidnappings made to look like abductions, cattle mutilations, disinformation campaigns—"

"Let's not forget the crop circles," Duncan added. "There's a congressman from Nebraska who is trying to get legislation through to get all those farmers reimbursed for the circles Majestic burned in their field."

"Jesus," Turcotte said. He took off his Class A green uniform jacket and threw it on the bed. He paused by the small brown refrigerator. "Want a beer?"

"All right."

Turcotte grabbed two cans and popped the top on one, handing it to her. "They've got the mothership, the bouncer, the guardian on Easter Island. What more do they want?"

Duncan took a sip. "A scapegoat."

"They've got General Gullick dead. They've got the surviving members of Majestic being held in the federal pen," Turcotte said. He opened his can and took a long, deep drag. "The list of charges against those guys is thicker than the phone book."

"Yeah, but people can't believe it didn't go higher than that."

"It did go higher than that," Turcotte said. "But that was fifty years ago. Seems like there's more important stuff going on right now."

"Speaking of what's going on," Duncan said, "I just found out that the guardian's ceased contact with Nabinger."

That was the first interesting thing Turcotte had heard in the past two days, since arriving in Washington from Easter Island. "Any idea why?"

"Nobody knows."

Turcotte rubbed his chin, feeling the stubble there. It felt strange to be in uniform after working classified assignments for so long. His jump boots, spit-shined this morning for his congressional testimony, now wore a layer of dust. His battered green beret was tucked into the back of his belt. He pulled it out and threw it next to his jacket as he sat down across from Duncan, next to the window.

A cannon barked a sharp report, followed by the faint strains of "Taps" as the post flag was lowered. Turcotte had heard that sound on many different posts around the world during his time in the army, but it never failed to touch him and make him think of comrades lost. Turcotte looked out at the bronze figures representing the Marines who'd raised the flag on Mount Suribachi.

Duncan shifted her seat slightly and followed his gaze. "Ahh, glory and honor," she said.

Turcotte tried to figure out if she was being sarcastic or serious. "They knew what they were doing," he said.

"Still looking for the bad guy wearing the black hat?"

"I don't feel particularly proud about what I've done," Turcotte said. "We met the enemy and they was us."

"Not all of us," she said.

Turcotte finished the rest of his beer. "No, not all of us."

"And General Gullick and the others were being controlled."

"Uh-huh." He crushed the empty can with one large fist. "I don't like it here."

"That's good," Duncan said, "because something else has come up. That's why I'm here."

"Oh?" Turcotte walked over to the bed and threw the can into a small garbage can. He picked up his dress green jacket and held it in his hand as she walked to the other side of the bed.

"We've received some information on a possible Airlia artifact site." She pulled a sheet of paper out of the small briefcase she'd had with her. "Here's the data. We'll be going soon to check it out."

"We?"

"We make a good team," Duncan said.

"Uh-huh." Turcotte took the paper but didn't look at it.

"I've got to go now," Duncan said.

Turcotte held the paper uncertainly.

"You're still willing to work on this?" Duncan asked, mistaking his hesitation.

Turcotte straightened. "Oh, sure."

"I'll see you tomorrow, then," Duncan said as she opened the door.

"Yeah, okay."

The door swung shut. Turcotte walked over to where Duncan had sat and picked up her beer can. It was almost full. He carried it to the window. The setting sun reflected against the bronze Marines. He watched Duncan walk down the sidewalk and get into a white sedan. As she drove away, he put the beer to his lips and drained it in one long swallow.

■ ■ ■

"You've finally given me an exclusive, Johnny," Kelly Reynolds whispered at the casket as she tossed a handful of dirt into the raw hole cut out of the Tennessee countryside. "I wished it had worked out otherwise."

Kelly Reynolds looked over the casket at the mass of media being kept at a distance by funeral personnel and local police.

"Did they get them all?" A woman's voice behind her caused Kelly to turn around. Johnny Simmons's mother stood there, a black veil covering her drawn features. Kelly had talked to her briefly at the funeral.

Kelly knew who she was referring to. "Yes. The ones who worked on Johnny in the lab in Dulce were killed when the Easter Island guardian destroyed it. The other members of Majestic are all being held for trial."

Mrs. Simmons was focused on the coffin. "They did things to him, didn't they? He wouldn't have killed himself. I knew he wouldn't have done that."

"No, Johnny wouldn't have killed himself," Kelly agreed. "They did really bad things to his mind. Johnny loved life too much. They hurt him so much, he couldn't remember that. He couldn't think straight."

Mrs. Simmons's gaze went past the coffin. "The news is making him into some kind of hero. They say he was the beginning of what brought what was going on in Area 51 into the open."

"He was a hero," Kelly agreed.

Mrs. Simmons reached out and her hand clutched Kelly's shoulder. "Was it worth it?"

"Yes." There was no hesitation in Kelly's voice. "Johnny dedicated his life to finding out the truth, and what he helped uncover is the greatest truth of our time. It was worth it."

"But is it a good truth?" Mrs. Simmons asked. "All these alien things they've uncovered; that message everyone is talking about—will everything turn out all right?"

Kelly looked at the casket once more. "Yes." Then she whispered to herself. "It has to."

Chapter 2

Deep Space Communication Center (DSCC) 10 was one of two dozen radio receiving systems placed around the globe by the United States government in conjunction with various research organizations to monitor radio waves coming in to the planet from outside the atmosphere. At DSCC-10 twelve large dishes were spaced evenly across the desert floor, 250 miles northeast of Las Vegas. The setting sun reflected off the metal struts and webs of steel that pointed to the sky, listening with the infinite patience that machines are capable of.

Cables ran from the base of each dish into the side of a large modern, one-story building. Inside the structure the two humans also had patience, that born of years of listening to the cosmos with no tangible results.

The recent discoveries on Easter Island and the disclosure of the alien mothership and bouncers secreted away just miles to the north in Area 51 had proven beyond the slightest doubt that there was extraterrestrial life in the universe and that that life had once had a colony on Earth. Humans were not alone, and while most of the planet focused its attention on what had been found, those in places like DSCC-10 were concerned with what was yet to be discovered among the stars.

The message sent out by the guardian computer had jolted everyone out of their daily humdrum. Now those at DSCC-10, and at other listening posts around the world, watched their computer monitors with mixed hope and fear. Hope that a message would come back in reply and fear about what the message would be and who would be sending it.

Jean Compton had worked at DSCC-10 for twelve years. Officially, and as far as her partner, James Brillon, knew, she worked for Eastern Arizona State University. In reality she worked for both EASU and the National Security Agency. Her job for the NSA was to have DSCC-10 ready as a backup to the Air Force's satellite dishes at Nellis Air Force Base. If the tracking station at Nellis went down, Compton was to use DSCC-10 to download classified data from the network of spy satellites that the U.S. had blanketing the planet as they passed overhead. The vast amount of data those satellites accumulated, and their limited storage space, made it imperative that each scheduled download be picked up or valuable intelligence could be lost.

Compton had yet to have to do that backup job, but she did appreciate the extra paycheck she received each month from the United States government, deposited directly and discreetly into her checking account. She also had a classified Internet address and code that she was supposed to use in case DSCC-10 ever picked up signs of intelligent alien life. All she knew about the organization on the other end was the designation, STAAR, and that the NSA told her to follow any instructions given by it.

She didn't know what STAAR stood for, and after receiving the briefing from the STAAR representative at Nellis four years ago, she'd had no desire to know more. The man giving the briefing had sent chills up and down her spine with his emotionless detailing of instructions she was to follow in case they found evidence of extraterrestrial life. He was a tall man, with blond, almost white, hair cut short, his face looking like it was carved out of pale marble. She wondered if the man's skin ever saw the sun, yet he had worn sunglasses throughout the entire briefing in an empty hangar at Nellis. Armed guards surrounded the hangar, hard-looking men in black jumpsuits. Their presence had further enhanced the significance and power of this mysterious organization.

Shortly after the guardian computer had sent out its message from Easter Island, she'd been contacted by STAAR and given a classified briefing by the same man and detailed new instructions. She didn't really believe that she would have to use those new instructions, as she hadn't the old ones from the NSA, until eight minutes before eight P.M. on this evening.

She was in the process of doing a loop scan, the dishes slowly rotating to get a clear radio picture of a section of sky, when the master warning light bolted to the beam running across the front of the control room snapped on and a high-pitched tone screeched.

At those two simultaneous occurrences, Brillon dropped his Coke, the can bouncing on the carpeted floor, dark fluid pouring out unnoticed as he stared at the flashing warning light. Compton was more practical. She immediately hit the record button on the console in front of her, which turned on every piece of monitoring machinery in the control center. Then she focused her attention on the large screen to her left, which had a series of electronic grid lines laid over the section of star map the radio scopes were currently aimed at.

"Off center, move quadrants. Left four, up two," she ordered.

Brillon shook his head, trying to get back in reality, and Compton had to repeat the order until he sat down at another console and began realigning the radio telescopes to be more on line with the incoming message.

Compton spun her chair to the left and looked at another screen. A jumbled mass of letters and numbers filled the entire display. "We've got data coming in," she said in a surprisingly calm voice. "Real data," she added, meaning it was not random radio waves generated by astral phenomena.

"Sweet Jesus," Brillon muttered, realizing what this meant. Contact. Not first contact as they had always dreamed—that had occurred with the discovery of the Airlia artifacts—but this was first live contact, beside which even those earlier discoveries paled.

Compton checked another display. "Damn, it's

a strong signal. Very strong." She glanced over at her partner. "Are you dead on yet?"

"I've centered up as best I can," Brillon reported, "but it's a very tight transmission beam and I can't seem to center."

"How do you make a radio transmission on a beam?" Compton asked. "They're not directional."

Brillon didn't have time to answer the hypothetical question as he continued to work. Compton quickly turned to another computer and accessed the secure Department of Defense Satellite Internet Link. She typed in the two addresses that she had long ago memorized but never used. As soon as she got a line and a prompt, she typed.

```
>NSA AND STAAR THIS IS DSCC-10.
WE'VE GOT A TRANSMISSION AT 235
DEGREES AND AN ARC OF PLUS 60 FROM ZERO.
```

Compton cursed to herself as she read the message. She quickly typed in more information.

```
>NSA AND STAAR THIS IS DSCC-10.
TRANSMISSION IS NOT RANDOM.
```

Compton sat back in the chair and waited while replies came back.

```
<DSCC-10 THIS IS NSA.
WE ARE ON-LINE.
```

```
<DSCC-10 THIS IS STAAR.
SOURCE AND DESTINATION OF TRANS-
MISSION?
YOU ARE RECORDING MESSAGE?
```

Compton shook her head in irritation at the STAAR questions.

```
>THIS IS DSCC-10.
WE ARE WORKING SOURCE AND DESTINA-
TION. WE ARE RECORDING ALL DATA. TRANS-
MISSION IS VERY POWERFUL. READS 10 BY
ON SCALE. HOWEVER THE BEAM IS DIREC-
TIONAL.
```

"Do you have a lock yet?" she asked Brillon.

"I've got a source lock!" Brillon yelled. "I'm sending it to your computer. Nothing yet on destination except it's west and south of here. This system wasn't designed to pinpoint a destination here on Earth for a transmission."

Compton accessed another program on her computer and put that box next to the one that was her dialogue with STAAR and the NSA. She transferred the source numbers to the dialogue box and transmitted them.

```
<DSCC-10 THIS IS STAAR.
WHAT ABOUT TRANSMITTED DATA?
```

Compton glanced at the other screen. More numbers and letters were still coming in.

```
>THIS IS DSCC-10.
I WILL FORWARD OUR TAPES AND COMPUTER
DATA ONCE SOURCE STOPS TRANSMITTING.
WE'RE STILL DOWNLOADING.
>THIS IS NSA.
ARE YOU SECURE?
```

Compton glanced over at Brillon. He was concentrating on what he was doing. Compton slid her hand under the edge of her desk. She felt the special switch the NSA had installed and flipped it on. It shut the center down from the outside world by severing all links except the one she was using.

```
>THIS IS DSCC-10.
WE ARE SECURE.
>ROGER DSCC-10. THIS IS NSA.
WE ARE DIVERTING RESOURCES IN YOUR
DIRECTION TO VALIDATE AND ENSURE YOUR
SECURITY.
```

"I can't get the destination," Brillon said. "Somewhere southwest a long way."

"Easter Island." Compton said it out loud before she could catch herself.

"Jesus!" Brillon said. "It's the answer to the guardian."

"Yeah, but I can't make any sense—" Compton began, but she was interrupted by a new message from STAAR.

```
<DSCC-10 THIS IS STAAR.
RECHECK SOURCE NUMBERS. WE HAVE NO
PLOTTED STAR SYSTEMS IN RANGE ALONG
THAT DIRECTIONAL TRACE. BASED ON POWER
IT MUST BE WITHIN RANGE OF RECORDED
SYSTEMS.
```

Brillon was now looking over her shoulder. "That's because it's coming from a spaceship, assholes," he muttered. "It has to, to be that strong. It's not coming from outside the solar system. It wouldn't be that strong," he repeated, "nor could they keep it directional over a distance of light-years." He frowned as something occurred to him. "Who the heck is STAAR?"

"NSA," Compton said, although she doubted very much that the pale blond man and STAAR really were part of the NSA. Why else, then, would she be sending the data to both of them?

"NSA? We work for the university."

"Not right now we don't," Compton said. "Check the numbers," she ordered.

Brillon grumbled something, but he sat down at his computer and did as she ordered. "Numbers are verified," he announced. "Whatever is transmitting is along that line." He cleared his screen and brought up a computer display of the solar system. "And I'll bet you my paycheck it's coming from a spaceship heading into our solar system on that trajectory. We've got to contact the university!" he said. "Professor Klint will be—"

"We can't contact anyone," Compton said. She was speaking from memory, seeing the pale blond-haired man in her mind. "This data and this facility are now both classified and closed by National Security Directive forty-nine dash twenty-seven dash alpha."

"Bullshit," Brillon said, reaching for the phone. He turned to her when he couldn't get a dial tone. "What did you do?"

"We're sealed off to the outside world, except for the NSA and STAAR," she said.

"Screw you!" Brillon said. "You sold out to the government." He stood, grabbing his jacket. "I'll drive and call it in on a pay phone, then. You people aren't going to pull another Majestic!"

"I wouldn't do that if I were you," Compton said in a surprisingly calm voice.

"Why not?" Brillon was tensed, his body leaning toward hers. "Are you going to stop me?"

"No."

"Then screw you and your national security directive."

"I won't stop you, but I think they will." She pointed to the ceiling. They could both hear the dull thud of helicopter rotor blades coming closer.

"Shit!" Brillon threw his car keys down.

Compton turned back to her computer and pulled up Brillon's display and looked at it for a moment before typing in a few commands. In a second an electronic green line reached out from the small dot representing Earth. It speared through space and intersected dead-on with a red circle.

"Goddamn," Compton muttered. She looked up at Brillon. "Besides owing me your life, you also owe me your paycheck. The message isn't coming from a spaceship. It's coming from Mars!"

Chapter 3

The screen of the laptop was difficult to read even though it was in the tent's shade, guarded from the fierce sunlight beating down on the rim of the volcano on Easter Island. Kelly Reynolds's fingers flew over the keys, her eyes slightly unfocused as her mind worked over the thoughts, fears, and questions she was trying to translate into the black-and-white of letters on screen so that readers back in the United States would understand the significance of what had been discovered here. Her quick trip to the mainland for Johnny's funeral had disconcerted her, as she saw that the major import of all that had happened seemed to be mixed up with the search for culprits over the entire Majestic-12 operation and fear over the message the Guardian had sent out into space:

> The discovery of the alien computer known as the ''guardian,'' hidden here on Easter Island at least five thousand

years ago, has been the most significant and most disappointing discovery in recorded human history. Significant because it conclusively tells us we are, or at least were, not alone in the universe. Disappointing because we can no longer access the wealth of information the computer contains. Like a hacker breaking into a top-of-the-line computer, we can read the file names but we don't have the code words needed to open those files and read the advanced secrets they contain. The guardian shut down less than forty-eight hours after transmitting a message up into the skies, toward whom or where we do not know.

The secret to the bouncers' drive system lies just a few inches away. The details of the mothership's interstellar engine lie just as near and just as far. The technology of the guardian computer is guarded with equal jealousy by the machine. Control of the foo fighters also rests inside the guardian. The answer to the mystery of where the Airlia, as the alien race called itself, came from and exactly why they were here on our planet also lies within.

We know some basics, the barest sketch of what happened five thousand years ago when the alien commander Aspasia decided to get rid of all trace of his people's, the Airlia's, presence here on Earth to save the planet from their mortal enemies, who we now know are called the Kortad. Upon making that decision, Aspasia had to fight rebels among his own people who did not wish to go quietly into the night and in doing so destroyed the land that in Earth legend we have called Atlantis, where the Airlia colony was home-based. By doing this he protected the natural development of the human race and for that we owe him a large debt of gratitude.

But beyond those few facts there are so many unanswered questions:

—What happened to Aspasia and the other Airlia?

—Why was an Airlia atomic weapon left hidden in the depths of the Great Pyramid of Giza? Indeed, as we now suspect, were the pyramids built as a space beacon by the Airlia?

—What really happened to Atlantis, site of the Airlia colony? What terrible weapon did Aspasia use to destroy it?

—And, perhaps most importantly, had fucto whom was the transmission directed that the guardian made four days ago when it was uncovered? And what did it say?

—And how do we turn the guardian back on?

Kelly Reynolds frowned at that last line. Her finger paused over the delete key. There were many who felt that no attempt should be made to access the guardian. Those people were the ones who looked to the skies full of fear of what the guardian might have called toward the Earth. In the last few days since the computer had been un-covered nothing had happened, but that had not allayed the fears of the Isolationists, as the media were calling them, but rather left them to stew in what was becoming a cauldron of paranoia. The United Nations had taken over the entire prob-lem and there were demands from isolationist groups in many countries to pull out of the UN and not to support the UNAOC, the United Na-tions Alien Oversight Committee.

Screw them, Kelly decided. It was more than likely that the message had gone to no one, since the Airlia outpost on Earth had been abandoned over five millennia ago. For all anyone knew, the Airlia's home planet, wherever that was, might have been wiped out by the Kortad, who might have become extinct themselves, their knowledge of the Earth returning to the ether.

As vocal as the isolationists were, there was an-other movement just as keen to gain the new technology and information held by the guardian, and they were pressing UNAOC to go forward. Dubbed the progressives, they believed the alien machine held answers for the multitude of com-plex problems the human race faced.

There was even a very strong argument made by the progressives to fly the mothership, some-thing that Reynolds and her comrades had raced against time to stop the Majestic-12 Committee in Area 51 from doing. At least by finding the guard-ian, they had discovered the reason the massive mothership shouldn't be flown: the interstellar drive, once activated, could be detected by the Kortad and traced back to Earth, which, accord-ing to records they'd uncovered, would lead to

Earth's destruction. That is, if the Kortad still existed, not a likely possibility in the opinion of the progressives.

Practically everyone on Earth had an opinion about what should be done with the alien artifacts, but the control of the guardian computer and all the technology the United hStateh has had kept hidden over the years at Area 51 in the Nevada desert outside of Nellis Air Force Base had been ceded to the Alien Oversight Committee, since this issue clearly transcended national boundaries. The bouncers, nine disk-shaped craft that operated inside of Earth's atmosphere, and the mothership had finally been opened to public scrutiny and international inspection after decades of secrecy.

Kelly typed on.

```
Ultimately it comes down to two key
questions, one looking back and the
other forward:
   1. What is the truth of Earth's
history now that we know an alien
outpost was established on our
planet ten thousand years ago and
disappeared over five thousand
years ago?
   2. What is our future now that we
have  uncovered  artifacts  from
those aliens, one of which has been
activated and has sent a message,
and what do we do with a large craft
capable of interstellar flight?
   Should humanity reach for the
stars before its natural time, and
if we do, who-or what-is waiting
out there for us? Or has the deci-
```

sion of first live contact been
taken out of our hands by the message the guardian sent and are
other interstellar craft like the
mothership already racing through
space, coming toward us in reply?
And who is piloting those ships if
they are coming? Peace-loving Airlia or the Kortad bent on destruction?

Kelly Reynolds stopped typing as a shadow filled the doorway to the army-issue GP medium tent that had been set aside for the press. Since the guardian had ceased contact, there had been little to report in the last two days. Kelly had been surprised this morning, when she'd arrived at the airfield, at how quickly the number of media people on the island had dropped. Most of the media's focus was now on Area 51, recording the Air Force flying the bouncers and wandering through the massive bulk of the mothership on guided tours of equipment Majestic-12 had jealously guarded for so many years.

Kelly smiled when she recognized the person entering. Peter Nabinger was the man who had made contact with the guardian and received from it the information about what had happened five thousand years ago. He was also the foremost translator of the Airlia high rune language, traces of which could be found at various ancient sites all over the globe, and had sent Kelly and her comrades on the right path to finding the guardian hidden under the volcano on Easter Island, arriving just before the Majestic-12 forces.

Nabinger was over six feet tall and heavyset. He

had a thick black beard below his wire-rimmed glasses. When he spoke, his thick accent showed his origins and employer, the Brooklyn Museum, where he was the head of archaeology. Kelly enjoyed his company and his unique take on things.

It was amusing, Nabinger often said, that people had always thought that first "contact" with an alien race would be done by astronauts or radio astronomers, but few people had ever considered that the most likely evidence of alien life would come in the form of the archaeological discovery of alien artifacts left here on Earth. Nabinger had argued long and hard that it was much more likely that Earth had been visited sometime in its millions of years of history rather than right now in the present and that those visitors could have left some form of evidence of their visit. Of course, Majestic-12, flying the bouncers out at Area 51 for decades, had fueled the UFO hysteria that Earth was currently being visited by aliens and directed attention away from more likely sources of contact.

"Hey, Kelly," Nabinger greeted her with a hug. "When did you get back?"

"This morning. I feel like I've been in the air forever." Kelly herself was short, just topping five feet, but she was large; not fat, but big boned. She had thick gray hair that she kept tied to the rear with a bright ribbon. Her skin was red and peeling from exposure to the harsh South Pacific sun. "I heard about you getting booted by the guardian."

"The whole world's heard," Nabinger said, sitting down on a folding chair. "Looks like you're going to have this tent all to yourself soon. We've suddenly become rather boring here."

"The major networks and CNN will keep a stringer here indefinitely," Kelly said. "They don't want to get caught flatfooted if the guardian does come back on-line. But the smaller outlets can't afford putting out this much money for nothing. They've filed all the stories they could dredge up on this island and taken all the shots of the guardian. It costs a lot to keep someone out here doing nothing, and they can get their feed off those of us who are here. I'm syndicated now in over sixty papers."

That was a far cry, Kelly knew, from where she had been just two weeks ago, when she'd been struggling to sell articles to any paper or magazine that would pay. But being part of the group that had uncovered the secrets of Area 51 and the guardian here on Easter Island had certainly bolstered her career, a thought that brought back an image of Johnny Simmons's casket.

Nabinger caught the look on her face. "How did it go?"

"The funeral was a media circus. I don't think the real feelings have caught up with me yet. And I'm not sure I want them to right now. I have too much to do. I owe Johnny that. He wouldn't want me to sit around crying when I could be hitting sixty papers with this"—she pointed at her laptop.

Nabinger nodded. "I understand."

"So," Kelly said, taking a deep breath. She forced a smile. "So. Since I have an exclusive with the man himself, why don't you tell me what's going on?"

"The guardian is still working," Nabinger said. "We know that because it's taking in power. It's just not talking to us."

"Why not?"

"Probably because it figured out we're not Airlia," Nabinger answered. "They hid it here in the first place to keep us homo sapiens from finding it."

Easter Island, known as Rapa Nui to the locals, was the most isolated island on the face of the planet. According to Nabinger's translations of the Airlia's high rune artifacts and interpretation of the information given him by the guardian, that was why Aspasia had chosen it to be the receptacle for the guardian computer. Underneath the lake in Rano Kau's crater, one of the two major volcanoes on the island, the Airlia had built a chamber and put their computer in place, leaving a small, self-sustaining cold fusion reactor to power it. Even the reactor's advanced workings were off-limits to the scientists, as the shielding guarding it was impenetrable. The dwindling power the reactor put out had recently been supplemented by numerous human generators flown in, and the guardian was at full power; but nothing was happening that could be detected.

"Hell," Nabinger said, "we don't even know if the guardian is a computer. We're calling it that because it's the closest piece of equipment we have that is like it, but the guardian can do so much more.

"They've tried everything in the last two days, including hypnosis, to get me back in contact with the guardian. The UNAOC people are banging their heads down there, trying to get that thing to work," Nabinger said. "I'm about ready to tear my hair out." Nabinger shrugged. "Maybe I was just lucky. Maybe it was set to be activated by anything living, but only long enough to ascertain the situation. Once it figured out that we weren't Airlia, it cut us out."

"Not before having its foo fighters obliterate Majestic-12's biolab at Dulce and the rebel computer in there," Reynolds noted. In the course of their search for the truth, Kelly and those with her had broken into the secret government lab at Dulce, New Mexico, where another, smaller guardian-type computer had been placed by the government after being uncovered under a massive earthen mound at Temiltepec in Central America.

They both looked up as a strong offshore breeze hit the tent and caused the canvas top to snap back and forth. The wind, the lack of trees, and the ocean completely surrounding them on all sides lent a disturbing air of isolation to the location.

Nabinger nodded at her comment. "Yeah, that's true. But there have been no foo fighter flights since then. We know the foo fighters are based under the ocean a couple of hundred miles to the north of here. I think the Navy is discreetly poking around out there, trying to pinpoint where exactly. You can be sure they're interested in that ray that was used to destroy Dulce."

"I haven't heard any of that," Reynolds said. "Does the Alien Oversight Committee know the U.S. Navy is doing that?"

"At first I thought the U.S. Navy was working *for* the Oversight Committee," Nabinger said, "but the UNAOC rep here says he doesn't know anything about it. I've only heard rumors, but I think either someone in the U.S. government is poking around with UNAOC's knowledge and tacit approval, or something else fishy is going on and they're cutting UNAOC out."

That brought a momentary silence to the tent, allowing them both to hear the nearby crash of waves on the rocky coastline. Nabinger shifted uncomfortably. "There's more going on than UNAOC is letting out to the media," he said. "The Oversight Committee is trying to track down any other artifacts from the Airlia that might have been left here. It appears Majestic-12 wasn't the only ones keeping secrets. There's some talk the Russians might have had a crashed Airlia craft all these years and that some countries and perhaps even some international corporations uncovered other things the Airlia left behind and have been working on them in secrecy."

"Damn, I thought we were past that secret stuff." Reynolds looked at him. "You haven't been taken over by the guardian, have you?" She had a grin on her face, but there was an undercurrent to her words.

"If I was, would I know it?" Nabinger said. "General Gullick and the others on Majestic thought they were acting for the good of the country. According to the MRI scans of my brain nothing seems amiss."

"You said there's word others have artifacts?" Kelly asked. "How come they're not coming forward now that everything's in the open?"

"They, whoever they are, lose control if they do that. Think of the economic potential if someone cracks the secret to some of the Airlia technology. UNAOC is trying, but it's not getting the greatest cooperation. I think the Navy is trying to uncover the foo fighter base because after what the fighters did to the lab at Dulce, anyone who controlled that power would be top dog on this planet. Also, the isolationists are pretty strong in some countries and they feel UNAOC leans too far toward the progressives."

Reynolds shook her head, but she knew that was the way people were, particularly people in power. "So what have you been doing when the oversight people haven't been trying to use you to turn on the guardian?"

Nabinger held up a file folder stuffed with pictures and computer printouts. "I still have the high runes as a source of information. Getting access into the guardian would certainly be nice, but, remember, I'm an archaeologist." He paused, then looked at her. "I think everyone is too worried about the future and not enough about the past."

"That's because we're going to live the future," Reynolds noted.

"But you can't understand the present if you don't understand the past," Nabinger argued.

Reynolds frowned. "I thought we had a pretty good lock on the past from what you learned when you accessed the guardian. Aspasia and the rebels and the Kortad and all that."

Nabinger slapped a photo on the cot between them, pinning it down with a coffee mug. "That's an underwater shot off Bimini, where Atlantis, or Airlia Base Camp if you want the unromantic term the Oversight Committee has adopted, was located. I was interested in it because that must have been where the Germans got their information about the bomb in the Great Pyramid.

"The runes had been damaged, but I've had one of the UN's computer experts reconstruct and digitally enhance it. I've got enough to work on a partial translation now."

"And?" Reynolds asked. "What's it tell you?"

"It makes mention of the Great Pyramid. And there may have been a drawing that showed the lower chamber where the bomb was hidden. But it also makes mention of the Kortad," Nabinger said.

"I take it that it's not good news?" Reynolds asked.

Nabinger frowned. "It's kind of funny. The more I study the high runes the more I think I understand the language and the syntax, but some things just don't make sense."

Reynolds waited, sensing the uncertainty in her friend.

"This one panel talks about the coming of the Kortad. And the next panel gives information about the atomic weapon hidden inside the Great Pyramid. But there's more than references to just the pyramid and the Kortad. The panel refers to other places, but I can't understand the geographic code system the Airlia used for our planet. It's more complex than latitude and longitude."

Nabinger had picked the photo up again and was fingering it. "Oh, I don't know. It's just so frustrating, uncovering one word after another, not being exactly sure of the meaning of the word, its tense, its proper syntax. Now I've uncovered a system I can't crack. When I thought I was dealing with ancient artifacts and dead cultures I could bear being patient, but this is different."

"You're still dealing with a dead culture," Reynolds noted.

"What makes you so sure of that?" Nabinger cut in. "One thing that no one seems too concerned about that concerns me greatly is what happened to the Airlia? Did they just disappear? Commit mass suicide after secreting away the mothership, the bouncers, and the guardian computer? Why'd they leave the guardian on, then?

"And what about the rebels? What happened to them? We know they directed the building of the Great Pyramid as a space beacon, so maybe they were the pharaohs. Maybe their descendants still walk the Earth?"

Kelly Reynolds smiled. It had been a favorite topic of speculation around the press tent. "Maybe we're all descended to some degree from the Airlia," she said. "We don't exactly know what they looked like other than that they had red hair and a humanoid form. The statues on this island weren't exactly built to scale."

"I don't know," Nabinger said. "But what I do know is that whatever the UN's Alien Oversight Committee decides to do about the guardian and the mothership is going to affect the course of human history more than anything else that has ever happened. And I'm not sure I feel much better about these UN people than I did about Majestic. The big players on the Security Council have loaded the committee with their people, and they seem to be doing a lot of talking in secret."

"That's why I'm here," Kelly Reynolds said, tapping her laptop. "To make sure the truth gets out. Majestic worked in total secrecy; at least here we have some openness."

Nabinger snorted. "You've got openness at least until something happens. Then see how fast this place gets locked down tight."

"That's the big question," Reynolds said. "What is going to happen next?" She was looking down at the photos. "I've got a stupid question, but why did the Airlia bother to write all this high rune stuff down if the guardian computer has a record of it all? Seems kind of primitive for a race as highly developed as they were."

"I've been asking myself the same question," Nabinger said.

"And what have you come up with?" Reynolds asked.

"I don't know," Nabinger replied. "I think the high rune language in many places was written by humans copying the Airlia, but I'm not sure." He gathered up the photos. "By the way, do you know where Mike is?"

"No. He was in D.C. with Lisa Duncan testifying, but when I tried to call him from the airport before I came back here, I was told he was off on a mission."

Nabinger nodded knowingly. "Yeah, well, I'd like to know exactly what *he's* up to now. You can bet he isn't sitting on his butt wondering, he's doing something."

Chapter 4

At the same moment that Peter Nabinger was wondering where he was, Captain Mike Turcotte was sipping a cup of coffee in one of the ready rooms on board the aircraft carrier USS *George Washington.*

Turcotte could feel the steady drum of the engines reverberating through the floor panels. The *George Washington* was the newest carrier in the American Navy's inventory. The most recent of the *Nimitz* class, it displaced over 100,000 tons of water and was cruising south at thirty knots from its normal duty station in the Persian Gulf. Off the starboard bow lay the coast of Ethiopia.

That the carrier had been taken off-station from the critical and volatile Persian Gulf told Turcotte how important this mission was, as much as what Lisa Duncan, seated to his left, had already told him. The presence of a British lieutenant colonel three seats over who sported the sand-colored beret of the elite British Special Air Service, SAS, also indicated a certain degree of

martial seriousness. On the other side of the British colonel was an American major in a flight suit,
the patch Velcroed to his left shoulder showing
the Grim Reaper of Task Force 160, the Night-
stalkers.

They were all prepared to listen to a briefing by
a former Soviet operative. The man, Karol Kostanov, spoke in clipped English, his accent polished
at one of the KGB's finishing schools during the
height of the Cold War. He claimed he had been
working freelance around the world since the
breakup of the Soviet Union. How the UN Alien
Oversight Committee had gotten hold of him,
Turcotte had no idea, but he imagined that it involved a lot of cash, based on the expensive suit
and custom-made shoes Kostanov wore.

"Please proceed, Mr. Kostanov," Duncan ordered once she made sure everyone was ready.

Kostanov had a carefully cultivated day's
growth of beard, framing his aristocratic face and
thin glasses, the frames made of some obviously
expensive metal. Turcotte wondered if Kostanov
even needed the lenses in the glasses or if they
were part of his costume, designed to impress.
Kostanov's skin was dark, his hair streaked with
gray.

"I was contacted a day and a half ago by a representative of the United Nations Alien Oversight
Committee," Kostanov began, but Duncan waved
a hand.

"I know about that," she said. "You claim you
know about a cache of alien artifacts in south-
western Ethiopia, guarded by people who work
for a South African business cartel. Since we are
closing on helicopter range of that area, I don't

have time to listen to your superfluous bullshit, as we will be launching a military strike force soon. Give me the facts."

Kostanov pursed his lips as he considered the diminutive woman who had just spoken so harshly.

"Ah, the *facts*," Kostanov repeated, just the slightest edge of mockery in his voice. "There are not many, so I will not waste your time.

"One. Before the breakup I worked at Tyuratam, a Soviet strategic missile test center. It was also headquarters to Section Four of the minister of interior. From what I have read recently in your newspapers, Section Four was the equivalent of your Majestic-12.

"We, however, were not so fortunate in our discoveries of alien artifacts as you Americans. We had the remains of one alien craft that had been severely damaged and that was all."

Turcotte leaned forward in his seat. He'd seen the bouncer that had crashed from a very high altitude at terminal velocity into the New Mexico countryside. There hadn't been a mark on it. What could have damaged the craft the Russians had?

"What kind of craft?" Duncan asked, showing that this was news to her also. "A bouncer?"

"Not a bouncer. Bigger than that but nowhere near mothership size either." Kostanov shrugged. "It was very badly damaged. The scientists worked at reverse engineering what we had, but there was not much success."

"Where was your craft found and when?" Duncan asked.

"Nineteen fifty-eight in Siberia. Best estimate

from the crash site was that it had been there for several thousand years. I believe the disclosure of that craft was used by the Russian government as part of their attempt to maneuver one of their people high on the UNAOC council. I would assume UNAOC is keeping that quiet for their own reasons and because there is little to be gained from the craft."

"Was it an Airlia craft?" Duncan asked.

"We didn't specifically know about the Airlia until just recently," Kostanov said, "but from what I have seen of your mothership, it was made of the same black material that the mothership is made of, so I would assume it was Airlia."

Duncan waved for him to continue.

"Despite the lack of success the head of Section Four felt that if there was one craft, there most likely would be others. The scientists postulated that this craft could not have crossed interstellar distances, therefore it had to have been ferried here. The unit I was part of was directed to search down other leads."

The Russian turned to the map and used a handheld laser pointer. "In 1988 we received word from KGB sources that someone had discovered something strange, here in southwest Ethiopia. I accompanied a Spetsnatz—Soviet special forces—unit," Kostanov added, with a glance at Turcotte's green beret and the colonel's sand-colored one, "that was sent in to do a reconnaissance."

"And you found?" Duncan prompted.

"We never made it to our target site. We were attacked by a paramilitary force. Since we were going in on the sly and did not have air support and could not risk an international incident, we were heavily outgunned. Half the team was killed. The rest of us were lucky to make it back to the coast and get picked up by our submarine."

"A paramilitary force?" Turcotte spoke for the first time.

"Well armed, well trained, and well led. As good as the Spetsnatz I was with and more numerous."

"Who were they?" Turcotte asked.

"I don't know. They weren't wearing uniforms with insignia. Most likely mercenaries."

"Get to the point," Duncan said. "What was at that location?"

"The word we received was that there were some sort of evidence of advanced weaponry," Kostanov said. "Alien weaponry."

Everyone in the room sat up a little straighter. The question of alien weapons had been raised many times in the closed chambers of the UN Oversight Committee. Given that the A-bomb had been partially developed from an Airlia weapon left in the Great Pyramid, there was a great deal of speculation about what other deadly devices might be secreted somewhere around the planet. The destruction of the Majestic-12 bioexperiment facility at Dulce, New Mexico, by a ray from a foo fighter indicated that there were weapons the Airlia had that many governments would dearly like to get their hands on. Weapons that the UN would like to get under positive control before an irresponsible party gained hold of them.

The message Professor Nabinger had received from the guardian about the civil war among the

Airlia indicated that they'd had a weapon powerful enough to have wiped the Airlia home base,
known in human legend as Atlantis, off the face
of the Earth so effectively that it had become only
a myth.

"More specifics," Duncan said.

"I don't have more specifics," Kostanov said.
"As I told you, we never made it to the target.
This happened in early 1989, and as you know
there was much turmoil and change in my country
that year. We were never able to relaunch another
mission. You now know as much as I do."

"And the target is?" the British lieutenant colonel asked.

Kostanov shrugged. "That is for *your* intelligence people to tell you. I gave them the location.
I assume they have better pictures than I had ten
years ago."

Duncan gestured at a woman in a gray three-
piece suit who had been sitting along the wall
while Kostanov spoke. She now stood up. She was
tall and slender with jet-black hair, cut tight
around her head, framing an angular face. She
appeared to be in her mid-thirties, but it was hard
to tell as her skin was perfectly smooth and pale.

"My code name is Zandra," the woman said. "I
represent the Central Intelligence Agency."

Zandra held a small remote. She clicked a
button. A long-range satellite photo appeared.
"Northeast Africa," Zandra oriented them
quickly. She clicked and the shot decreased in
scale. "Southwest Ethiopia, near the border with
Kenya and Sudan. Very inhospitable terrain.
Largely uninhabited and largely unexplored."

Turcotte nodded to himself. That fit the pattern. The Airlia had picked the most inaccessible places on Earth to hide their equipment: Antarctica, the American desert in Nevada, Easter Island. Always where it would be difficult for humans to get to and survive.

"The most significant terrain feature in this part of the world is the Great Rift Valley. It starts in southern Turkey, runs through Syria, then between Israel and Jordan where the Dead Sea lies; the lowest point on the face of the planet. It goes from there to Elat, then it forms the Red Sea. At the Gulf of Aden it splits, one part running into the Indian Ocean, the other going inland into Africa, to the Afar Triangle. The lowest point in Africa, the Danakil Depression, which is where our target is, lies directly along the Great Rift Valley.

"From there the Rift Valley goes south, encompassing Lake Victoria, the world's second largest freshwater lake, before ending somewhere in Mozambique."

Another click and there was a tiny square in the center of a deep valley, high mountains on both sides and a river running in the center. The next shot and they could see that the square was a fenced compound next to the river. The vegetation was sparse and stunted.

"That's your target. According to legal documents we've traced, that compound is owned by the Terra-Lel Corporation, which is headquartered in Cape Town, South Africa. They own a variety of interests, and they claim this compound is a mining camp. It's been there for sixteen years. Our satellites have never shown any mined material leaving. The only way in or out is by plane or helicopter or a hazardous three-day trip by all-terrain vehicle from Addis Ababa.

"The interesting thing about Terra-Lel is that the only sort of mining operation, if you could call it that, they've ever been associated with has been sending mercenaries into Angola to attack diamond mining camps. Terra-Lel's main business is arms; manufacturing, buying, selling, and exporting them to the highest bidder. They used to do quite a good business on the international black market until Mandela came into power."

Zandra used the laser pointer. "Here is the airstrip near the compound. This building"—she highlighted a three-story structure—"is where we believe the Airlia artifacts are stored. This is the barracks for the paramilitary mercenary forces guarding the compound. There are also surface-to-air missiles, here, here, here, and here. Several armored vehicles." Zandra gave a frosty smile. "Certainly they would not need such protection for just a mining compound."

"If these Terra-Lel people are out of South Africa, then why didn't they just move what they've found home?" Duncan asked.

"We don't know," Zandra said. "Our best guess is that maybe they can't move whatever it is they've found. Or perhaps the unstable political environment over the years in South Africa precluded that option. There was a discreet inquiry made through the United Nations Alien Oversight Committee to the South African government to get open access to the compound."

"And the answer, as you can tell by the fact we're heading there with a squadron of SAS on board," Duncan said, "was silence."

"So they know we're coming," Turcotte summarized.

"Most likely," Zandra confirmed.

"Bloody hell," the SAS colonel muttered, then asked, "What about the Ethiopian government?"

"What about them?" Zandra replied, her tone answer enough that that was not a factor here.

Duncan looked at the SAS officer. "Colonel Spearson, what's the plan?"

Spearson stood and walked to the front of the room. He looked at the American officer in the flight suit. "When can we launch, Major O'Callaghan?"

O'Callaghan pointed at a map of northeast Africa. "The ship's captain is pushing his engines to the max, so we're making good speed. Our launch point, where all aircraft will have enough fuel for a round trip plus fifteen minutes on-station, is here, forty kilometers from our present position—which means we will be able to launch in less than an hour."

Spearson didn't look happy about that timetable, and Turcotte knew why. It would be dawn shortly, and the SAS would hit the compound just before daylight. It was a tight window with a lot of room for disaster.

Spearson cleared his throat. "An American AWACS is in position off the coast. It will control all flight operations, coordinating O'Callaghan's helicopters and jets from your navy. I am the commander of all ground forces. I will be on board an MH-60 until the first air assault wave lands. At that time I will reposition to the primary target.

"The basic plan is a four-stage attack. Stage

one is to land a squad by parachute on top of the building you believe holds the artifacts. These troopers are to gain a foothold. Stage two is an attack by antiradar missiles launched by Navy planes to take out their surface-to-air missile sites. Stage three is the rest of my force coming in by helicopter with gunship support. Stage four is to secure the compound." Spearson looked at the others in the room. "Questions?"

"How is your airborne force going in?" Turcotte asked. "HALO or HAHO?"

"HAHO," Spearson replied, letting Turcotte know that the men would be jumping at high altitude and opening their parachutes almost immediately, flying them in to the target. The thin chutes wouldn't get picked up by radar like aircraft would, allowing them to arrive undetected.

"I'd like to go in with the jumpers," Turcotte said.

"That's fine," Spearson said.

Duncan stood up. "All right—"

"*I've* got some questions," Spearson suddenly said, looking directly at Duncan. "What if these Terra-Lel people have indeed uncovered some Airlia weapons?"

"That's why we're going there," Duncan said. "To find that out."

"But what if they can use these weapons against us?" Spearson clarified his concern.

"Then we're in big trouble," Duncan said simply.

"I doubt they have had any success in that area," Zandra interjected. "We've kept close tabs on Terra-Lel. You can be assured that if they had uncovered anything they could use, it would be on the international arms market in one form or another."

Spearson didn't seem much comforted by that. "What are our rules of engagement?"

"If you meet any resistance," Duncan said, "you are free to use whatever force is necessary to overcome that resistance."

Spearson frowned. "Your planes will be taking out their radio and radar facilities right after my initial forces land. There's bound to be some casualties from those strikes. That means we will most likely have fired the first shots."

Duncan's face was impassive. "We gave them their chance to cooperate. The United Nations Security Council has already considered this situation, and it is felt that the threat of Airlia weapons being in the wrong hands is too great a danger. UNAOC has been given the power by the Security Council to use whatever force is necessary to get all Airlia artifacts under UN control."

Spearson stared at her hard, then nodded. "Right, then. Let's get up to the flight deck and get going."

Turcotte stood and followed the SAS colonel. As he reached the door, Lisa Duncan put out a hand and tapped his elbow. "Mike."

"Yes?" Turcotte waited, surprised. That was the first time she had called him by his first name.

"Be careful."

Turcotte gave her a smile, but it was gone just as quickly. "Did you know about the Airlia craft the Russians found?" he asked.

"No."

"That's not good," Turcotte said. "Oh, well, I

guess it's not important right now. I'll be safe. I'll make sure I duck if I have to."

"Try to do better than that," Duncan warned.

Turcotte paused. They stared at each other in the narrow metal stairwell for a few seconds. "Well," Turcotte finally said, "I've got to go."

"I'll see you on the ground," Duncan said.

Turcotte turned and climbed the stairs that led to the massive flight deck of the *Washington*. There was a warm breeze blowing in from the seaward side. Looking across the flight deck, Turcotte could see SAS troopers rigging equipment. Some were doing a last-minute cleaning of their weapons, others honing knives or smearing camouflage paint onto their faces. Pilots from both the Army and Navy were walking around their aircraft, using red-lens flashlights to do a final visual inspection.

A figure loomed up in the dark and a rich British accent rolled across the flight deck. "You Turcotte?"

"Yes."

"I'm Ridley. Commander, HAHO detachment, Twenty-first SAS. I understand you're coming with us?"

"That's right."

"Well, I'll assume you know what you're doing. You jump last and don't get in anybody's way or you're bloody well likely to get shot, and you won't catch me crying in my tea over that. Clear?" Ridley was already walking toward their aircraft.

"Clear."

"Turcotte," Ridley said. "Sounds fucking French."

"I'm Canuck," Turcotte said. They came up to a C-2 cargo plane.

Ridley handed him a parachute. "Packed it myself. What the bloody hell is a Canuck?"

"French-Indian," Turcotte said. "I'm from Maine. There's a lot of us in the backwoods there." He put the chute on his back.

Ridley was behind him, reaching between his legs with a strap. "Left leg," he announced.

"Left leg," Turcotte repeated, snapping it into the proper receiver. He felt comfortable around Ridley's gruff manner. He'd met many men like that in his years working special operations. Turcotte had even worked with the SAS before in Europe, when he'd done counterterrorism work. He knew the Special Air Service to be top-notch professionals who got the job done.

Quickly Turcotte rigged and climbed into the plane. The C-2 was the largest aircraft the *Washington* had in its inventory. It normally moved personnel and equipment from the vessel to shore and back. Right now the small cargo bay held sixteen heavily armed SAS troopers in tight proximity to each other.

Turcotte smelled the familiar pungent odor of engine exhaust and JP-4 jet fuel, reminding him of other missions in other parts of the globe. The back ramp to the C-2 closed and the plane taxied to its takeoff position. The engine noise peaked and then they were moving, rolling across the steel deck. There was a sudden, short drop, then the nose of the plane tilted up and they were climbing in altitude. Below and behind them, like fireflies in the dark, helicopters lifted and followed.

■ ■ ■

"Ten minutes!" the SAS jumpmaster said. The message was picked up by the throat mike wrapped tightly around his neck and transmitted to the earpieces of all the jumpers, Turcotte included.

Turcotte did one last check of his gear, making sure everything was functioning properly. He looked around at the other men in the cargo bay. He was the only one in a single rig. The SAS troopers were wearing dual rigs—two people hooked together in harness with one chute. Turcotte had never seen that used for military purposes before. Usually such rigs were used by civilian jump instructors to train novice jumpers.

The jumpmaster continued, pantomiming the commands with his hands. "Six minutes. Switch to your personal oxygen and break your chem lights."

Turcotte stood up at the front of the cargo bay. He unhooked from the console in the center of the cargo bay that had been supplying his oxygen and hooked in to the small tank on his chest. He took a deep breath and then broke the chem light on the back of his helmet, activating its glow.

"Depressurizing," the crew chief announced.

A crack appeared at the back of the plane as the back ramp began opening. The bottom half leveled out, forming a platform, while the top half disappeared into the tail section. Turcotte swallowed, his ears popping.

"Stand by," the jumpmaster called out over the FM radio. He moved forward until he was at the very edge, looking into the dark night sky.

Turcotte knew they were over fourteen miles off-set from the Terra-Lel compound and should be attracting no interest from ground-based radar at this distance.

"Go!" The jumpmaster and his buddy were gone. The others walked off, the pairs moving in unison. Turcotte went last, throwing himself into the slipstream and immediately spreading his legs and arms and arching his back, getting stable.

He counted to three, then pulled his ripcord. The chute blossomed above his head. He slid the night vision goggles down on his helmet, checked his chute, then looked down. He counted eight sets of chem lights below him. He turned and followed their path as the SAS troopers began flying their chutes toward the target. With over six miles of vertical drop, they could cover quite a bit of distance laterally using their chutes as wings. Turcotte didn't know what the current record was, but he had heard of HAHO teams covering over twenty-five lateral miles on a jump. He felt confident that with the sophisticated guidance rigs the front man of each pair of jumpers had on top of his reserve chute, they would find the target. All Turcotte had to do was follow. And, as Ridley had warned, stay out of the way as the SAS did its job.

Turcotte was cold for the first time in weeks since leaving Easter Island. Even at this latitude thirty thousand feet meant thin air and low temperatures. Turcotte's hands were on the toggles that controlled the chute, both turning and descent rate. He adjusted as the line of chem lights below him changed direction slightly. He checked his altimeter: twenty thousand feet.

■ ■ ■

Fifty kilometers away the first wave of the air assault element was flying toward the target. Four Task Force 160 AH-6's—known as Little Birds—led the way. They were modified OH-6 Cayuse observation helicopters. The AH-6 was designed as one of the quietest helicopters in the world, capable of hovering a couple of hundred meters from a person and not being heard. The two pilots both wore night vision goggles and used forward-looking infrared radar to fly in the night.

Two Little Birds carried 7.62mm minigun pods and the other two 2.75-inch rocket pods. In the backseat of each aircraft SAS snipers armed with thermal scopes provided additional firepower. The SAS troopers wore body harnesses and could lean completely out of the helicopter to fire their rifles.

Ten kilometers behind the Little Birds, four Apache gunships followed. Besides the 30mm chain gun mounted under the nose, the weapons pylons of each bristled with Hellfire missiles. A Black Hawk helicopter was directly behind the Apaches: Colonel Spearson's command aircraft. And ten kilometers behind the Apaches came Spearson's main ground force: eight Black Hawks carrying ninety-six SAS troopers ready for battle.

At a higher altitude and circling, the air strike force from the *George Washington* was poised. It consisted of F-4G Wild Weasels to suppress air defense and F-18 Tomcats with laser-guided munitions. And circling high above it all off the coast was the AWACS, coordinating carefully with

Colonel Spearson to make sure that everything arrived on target at just the right moment.

Next to Colonel Spearson, in the command Black Hawk helicopter, Lisa Duncan felt reasonably calm. She had always handled stress and crisis well, and this was to be no exception.

She'd moved up in Washington for years until getting her last assignment, as presidential science adviser to Majestic-12. The fact that when she had been given the assignment she had only known of that organization as a rumor, had been the very reason the President had picked her. Even *he* hadn't known exactly what Majestic-12 was, having been briefed when coming into office that MJ-12, as insiders called it, was a committee established after World War II to look into the discovery of various alien artifacts. At the briefing the head of MJ-12, General Gullick, had not told the President exactly what it was they had hidden at Area 51 in Nevada that required over $3 billion a year in black budget funding, other than to hint that they had recovered several types of alien craft, all in nonflying condition.

Unlike his predecessors this President had wanted to know more, and he'd tapped Lisa Duncan to get that information for him when the presidential-scientific-adviser slot had come open upon the death of the man who'd held it for thirty years. The President had listened to those who told him that there were rumors Majestic had more than just nonoperational craft at Area 51 and that he was being kept in the dark. He wanted the truth and Lisa Duncan was the one he had chosen to get it for him.

Receiving the assignment, Duncan had gathered as much information as she could about MJ-12 and Area 51. One disturbing bit of information she was given by a senator, one of those who had pushed the President, indicated that MJ-12 had employed former Nazi scientists brought to America under the classified auspices of Operation Paperclip after the end of the Second World War.

Sensing that she was going into unfriendly waters, Duncan had intercepted Turcotte a few weeks ago on his way to a security assignment at Area 51 and coopted him to spy for her before she traveled there for the first time.

She had been shocked upon arrival at Area 51 to find out that MJ-12 was flying nine alien-made bouncers; disk-shaped craft that used the Earth's magnetic field to power their engines. And that MJ-12 planned on flying the mothership, a massive craft capable of interstellar flight, hidden in a cavern inside Area 51.

That dangerous plan had dissolved with the help of Turcotte, Kelly Reynolds, Peter Nabinger, and Werner Von Seeckt, one of the original Nazi scientists. Von Seeckt's physical condition had deteriorated shortly after they'd succeeded in stopping General Gullick's attempt to fly the mothership, and he was now in the intensive care unit at the Nellis Air Force Base hospital.

Duncan felt that being in this Black Hawk, flying toward an unknown site in Ethiopia, was simply continuing to do her duty to her country, and to the human race as a whole. If there was something alien out there, she felt it was her job to help find it. There had been too much secrecy for too long all over the world.

But she wondered how many more people would die. She listened to the pilot of the C-2 report that all jumpers were away, and her thoughts went to Mike Turcotte.

■ ■ ■

Turcotte understood the tandem rigs now. The man in the rear was flying the chute. The man in front, not having to bother with controlling the toggles for maneuvering, held a silenced MP-5 submachine gun in his hands with a laser scope.

Turcotte checked his altimeter and the glowing numbers told him they were just passing through ten thousand feet. He looked around, now able to make out some details on the ground. There were mountains to both sides, some as high as his present altitude. Turcotte remembered the warning that the compound was in a depression, the deepest in Africa, Zandra had said, and they had to descend twelve hundred feet below sea level.

Turcotte pulled his oxygen mask aside and breathed in the fresh night air. He had a moment now to collect his thoughts, and one thing still bothered him from the briefing: Why had Zandra given so much information about the Rift Valley? It was Turcotte's belief that people never did things for no reason at all. Zandra had to have had a conscious, or perhaps subconscious, reason for going into detail about the geographical formation. There was no doubt, looking about through his night vision goggles, that the terrain of the valley was spectacular. Jagged mountains rose on either side, framing a twisted and torn valley floor.

The formation changed directions, curving to

the left, and Turcotte brought his mind back to the task at hand, pulling his left toggle and following the stream of glowing chem lights below.

The jump formation broke apart two hundred feet above the roof of the research building. Turcotte knew the guards on the roof had to be awake, but would they be looking up?

There was a brief sparkle to one side and below. One of the SAS troopers was firing. Through his earplug Turcotte could hear the men call in.

"Guardpost one clear."

"Guardpost two clear."

"Team one down."

The first troopers were on the roof and it was clear of opposition without any alarm being sounded. Turcotte let up on his toggles and aimed just off the center of the roof. He could see the SAS men clearing themselves of their parachute rigs.

Turcotte pulled in on his toggles and braked less than three feet up. His feet touched and he immediately unsnapped his harness, stepping out of it even before the chute finished collapsing. He turned, looking about, MP-5 at the ready. He could see several bodies; guards dispatched by the SAS.

"This is Ridley. We're landed and secure," the squad leader's voice announced over the radio.

"Air wing, in now," Colonel Spearson ordered.

■ ■ ■

The F-4G Wild Weasel was the only remaining version of the venerable F-4 Phantom still in the U.S. inventory. It had one very specific job—kill enemy radar and antiair systems.

Two Weasels came in on Spearson's orders fast and high out of the east. The radar systems of the Terra-Lel compound picked them up and locked on, which was exactly what was desired. Missiles leapt off the wings of the Weasels—Shrike, AGM-78, and Tacit Rainbows—fancy names for smart bombs that caught the radar beams and rode them down to the emitters.

The pilots of the Weasels banked hard and were already one hundred and eighty degrees turned when the missiles struck. All of the compound's air defense went down in that one strike.

Right behind came the first air assault wave.

■ ■ ■

The SAS demolition's men had been carefully placing shaped charges on the roof; four different charges, evenly spaced. They had run out their detonating cord and were waiting on the order to fire.

As the sound of helicopters came from the east Colonel Spearson gave the order to Ridley.

"Fire in the hold!"

The charges blew, searing the night with their explosive crack and brief flash. Four holes appeared in the roof, and soldiers jumped down into each one.

Turcotte paused, head cocked to the side. A roar of automatic fire reverberated out of the southwest hole. Turcotte sprinted over. A jagged opening, four feet in diameter, beckoned in the concrete. He looked down. The four SAS men who had gone into the hole lay motionless on the floor.

Turcotte pulled a flash-bang grenade off his

vest and tossed it in, counted to three, then jumped in, just as the grenade went off, stunning anyone inside. Turcotte was firing even before he hit the ground. He landed on the body of one of the SAS men and fell to his right side. A string of tracers ripped by, wildly fired just above his prone body.

Turcotte stuck the MP-5 up and blindly returned the fire, spraying in the direction the tracers had come from. He heard the sound of a magazine being changed and was just about to move when he froze. That was too obvious. He rolled onto his stomach and peered about. All the SAS men were dead. There was a desk to his left in the direction the bullets had come from. That was where the man was. Whoever he was, he was using the mirror on the wall behind the desk to aim. Turcotte fired, shattering the glass. Turcotte put a couple of rounds into the desk, confirming what he'd suspected. He wouldn't be able to shoot through it.

Turcotte heard just the slightest sound of someone moving over broken glass. The other man could come from around either side of the desk and if Turcotte picked the wrong one, the other man might get the first shot.

Turcotte fired at the lights, shattering them and throwing the room into darkness.

A small object came flying over the top of the bar. Grenade, Turcotte thought, and reacted just as quickly, rolling away. The man was right behind the object, vaulting the desktop—which didn't make any sense if it was a grenade. Turcotte knew he'd made a mistake as he fired offhand with the MP-5, still rolling.

The other man was also firing in midair, his bullets trailing Turcotte's rolls by a few inches, Turcotte's winging by him.

Turcotte slammed into the wall just as the bolt in his MP-5 clicked home on an empty chamber. He dropped the submachine gun and drew his pistol, firing as he brought it to bear. In the darkness it was his night-vision goggles that gave him the advantage over the other man, and his rounds hit the other man in the chest, knocking him down.

Turcotte stood, listening to the radio, hearing the SAS clearing the building from top floor down. There was no sign of any Airlia artifacts yet. He called in his own location and that the room was secure as he moved to the door, and carefully opened it.

At the end of the hallway a searchlight came in the window from an AH-6 helicopter hovering just outside. Turcotte could see SAS sharpshooters hanging out the doors and the small laser dots creeping around the hall, searching for targets. He flipped a switch on the side of his night-vision goggles and they emitted an infrared beam, identifying him as friendly.

■ ■ ■

From five thousand feet Colonel Spearson was orchestrating the assault over five different radio nets. The airborne force was in the main building. The Little Birds were flitting about the compound, searching for targets. He turned to Duncan.

"All or nothing, now, miss," he said.

"Let's go in," Duncan said.

Spearson gave the orders for the main assault force to land.

■ ■ ■

Turcotte kicked open the door at the juncture of the hallway, his reloaded MP-5 in his left hand. He spotted two men in khaki with their backs to him, firing around the corner. Turcotte killed them with one burst.

"Who dares, wins!" he called out the SAS motto, moving down the hall. Turning the corner he met four SAS gathered by the stairwell, one of them holding his muzzle inside the door, firing an occasional shot to keep more security men from coming up.

Ridley came around the corner with more men. Turcotte stepped back and let the professionals do their job as they began to clear down the building.

■ ■ ■

The Little Birds were also going down the building one floor ahead of the SAS inside. The two armed with 7.62 miniguns were firing through windows. The snipers hit anything they saw moving. Windows shattered out and tracers crisscrossed the floor. The men inside lay low, hiding from the carnage as best they could.

The two Little Birds with rockets were firing up the barracks buildings nearby as security personnel poured out of them. As the first armored vehicles began appearing, they switched to those.

The four Apaches arrived just in time and fired a salvo of eight Hellfire missiles at the armor. Each one was a kill, ending that threat.

■ ■ ■

A pair of SAM-7's—shoulder-fired heat-seeker missiles and thus not affected by the Weasel attack—streaked up at one of the Apaches. It exploded in a ball of flame.

■ ■ ■

"Bloody hell," Colonel Spearson muttered as he saw the signal for the Apache disappear and heard the pilot screaming before the radio went dead. He ordered in the F-18's, directing the Apaches to laser-designate targets for the smart bombs the fast-moving jets carried.

Lisa Duncan watched the chopper go down, knowing that meant two men dead. "Let's land," she told Spearson, who looked like he was going to argue with her, then changed his mind.

■ ■ ■

The SAS soldiers were quickly overcoming their opposition in the building. Surprise, superior firepower, and superb training were winning the day. Turcotte followed them down, floor by floor, until the entire building was clear except for whatever was hidden behind a set of steel doors on the ground level.

■ ■ ■

One of the Little Birds was hit by ground fire and autorotated down. Once it was on the ground, the four men got off and immediately became embroiled in a gun battle with ground forces.

The Apache pilots were also firing now, trying

to suppress any SAM fire from shoulder-fired missiles. They would be out of ammunition in another minute at their current rate of expenditure.

The F-18's came in, their bombs riding the laser beams down with pinpoint accuracy. The effect was devastating.

$$\bullet \; \bullet \; \bullet$$

"One minute!" the pilot said.

Colonel Spearson keyed his mike. "Put us in with the first wave!" he ordered. The pilot glanced over his shoulder at Duncan and she nodded. The Black Hawk swooped down, heading toward the secondary explosions in the compound on the valley floor.

The Black Hawk touched down and Duncan jumped off, following Colonel Spearson. The chopper was back up and gone just as quickly.

"How are the men inside?" she asked.

Spearson had the handset for the radio his batman was carrying pressed to his ear. "They're in the basement. Took some losses, but they've cleared the building."

$$\bullet \; \bullet \; \bullet$$

Turcotte watched as Ridley examined the steel doors. "Okay, men, let's get through this thing."

A demolitions expert took a heavy backpack off and pulled out a three-foot-long cone-shaped black object. He placed the shape charge up against the doors and ran out the firing wire.

"Fire in the hole!" he yelled, causing everyone to scatter and take cover.

$$\bullet \; \bullet \; \bullet$$

On the surface the battle was about over, disheartened mercenaries surrendering now that they saw that there was only one possible ending to this conflict. Spearson's men rounded them up, while they searched for the scientists who had been working at the site.

Spearson had been listening to the force inside the building, and he knew that they were getting ready to blow the doors. "They must be underground," he told Duncan when she asked where the scientists were.

"Let's get inside," she told him.

"Oh, yeah," Spearson added as they headed for the main doors to the building. "Your buddy is okay."

The only acknowledgment Duncan made was to slow her walk slightly.

■ ■ ■

Turcotte's head rang from the explosion, and swirling dust choked his lungs. SAS men with gas masks on ran through the hole in the twisted metal.

Turcotte forced himself to wait. He turned as Lisa Duncan and Colonel Spearson came down the hallway and joined him.

"This has got to be it," he said.

"We wait on my people to clear," Spearson said.

"Fine," Duncan acknowledged. She turned to Turcotte. "You all right?"

"I'm getting too old for this," he said, earning a laugh from Spearson.

The minutes stretched out. Finally, after almost a half hour of waiting, a dust-covered Major Ridley crawled back out of the hole. He pulled his gas mask off and wiped his eyes.

"Did you find any of the scientists?" Duncan asked.

Ridley looked slightly disoriented. "Scientists? They're all dead in there. All dead."

"How?" Colonel Spearson demanded.

Ridley shrugged, his thoughts elsewhere. "Gas, most likely. Must have been set off by the guards when we attacked. It's clear in there now. The merks were just delaying us until the gas worked. The scientists were trapped in there like rats. Looks like they hadn't been allowed out in a long time. Probably lived down there for years. There's plenty of tunnels full of supplies. Living quarters. Mess hall. All that."

"What about Airlia artifacts?" Turcotte asked.

"Artifacts?" Ridley's laugh had a manic edge that he was trying hard to control. "Oh, yeah, there's artifacts down there, sir." He slumped down into a chair. "But you best go see for yourself."

Spearson leading the way, they went through the destroyed doors. They were in a large open tunnel with concrete walls and a floor that sloped down and to the right, disappearing around a curve a hundred meters away. Ridley had been correct about the supplies, Turcotte noted as they walked down. There were numerous side tunnels cut into the rock, full of equipment and supplies. Several of the side tunnels housed living areas, and as Ridley had noted, one was a mess hall. SAS soldiers stood guard at each door and told the colonel that there was no one alive inside.

Bodies were strewn about here and there,

wherever the poison gas had caught them. Whatever Terra-Lel had used on its own people must have been fast acting and had dissipated quickly, Turcotte noted, but also appeared to have been painful. The features of each corpse were twisted in a grimace and the body contorted from violent seizures.

As they went around the bend, the three stopped momentarily in surprise. The wide walkway expanded to a sloping cavern, over five hundred meters wide, the ceiling a hundred meters over their heads hewn out of the volcanic stone. As far as they could see it descended at a thirty-degree slope. Rubber matting had been placed over the center of the smooth stone floor to form a walkway and there was a cog railway built next to the rubber matting.

"Bloody hell," Spearson whispered.

"Look," Duncan said, pointing to the right. A black stone stood there, like a dark finger pointed upward into the darkness. It was ten feet high and two in width, the surface a polished sheen except where high runes were etched into the stone.

"Hope it doesn't say, NO TRESPASSING," Turcotte said.

An SAS sergeant stood next to the small train and passenger cars. He saluted Spearson. "Already been down there, sir, with the captain," he reported, pointing into the unseen deep distance where a row of fluorescent lights next to the rail line faded into the dark haze. "Left a squad on guard." The sergeant swallowed. "Never seen nothing like it, sir."

"Let's take a look for ourselves," Spearson said, climbing into the first open car.

Duncan and Turcotte joined him while the sergeant got in the cab and pushed the throttle into the forward position. With a slight jolt they began rattling down the cogs, descending farther into the cavern. As they went down, the cavern widened until they couldn't see an end to either side, just the meager human light fading into the darkness ahead and behind. Turcotte pulled the collar of his battle-dress uniform tighter around his neck, and he could feel Duncan pressing closer to him. There was the feeling of being a tiny speck in a massive emptiness. Turcotte glanced over his shoulder back the way they had come. Already the brighter light of the cog railway terminal where they had boarded was over a mile behind them. The train was moving at almost forty miles an hour now, clattering over the cogs, but there was no sense of movement other than the fluorescent lights strung on poles next to the rail line flashing by.

After five more minutes they could all make out a red glow ahead. At first it was just the faintest of lines across the low horizon. But as they got closer, they could see the line grow clearer and larger over a mile ahead, perpendicular to their direction of travel. Turcotte had no idea how deep they were, but the temperature was starting to rise and he could feel beads of sweat on his forehead.

Turcotte looked down and could see that the floor of the cavern was still perfectly smooth. He'd seen Hangar Two at Area 51 where the mothership had been hidden, but this cavern dwarfed even that massive structure. He couldn't imagine the technology that would be needed to carve this out. And for what purpose? he wondered. Directly ahead there was a red glow coming out of a wide crevice that split the cavern floor. Turcotte spotted several smaller glowing lights, the flashlights of the SAS squad at the end of the railway. As they slowed down, Turcotte could see the far side of the crevice, over half a mile away, but he couldn't see down into it because they were still over a hundred meters from the edge when the train stopped at the end of the line.

"Sir!" An SAS trooper nodded at Colonel Spearson as they got out.

They walked together toward the edge and stopped where the smooth stone, which had been sloping down at thirty degrees, suddenly went ninety degrees straight down. Duncan gasped and Turcotte felt his heart pound as he carefully peered over the edge. There was no bottom that they could see, just a red glow emanating up from the bowels of the Earth. Turcotte could feel heat washing over his face, accompanied by a strong odor of burning chemicals.

"How deep do you think that goes?" Spearson asked.

"We must be at least seven or eight miles underground already," Duncan said. "If that red glow is the result of heat generated from a split in the Mohorovicic discontinuity—"

"The what?" Spearson barked.

"The line between the planet's crust and the mantle—then we're talking about twenty-two miles altogether to the magma, which is what's giving off that red glow."

"Jesus," Turcotte exclaimed.

"Look over there," Colonel Spearson said, drawing their eyes from the spectacle of a doorway into the primeval inner Earth. To their right, about two hundred meters away, a series of three poles stretched across the chasm to the other side. Suspended from the cables, directly in the center, was a large, bright red, multifaceted sphere about five meters in diameter.

They walked along the edge of the crevice until they came to the first of the poles that held the sphere in place. The pole ran right into the rock face several feet below the lip. Turcotte had seen that black metal before. "That's Airlia," he said. "Same material as the skin of the mothership. Some incredibly strong metal we still haven't been able to figure out."

"What the bloody hell is that thing?" Spearson was pointing at the ruby sphere. It was hard to tell if the sphere itself was ruby or if it was reflecting the glow from below.

Duncan didn't answer, but she led the way farther right where a group of low structures had been erected. It was obvious most of them had been built by the Terra-Lei scientists who'd been working down here. But in the center was a console that immediately reminded Turcotte of the control panel in one of the bouncers. "That's Airlia too," he said, walking up the panel.

The surface was totally smooth. There was high rune writing etched on it and Turcotte imagined that once it was powered up, more rune writing would appear, pointing to various controls that could be activated with just a touch on the surface. He wished Nabinger were here to give them an idea what they were looking at.

"This"—Duncan was pointing at the panel—"controls that"—she pointed at the ruby sphere.

"And what does *that* do?" Spearson asked.

Duncan was looking about the great cavern. "I'm not too sure what more it can do, but I do believe it might have done this." Her hands were spread wide taking in the space they were in.

"That thing blasted this out?" Spearson was incredulous.

"*Something* made this cavern," Duncan said. "It isn't a natural formation. The Airlia had technology beyond our imaginings, so I think it's safe to say something of theirs made this cavern. And the Terra-Lel people spent a lot of years down here trying to figure this out. Now we know why they never moved this to South Africa."

"They couldn't move it," Turcotte agreed. "That metal in those poles took the guys at Area 51 over fifty years to get through, and then only after they were taken over by the rebel guardian and given the information needed."

"And the South Africans must have been scared of what they were working on," Duncan added.

"Scared?" Colonel Spearson repeated.

"They killed all their own people," Turcotte noted. "The guys we fought upstairs were just mercenaries who I'm willing to bet don't have a clue who really hired them or what was in here."

Spearson was looking about. "Why do you think it's here? Over a crack in the Earth's crust?"

"It picks up thermal energy?" Turcotte suggested.

Duncan didn't appear to hear him. "I think I've

just figured out what this is and I think they did too. And they had sixteen years to sit here and look at it. No wonder they were scared."

"What is it?" Turcotte asked.

Duncan was staring over the massive crevice in the Earth at the ruby sphere. "I think it's a Doomsday device set there to destroy the planet."

Chapter 5

The command center for the United Nations Alien Oversight Committee, or UNAOC, as it was being referred to, on Easter Island was set inside four connected communications vans that had been flown in from the mainland aboard a massive C-5 cargo plane. Two of the vans retained their original function, connecting Easter Island UNAOC with New York UNAOC. The other two had had the connecting wall removed and now housed banks of computers, a large display screen along the front wall, and several desks where the ranking members sat.

Peter Nabinger had spent many hours inside the command center. There were live television feeds to the cavern below the volcano that housed the guardian computer. He always felt a strange sensation slither up his spine each time he looked at those screens and saw the large golden pyramid. He'd gone down to the cavern several times, attempting to reestablish his mental communication with it, but to no avail.

Today, though, he was in the CC for a different reason. The director of operations for UNAOC on the island had called him in for a conference meeting with the main UNAOC council in New York. The purpose of the meeting had not been disclosed.

Nabinger hated video conferencing. He felt strange sitting in front of a computer screen that showed him the others in the conference and having to look into the small camera on top of the screen that beamed his image to them.

As he took his seat, the man who had called him in took the seat to his left. Gunfield Gronad was the ranking representative from UNAOC on Easter Island, and Nabinger knew that so far his tour of duty had been one large bust. The guardian was still inactive, there was no more information flowing, and the world media, not to mention UNAOC headquarters, were less than pleased. Nabinger felt sorry for the young Norwegian, who had to report failure even though they had no control over the guardian.

Nabinger knew Gunfield was further distressed to see the face of Peter Sterling fill up the screen on the computers in front of them. Sterling was the chief commissioner of UNAOC. He was the former head of NATO, who had been coopted to lead UNAOC by the Security Council three days ago. Sterling was a distinguished-looking man who had been very high profile in the media for the past several days. His enthusiasm for the UNAOC position and what they were uncovering was unbounded, and he most definitely was in the camp of the progressives.

Nabinger leaned back in his seat and waited as

Sterling reached down and did something with his keyboard and his image grew smaller. Now Nabinger could see that they were connected to the main UNAOC conference room on the top floor of the UN Building. He could see the second-in-command of UNAOC, Boris Ivanoc, seated to Sterling's left and the other members of UNAOC arrayed around the table, their own teleconference computers in front of them. Ivanoc was a concession to Russia, an attempt to balance the immense power that UNAOC would hold if they could get back into the guardian and gain access to the knowledge secreted there. The camera zoomed back in, and Sterling's patrician face stared at both Nabinger and Gunfield.

"Anything to report, gentlemen?" There was the hint of a smile around Sterling's lip.

"No, sir," Gunfield said. "The guardian is still inactive and—"

"No sign that the guardian transmitted or received a transmission?"

"No, sir."

"You need to be alert," Sterling eagerly interrupted. "We've received a reply."

Nabinger leaned forward. "To the message?"

"Of course to the message," Sterling said. "It came in yesterday. Several tracking stations picked it up and recorded it."

"I've heard nothing from the media," Nabinger began, but again he was cut off.

"We're not releasing this information quite yet, but we will shortly, I can assure you. We're still coordinating with the various governments that picked it up. Are you certain that the guardian did not receive the message?" Sterling asked once again.

"Sir," Gunfield replied, "the guardian may well have received this message. There is no way for us to know. Reception is a passive action. Now, if the guardian sends a reply, our tracking instruments will certainly pick it up."

"In what format is the message?" Nabinger asked.

"Most of it is very complex, and we can't make heads or tails of it," Sterling said. "We think that part was directed to your guardian. Some sort of special code."

Nabinger leaned forward. "And the other part?"

"It's digital. Basic binary." Sterling's face was flushed. "That part was directed to us. Humanity."

"What does it say?" Gunfield asked.

"We'll send you the text via secure SATCOM. You'll have it when we release it publicly. It's not long."

"The basic gist?" Nabinger asked.

"You'll see," Sterling said mysteriously, like a child holding on to a secret. "I'm not authorized to tell anyone in advance, as it has to be released simultaneously around the world. But I can tell you one thing, gentlemen; things have changed and are going to change even more."

Nabinger raised a hand. "Where did the message come from? Is there a mothership coming?"

Sterling's eyes shifted, looking about his conference room, then settled back on the camera. "Mars."

Gunfield couldn't help himself. "Mars?"

Nabinger nodded as he made a connection in his mind.

"What are you thinking, Professor?" Sterling asked, catching the movement.

Damn, Nabinger thought. He could never get used to being watched by a machine. "Mars makes sense, at least from an archaeological viewpoint."

"Explain," Sterling ordered.

"We found the Airlia atomic weapon in the Great Pyramid at Giza, just outside Cairo," Nabinger said. "Some Egyptologists define the word *Cairo* as meaning 'Mars.' Quite a coincidence, I would say. Do you have an exact fix from where on Mars this message was broadcast?"

"The Cydonia region on the north hemisphere," Sterling said.

"You know what has been photographed at Cydonia, don't you?" Nabinger said.

"Why don't you tell us?" Sterling said.

"Well, first there's what appears to be the thrust-up outline of a large face on the surface of the planet there," Nabinger said. "It was discovered in July 1976 by NASA personnel studying the images sent back by the Viking probe."

Nabinger paused but no one interrupted, so he continued. "In 1979 some computer engineers at the Goddard Space Flight Center reexamined the digital frame that held the face, then expanded the search, checking out the imagery of the immediate area.

"They found what appeared to be a pyramid close by. A pyramid, that as nearly as they could tell, was over five hundred meters high and about

three kilometers long on each base, easily dwarfing the Great Pyramid at Giza."

"How do you know all this?" Sterling asked, a
frown on his face—whether from the fact that
Nabinger had stolen his thunder or wondering if
Nabinger had learned more from the guardian
than he had told UNAOC, Nabinger neither knew
nor cared.

"I have a friend in the most unique field of
archaeoastronomy: the study of archeological objects in space. Since most people believed there
were no archeological objects in space, he was
rather, shall we say, ignored by the other scientists. I would imagine now, though, that his expertise is in rather strong demand. We met at a
conference, and since there were some similarities
between what he thought he saw on the surface of
Mars and what I was investigating on the surface
of the Earth at Giza, we spent some time ex-
changing notes."

"Go on about Cydonia," Sterling ordered.

"The face, if I remember rightly, was estimated
to be about two and a half kilometers long by two
wide, and I think five hundred meters high also."

"More like four hundred meters high, from
shadow analysis," Sterling said.

"Four hundred meters, then," Nabinger said.
"Obviously you have access to data about this. Do
they have any better idea about the City?"

"City?" Gunfield asked.

Nabinger turned in his seat. "Yes. Besides the
Face and the Pyramid, there was a group of what
appeared to be smaller pyramids to the southwest
of the face. And an object that was called the
Fort: four straight lines like walls, surrounding a

black courtyard. The men looking at this dubbed those pyramids and the Fort as the City."

Nabinger turned back to Sterling. "So now we know that what NASA dismissed as just shadows and natural objects, are really artifacts from the Airlia. Another Airlia colony, perhaps."

"It appears that is so," Sterling admitted. "If there was an Airlia outpost on Mars, it would also explain some facts that were dismissed as coincidence. The fact that the Russians have launched ten unmanned missions to explore Mars with very little success. Several exploded on takeoff. They lost control of two and couldn't get them out of their intermediary orbits around Earth. Two missed Mars when their guidance systems went haywire. Three made it to Mars but their probes went dead. There was one lander that the Russians managed to get there and send down. They lost data link with it as it was descending for a landing while relaying back some very confusing data."

"How about American missions to Mars?" Nabinger asked.

"Suffice it to say that they had many failures also, some public and some not so public. The Americans did manage to get their two Viking missions to the Red Planet in 1976 and get both landers down. The interesting thing about that, though, is that those landers went down a long way from Cydonia and the orbiters never went directly over that site. The one Viking satellite that is still up there does not go over the Cydonia region in its present orbit."

"What about *Pathfinder*?" Nabinger asked. "That was all over the news last year."

"Yes, indeed," Sterling said. "But it landed very far away from the Cydonia region. And the range of the Rover is so limited that it would take several lifetimes for it to make it there and it would run out of power long before it got a tenth of the way."

"There were many requests by my friend and others to get the orbiters to take a picture of Cydonia," Nabinger noted. "Those requests were never acted on." Nabinger had to wonder if Majestic-12 had known anything about Cydonia and the connection with the Airlia and that was the reason NASA had so blithely ignored the Face and Pyramid and the entire region even though they had pictures of it. And if that had had anything to do with the selection of the Mars landing site for *Pathfinder*.

"That action is being taken by NASA as we speak," Sterling said. "They are going to use the last reserves of fuel *Viking II* has to reposition it so that it can take a closer look at Cydonia.

"The issue is, what is there? Is there any hint from what you received from the guardian when you were in contact that the Airlia had left an outpost on Mars?"

Nabinger shook his head. He had told no one of the last vision he had had, and he didn't see that it applied here. "No. But you have to remember that there was much that was left out of what the guardian gave me. So many unanswered questions. What about the message? Didn't it give you more information?"

"You'll see for yourself when it gets released," Sterling said. "I want you to stay alert. We need to know if there is communication between the

guardian and whatever is at Cydonia. We suspect
it is most likely another computer left by the Airlia, but if we can get a dialogue going with the
Mars guardian, perhaps we can access the Airlia
data base by tapping in. Just think of that!

"Besides, the one on Mars has made communication with us now. There's no reason to think it
won't continue to do so. Also," Sterling continued, "you are not to release any news of this message to the media quite yet."

"I thought—" Nabinger began.

"I have to go now. That is all." The screen went
blank.

■ ■ ■

In the eastern slope of the Rocky Mountains,
eight hundred feet underground, a system that
had originally been developed to detect ICBM
launches during the Cold War suddenly sprang to
life.

"Sir, we've got activity in the Pacific. Sector
four-six-three."

The Warning Center watch officer, Major
Craig, looked over his shoulder. "Can you identify
the signal?"

The screen watcher stared at the information in
front of him: infrared maps of the Earth's surface
and surrounding airspace downloaded every three
seconds from satellites in geosynchronous orbit
twenty thousand miles up.

"Multiple contacts. Very small." He took a
deep breath. "Signature matches foo fighters."

The term *foo fighter* came from World War II,
when American airmen reported small, glowing
spheres that they occasionally spotted on mis-

sions. What had not been generally reported was that the first several times foo fighters had been spotted and aircrews attempted to engage the flying spheres, the planes had been knocked out of the sky. That had led to an Air Corps–wide policy ordering crews to ignore the foo fighters, which in turn had led to no more fatal incidents. What had been particularly intriguing was that during the *Enola Gay*'s run in to Hiroshima it had been shadowed the entire way by two foo fighters, almost leading to a cancellation of the mission. The consensus now was that the foo fighters were the guardian's way of gathering information and, when needed, directing force.

"What about the Navy ships there over the site?" Craig asked. "They pick anything up?"

"The fighters are coming up fifty miles west of where the ships are, over the horizon from their radar."

"Send the Navy the data," Craig ordered. He knew it was too late for the Navy to do anything, but at least they couldn't complain that they hadn't been informed as quickly as possible.

"Put it on the screen," Craig ordered. The large screen in front of the room displayed a Mercator conformal map of the entire world's surface. With a few commands the data that was being downloaded from DSP could be selectively displayed on the screen. Several glowing dots appeared.

"I count three foo fighters," the operator said.

Craig could clearly see them. One glowing dot heading due east toward the coast of South America. One heading west across the Pacific, and a third heading northeast toward Central America.

"Damn, those suckers are booking," one of the men in the center muttered.

Craig looked down at his own computer and cleared it, then put the tracking data the other man had on his screen. He chewed absently on the nail of his right forefinger as he considered the data, then did what he knew he had to do.

He entered a code and transmitted the data to the UNAOC operations center in New York and on Easter Island along with the Pentagon, NSA, and CIA in his own government. Then, glancing around and making sure no one was watching, he entered another code consisting of the five letters STAAR, and transmitted the data to that destination. He breathed a sigh of relief as soon as the message was sent and his screen was clear again.

He looked up and watched. One of the foo fighters hit the shore of South America over Chile, then cut hard left and followed the coast north. It followed the entire coastline up to Central America and then looped back.

Meanwhile, the second one had crossed Central America and was over the mid-Atlantic while the third was passing New Guinea. The first dot returned to the spot it had originated from and disappeared.

The second foo fighter passed straight through the Strait of Gibraltar and flashed across the Mediterranean. The third had passed Taiwan and was doing a loop over mainland China.

The second reached the far end of the Mediterranean and curved right over Egypt before heading back. The third had done a large figure eight over the entire length of China and was now also heading back. At speeds in excess of thirty thousand miles an hour, the blips on the screen ate up large chunks of distance quickly and shortly all were back down underwater at the point where they had come up.

"What the hell was that all about?" someone asked.

Craig was tapping his forefinger against his lips in thought. "Reconnaissance," he said.

"Looking for what?"

"Damned if I know," Sinclair answered.

Chapter 6

The pebble hit the bricks, then slid down to the turf at the base of the Wall. Che Lu bent to pick up another one, then paused, her back aching with pain. She straightened, as much as a wizened seventy-eight-year-old woman could, to her full height of four inches over five feet.

"Never works for me," she muttered as she turned from the crumbling remains of the Great Wall.

"What doesn't work, Mother-Professor?" her assistant, Ki, asked. He was young, just out of the university, and it was her opinion that he had taken the job more out of desire not to be arrested in Beijing than interest in her work. He used the term her students had used for her for many years. It was a sign of respect for both her age and her status as chief archaeologist at Beijing University.

"The tradition." She peered at him, her eyes a bright blue and, despite her years, not needing glasses of any sort. "You need to know traditions.

They are very important in archaeology. They can guide you to what you look for."

She waved her hand at the serpentine mound of rubble that extended left and right as far as the eye could see. This portion of the Great Wall was not what was shown on documentaries to the outside world. The fools in Beijing would want the world to believe that the entire fifteen-hundred-mile length was in pristine condition, but this pile of rubble and decaying brick was more the norm, left to the ravages of nature and the needs of generations of peasants who had used the bricks to build their hovels.

"The tradition is that a traveler going through the Great Wall should throw a pebble against the brick. If it bounces back, then the journey will be a good one. If it simply falls to the ground, then it will be not so good."

"So we will have a not-so-good expedition?" Ki said with a worried smile.

"It has been not so good from the very beginning," she said. "I don't see why things should get any better." She turned from the wall and headed toward the battered American Jeep that she had been using for so many years. A Russian truck, also Korean War vintage, was puffing large clouds of diesel into the air directly behind the Jeep. It held the other five students in her group and their equipment.

Her great expedition, Che Lu thought to herself as she allowed Ki to help her into the passenger seat. He scurried around and got behind the wheel, throwing the ancient transmission into gear. They continued on their way, now paralleling the Wall, heading toward their work site many miles distant in the vastness of the western provinces of China.

Despite the pebble and paucity of people and equipment allotted her, Che Lu was as excited as she had been in many years. She had finally received permission to dig into Qian-Ling, the mountain tomb of the third emperor of the T'ang dynasty. Inside the massive hill that made up the tomb were buried the Emperor Gao-zong and his empress, the only empress ever to rule in China.

She knew it was the confusion of the current turmoil in China, of course, that had gotten her the permission. Some fool in the Antiquities Division of the government had made a mistake and stamped APPROVED on her request after twenty-two years of her resubmitting it every six months. She'd changed the wording on each submission, obscuring in scholastic language the fact that she wanted permission to actually enter the tomb.

She'd known they had to get to Qian-Ling quickly and get to work before someone else at the division discovered the error. There were two things working against her, and both were significant. One was tradition. The Chinese people revered their ancestors and thus their dead. Grave robbing was unknown in the country, and archaeological digging was considered practically the same: defiling the burial place of someone's ancestors. The second reason was that the present Communist government was walking a very tight rope in how the past was treated. There was fear, foolish fear in Che Lu's opinion, that there might be desire among the peasants for a return to the old imperial days.

Che Lu understood respect for ancestors. But

she thought it was carried a bit too far in China, denying the world, and most particularly the Chinese people, a look into the splendor that had once been the Middle Kingdom. If China was ever going to take its rightful place in the present world order, Che Lu felt it had to acknowledge its power in ancient times *and* understand how that power had been eroded and destroyed by the ignorant and small-minded people who had ruled.

Che Lu had given much to China, and she wanted to see her country regain some of the stature it had held in ancient times. She had participated in much of the history of modern China, often at the cutting edge. Just twenty-six women had started the Long March with Mao sixty-four years ago. Only six had made it to the end alive, Che Lu being one of them as a young fourteen-year-old girl. Over one hundred thousand men had also been there at the start, less than ten thousand remaining alive when they arrived at Yan'an in Shaanxi Province in December 1935 after walking over six thousand miles.

Such a feat should have assured Che Lu a revered place in Communist China, but such were the shifting vagaries of power and influence that she had long ago fallen out of favor with newer regimes. At least she had been able to get schooling and earn her degree in archaeology before she was put on the blacklist.

The Jeep hit a pothole in the dirt road and she felt pain shoot up her spine, a fiery red explosion in the back of her head. Ki turned to make an apology and she waved him to remain silent. Young fools. They knew nothing of suffering.

The two-vehicle convoy was heading west from

Xi'an, the city that had been the first imperial capital in China and the eastern terminus of the Silk Road that had stretched from western China across Central Asia to the Middle East and on to Rome. Che Lu and her associates had arrived there three days earlier and checked in with the local authorities. Things were not much calmer here, a thousand miles away from the turmoil that was brewing in Beijing. The students were growing restless and now the workers were also. The UN disclosure of aliens visiting Earth had seeped its way even into tightly controlled China. Change was in the air all over the globe, and Che Lu feared and hoped that it was coming in China.

She reached into the old straw bag between her legs and pulled out a leather sack. She emptied the contents into the cloth of her skirt that was stretched wide between her legs and looked at the four pieces of bone that lay there. She picked one up and turned it, staring at the marks etched into the white material. The bone was from the hip of some animal, perhaps a deer, triangular in shape, with two long flat sides.

"What are those?" Ki asked.

What did they teach young people at the university? Che Lu wondered. Of course, Ki was a geology major, not archaeology. Most of the students she usually worked with had preferred to remain in Beijing, prepared to participate in whatever happened in the upcoming weeks. That there would be another event like the Tiananmen Square massacre Che Lu had no doubt. She had lived through too many purges and bloodlettings in seventy-eight years to be optimistic that this turmoil would end peacefully. The key issue was would everyone behave like sheep and go back to the status quo after the blood had flowed, like they had in 1989? Che Lu, from listening to her students who politely but firmly declined to come with her, felt this time it would be different.

"They are oracle bones," she answered.

Ki raised an eyebrow, inviting more information. At least he was curious, she would give him that. "They were used in ancient times by diviners to communicate with ancestors." She felt the smooth bone under her wrinkled fingers. "In the beginning was not the city, but the word," she murmured.

"Excuse me?" Ki politely asked.

Che Lu looked up. "Every other developing civilization on Earth was based on the growth of the city. In China, our civilization is based on the written word. In fact, our word for *civilization, wenha,* means 'the transforming influence of writing.'" She held one of the bones closer so he could see the marks on it. "The interesting thing about these bones is that no one can read the writing. Most curious. After all, we had writing long before the rest of the world. But this writing, it predates even our own language."

"Perhaps it is just some form of drawing, Mother-Professor," Ki ventured.

"No, it is writing," Che Lu said.

"Where did you get those?" Ki asked.

"From an old friend."

"And are they important?"

Che Lu nodded but didn't say anything. She didn't trust anyone else yet, although she knew that there was a call she was going to have to make. She wanted to be clear of the monitored phones in Xi'an, though, before doing that.

"Do they relate to Qian-Ling?" Ki asked.

"They were found near the tomb," Che Lu acknowledged. She saw a small town approaching. Tracking the single telephone line to a small store, she indicated for Ki to stop there.

She walked inside and greeted the proprietor. She held out a wad of cash, and asked to use the phone to make a most important call. The cash was more than the proprietor saw in a month, and the old man was most happy to oblige this strange woman.

Che Lu dialed on the old rotary device, getting the local operator. Slowly she worked her way through until she had an international operator in Hong Kong who could make the final connection.

Che Lu stood still in the dilapidated store, watching her young charges buy food for the journey, as she listened to the faint echo of a phone ring on the other side of the world. Finally there was a click, and a distant voice spoke in English.

"This is Peter Nabinger. I'm away from my office, but I do check my machine daily. Please leave your name, number, and a short message and I'll get back to you as quickly as possible."

There was a beep and Che Lu spoke in hushed English. "My name is Professor Che Lu. I am the head archaeologist with the Imperial Museum in Beijing. I understand you can read the high rune language. I have oracle bones in my possession that I believe are inscribed in that language. They were found near the Imperial Tomb of Gao-zang at Qian-Ling. I am going into that tomb. I believe

the tomb may be connected with the Airlia some-
how. If you wish to find me, I will be there."

She put the phone down and turned to her students. "Let us continue on our way."

Chapter 7

It had analyzed the data, received a little over three days ago, quickly, in less than four seconds. The various courses of action, though, were more difficult to determine. More data had been needed. Power had been allocated to sensors, and the wealth of transmitted electronic material that flowed out of Earth's atmosphere had been the target. That took time, and when it was done, there was no clear-cut answer, only probabilities.

The probabilities were weighed and the machine made a decision. A message had been sent to Earth in reply, then the master program was activated. It would take time for the program to run its course.

Waiting didn't bother it. First, because it wasn't alive and second because it had spent millennia waiting to activate the master program. A few more days would not matter.

Chapter 8

Lisa Duncan handed a file folder with a red top-secret cover to Mike Turcotte, then took the seat across from him. They had the entire forward section of the specially modified Air Force 707 to themselves. Behind them the bulk of the aircraft was filled with communications equipment and the military personnel who manned it.

Turcotte picked up the folder and thumbed through. He glanced up as he read the first sheet. "When did you find out there was a transmission to the guardian?"

"Just now," Duncan said. "I've been so busy reporting our find to UNAOC and getting us this flight back to Easter Island that it was my first chance to catch up on things."

The plane was currently somewhere over the Indian Ocean and flying east. They'd left UN Forces securely holding the Terra-Lel compound and UNAOC scientists cautiously puzzling over the strange ruby sphere.

"It just got released worldwide," Duncan added.

"Great," Turcotte said. "Sometimes I think we'd get better intelligence if we just watched CNN."

Turcotte looked at the second page and read the block letters of the message from Mars.

```
GREETINGS
WE ARE OF PEACE
ASPASIA
END
```

"What the hell does this mean?" Turcotte asked.

"That's the part of the message that was in binary and obviously meant for us," Duncan said.

"Aspasia?" Turcotte read out loud. "He's long gone."

"Maybe the computer on Mars doesn't know that. Maybe it's just reacting to the message the guardian sent out and playing back a recording. The important thing, though, is that we now have communication with the computers."

Turcotte turned the page and looked at the photo of the Face on Mars. The next page had a summary of information about the Cydonia region.

"This is some weird stuff," he said.

"Certainly not what anyone expected," Duncan said. "Another guardian computer on Mars?"

"Besides the one we know about under Easter Island," Turcotte said, "there was one from Temiltepec that got destroyed in Dulce. Who knows how many of these things there are? Why did we have to wait to get this?" Turcotte asked.

"Why didn't we get informed before UNAOC made it public?"

"UNAOC didn't want any leaks."

"So they don't trust us."

"You keep talking as if you weren't part of UNAOC," Duncan said, leaning back in the swivel chair bolted to the thinly carpeted cabin floor.

"I'm a soldier in the United States Army and I've been ordered by my chain of command to do this. I'm not happy about it, but there wasn't a happiness clause in my enlistment contract." He looked at her. "You had a seat on Majestic-12. Were you a part of that?"

"You know I wasn't," she answered, a dark line appearing across her forehead.

Turcotte held up his hand. "Hey, don't get upset. I'm just a dumb soldier and that was a rhetorical question. I know you weren't part of what Majestic was doing. But in the same manner I'm not part of what UNAOC is doing." He pointed at the top-secret cover sheet. "This tells me UNAOC is starting to do the same thing Majestic did; thinking it knows better and keeping the truth a hostage to their own aims, even if those aims are public relations."

"You don't trust UNAOC?" Duncan asked.

Turcotte stared at her hard. "Do you, Lisa?" It was the first time he had ever used her first name. If she noticed, there was no indication.

"No, I don't. They didn't bother to brief me on the crashed craft the Russians gave up to UNAOC. Now, that simply might have been a bureaucratic oversight, but then again it might not have. Our experiences the last two weeks have made me a bit more paranoid than I was."

Turcotte laughed. "You were pretty paranoid when I first met you."

"I was doing my job." She pointed at the folder. "I'll tell you one thing about that message, though. It will give the progressives a shot in the arm, and UNAOC is solidly in their camp."

"Why?" Turcotte asked.

"The UN has to be. It's an organization that's trying to bring the world closer together and foster peace. This whole Airlia thing could be the catalyst for that."

Turcotte snorted. "What, a computer says 'We are of peace' and we're supposed to believe it?"

"We'll be at Easter Island soon," Duncan said. "Let's see what's going on when we get there. I don't know if it's going to matter much whether the computer says it's of peace or not, since there's not much it can do on Mars."

"Yeah, well, the one on Easter Island sure did a number on the lab in Dulce using the foo fighters," Turcotte said, "and they're talking to each other."

"Better look at the last page of the report," Duncan said.

Turcotte flipped the page. "Hell, the damn things are flying again," he remarked as he noted the report on the strange flight of the three foo fighters. He reflexively looked out the small round window next to his seat, half expecting to see a foo fighter flying off the plane's wing, but there was nothing but blue sky.

An officer stuck his head in the compartment.

"Ma'am, there's been a reply from the Easter Island guardian to the message from Mars."

"The text?" Duncan asked.

"The entire message was in the same cryptic format that we still haven't been able to figure out from the first message," the officer said. "No specific message for us. Humankind, I mean."

"Great," Turcotte muttered. "So now they're talking to each other and we have no idea what they're saying."

■ ■ ■

Peter Nabinger was looking at the explosion of data the sensors ringing the rim of Rano Kau's crater had just picked up from the Guardian. This message was much longer in duration than the first one, lasting almost a full three minutes of highly compressed data.

Nabinger paused as he reviewed the incomprehensible numbers and letters of the reply. They still hadn't deciphered the first one yet. Nor had they been able to decipher the message sent from Mars, other than the binary part. Nabinger stared hard at the screen, scrolling through, looking for anything that might be familiar or indicate that the computers were using the high rune language.

After twenty minutes he pushed back from his desk in disgust. This wasn't his field and wasn't what he should be doing. He felt like he was missing something important. He shoved his spiral notebook of high rune translations into his leather backpack and stood up. He walked out of the UNAOC operations center and went to the press tent, his mind a fog of swirling letters and numbers.

"Things seem to be jumping," Kelly Reynolds greeted him as he came up to the entrance to the tent. The other reporters were at the UNAOC operations center, waiting to hear the official word if anything broke on the latest message. Kelly knew that any official word would come out of the UN in New York, so she'd stayed at the tent, hoping that Nabinger would show up.

She joined him and they walked toward the rim of the crater overlooking the Pacific. From their vantage point they could see the entire island. Roughly triangular in shape, Easter Island was less than fifteen miles across at its widest point. It had been given its English name by a Dutch explorer who happened to land there on Easter Day. Looking down, Kelly could see one of the *ahu*s or stone burial platforms that supported a row of four of the large megaliths. Each was over thirty feet high and weighed over twenty tons. It had always been a great mystery not only how the statues had been moved to their locations from the sides of the volcano where they were carved, but why they were carved in the first place.

"Do you think the Airlia helped move the statues?" Kelly asked, sensing Nabinger's dark mood.

"Huh?" Nabinger looked down. "No. It's been proven that using trees as rollers and ropes and a system of pulleys, the early islanders could move them."

"But they do represent the Airlia?"

"A legend of the Airlia," Nabinger said vaguely. "You've seen the Mars message?" Nabinger said, changing the subject.

"UNAOC just released it worldwide out of New York," Kelly said.

"You know our guardian sent a reply a little while ago?"

"Yes, but UNAOC is controlling all information. Plus, there's not much to report on that, is there?"

"No," Nabinger agreed, "there isn't."

"What about the foo fighters flying again?" Kelly asked.

"Two of the flights I can figure out," Nabinger said.

"What do you mean?"

"Their flight paths. One checked out the Great Pyramid at Giza where the rebels left the nuclear weapon, and the other overflew Temiltepec where the rebels left their computer. The guardian is taking a look-see at where the rebels once were."

"What about the third flight over China?"

"I don't know about that," Nabinger said. "There may be something hidden there we haven't uncovered yet. I've tried correlating those two specific sites with the general area in China against the Airlia 'coordinates' I have, but it doesn't work. I need a specific site in China to be able to do it." Nabinger rubbed a tired hand along the stubble on his chin. "What's the reaction in the outside world?" he asked. "I've been so busy in the op center, I haven't had a chance to see or hear anything."

"Mixed," Kelly said. "On one hand people are happy about the peace thing, on the other they're disappointed that it just appears to be an old recording by a machine on Mars."

"It's not an old recording," Nabinger said.

Kelly perked up. "Why do you say that?"

"Because it was in binary that we understand

with our present technology," he said. "That message was directed toward humans. My best guess is that our guardian here sent the first message to Mars four days ago, including information it had gathered about us. The computer on Mars analyzed the information and sent a reply back to us and the guardian."

"Guardian Two is what they're calling the one on Mars," Kelly noted.

"Hmm, yes," Nabinger said, but his attention was obviously elsewhere.

Kelly considered calling in to the news service that the message wasn't old, but she realized someone else had to have figured that out already and it would hardly be news.

"Hey," Kelly said, tapping him on the arm. "What's the matter?"

"Huh? Nothing."

"You've been wandering around in a fog for the past couple of days. Something's up."

Nabinger shrugged. "I don't know. I'm just bothered by . . ." He paused as they saw several people running toward the press tent.

"Something's happening," Kelly said. The two of them ran toward the green canvas tent. They pushed their way in behind the other people staring at the small TV set. A broadcast of CNN relayed from the American naval task force offshore was playing. They caught the broadcaster breathlessly repeating her news:

"This just released from UNAOC in New York City. There has been a second message from the Guardian Two computer on Mars. The entire text of this new message is in the binary form that part of the first was in. We are waiting on the translation of the message that has been promised us by a UNAOC spokeswoman. It will . . ." The announcer paused. "Yes, it is coming in now. We will put it up on the screen for you to read as we get it."

In bold black letters, words began to scroll up the screen.

```
GREETINGS
WE ARE OF PEACE
WE HAVE WAITED LONG FOR THIS
BUT NOW WE CAN COME BACK
NOW THAT YOU ARE READY
TO JOIN US
WE WILL AWAKE
AND COME BACK TO YOUR PLANET
ASPASIA
END
```

"Oh, my God," Kelly muttered as the inside of the tent broke out in bedlam. She staggered outside with Nabinger. "They're up there," she said, looking into the sky. "They've been up there all this time. That's where they went!"

Chapter 9

"**T**hose are the statues of the sixty-one foreign ambassadors and rulers who attended the funeral of Gao-zong," Che Lu said as they slowly drove down the wide dirt road that led to Qian-Ling.

"How come their heads are gone, Mother-Professor?" Ki asked, staring at the large stone figures that stood in rows at the side of the road.

"No one knows," she said. Her attention was focused on what lay directly ahead. Rising up in front of them, over three thousand feet high, lay the mountain that was Qian-Ling. It was the largest tomb in the world, dwarfing even the pyramids of Egypt and the large dirt mounds in the Americas. The sides of the mountain were covered in trees and bushes, but it was easy to see that it was not a natural formation, as the sides had a uniform slope leading up to a rounded top.

They were traveling down the same road the funeral procession for the Emperor Gao-zong had taken so many years ago. Che Lu felt the familiar tingle of touching the past, the feeling that had determined her destiny for her so many years ago when she'd first passed through the Great Wall in the company of Mao.

Her attention was distracted from the massive hill, though, by the sight of several trucks and tanks parked across the road a kilometer ahead. She could make out the men in the green uniforms and the guns in their hands clustered around the vehicles.

"What should I do?" Ki asked, slowing the Jeep.

"Go up to them. We have permission," Che Lu said. The immediate area for several kilometers around was unpopulated, being designated a historic district. She could think of no reason why the army would be here unless someone in Beijing had wised up. If that were the case she knew from hard experience it would be better to face this head-on than run.

But as she slowly stepped out of the Jeep and met the soldiers, she noticed that they seemed as surprised by her presence as she was by theirs. The officer in charge of the checkpoint carefully read the letter from the Ministry of Antiquities giving Che Lu permission to be here.

"Will you be entering the tomb?" he asked.

Che Lu shook her head. "We will be doing some measurements on the outside. That is all."

The officer frowned but the letter had the proper signatures and seals. "Be careful. There are bandits in the area. I take no responsibility for your safety on the mountain."

"Bandits?" Ki asked. They drove away from the checkpoint, beginning their ascent up the side of the mountain toward the entrance, leaving the soldiers behind and out of sight as they went around the western shoulder.

"Anyone the government does not like is a bandit," Che Lu said. "I was a bandit once myself." She smiled. "And there is one now," she added, pointing at a wizened old man who had just materialized on the road in front of them, standing as still as one of the statues.

He wore a faded blue shirt and black pants. He carried an AK-47 in his gnarled hands and battered army-issue pack on his back.

"My dead friend, Lo Fa!" Che Lu cried out as Ki stopped the Jeep.

"Ah, you old hag," Lo Fa spat into the dirt.

"You old goat," Che Lu returned as she hugged him. She looked past him, where the road disappeared between two large boulders. "Are we ready?"

"I have removed the earth," Lo Fa said. "I did it at night. Those fool soldiers wouldn't know it if you dropped a rock on their heads. I had friends help. But their friendship only goes so far," he added. He had one eye that was dead, completely white, so he spoke with his head twisted, good eye forward.

"You have no friends," Che Lu said. "Only scoundrels you keep company with." She held out a small packet filled with bills and it disappeared into Lo Fa's tunic. "For your friends."

"They will remain my friends now." Lo Fa smiled, revealing broken and yellowed teeth. "Let us go, quickly, and get off this road. You have permission to break the seal?" he asked as he jumped into the back of the Jeep.

"Yes."

With Ki driving slowly, the truck following, they went between the massive boulders. There were statues of tigers perched on top of each one. The boulders enclosed a small courtyard, about thirty meters wide by fifteen long. The side of the mountain was cut into, revealing two massive bronze doors covered with writing. A large pile of dirt was pushed to the side, Lo Fa's work for the past two weeks since Che Lu had contacted him. She knew they wouldn't have much time and she hadn't wanted to waste it digging to the doors.

"This way." Lo Fa was out of the Jeep, surprisingly agile. He walked up to the doors, Che Lu and the others following. He pointed at the barely visible seam between the two panels. "The Old Ones sealed it with molten bronze."

One of Che Lu's students was filming the doors with a videocamera, recording them for posterity. They had not seen the light of day for over two thousand years.

"How do we open them?" Che Lu asked.

"It is not my problem," Lo Fa said. "You told me only to uncover the doors."

"I told you to get me in," Che Lu said.

Lo Fa spit again, then gave a crooked grin. "Yes, that you did." He slipped off his backpack. He reached in and pulled out a long line of blue cord. "Have your students tape it to the seam, from top to bottom."

"What is it?" Che Lu asked as she waved a couple of her male students to do as he bid.

"Detonating cord. Explosive," Lo Fa said.

The students paused, looking at the cord in their hands in fear.

"Ah, it won't explode until I put a blasting cap in the end," Lo Fa snarled.

"And where did you get that?" Che Lu asked.

"The army is very careless," Lo Fa said. "It always surprises me when they manage to put their boots on the correct feet."

"Why is the army here?" Che Lu asked him as he prepared the detonator.

Lo Fa spit. "This time the trouble is not just students in Tiananmen Square. There is real trouble. People are tired and they want change." He pointed at the mountain tomb that dwarfed them. "This once was China, the center of civilization. Now with this talk of aliens, people no longer know what to believe and the agitators are seizing the opportunity to push for change, to regain China's place in the world. It is easier said than done."

"But you have not said specifically why the army is here," Che Lu chided him.

Lo Fa straightened and stared at her with his good eye. "They are here specifically, old woman, to fight rebels."

"Rebels?" Che Lu wondered if she had spent too much time in the library at the university. "There is open rebellion?"

"There is fighting. Especially among the Muslim people who live in this province. They owe no loyalty to Beijing."

"I have heard nothing."

"That is the government's desire." Lo Fa had a small metal cap in his hand that he was attaching to the end of the blue cord. "It is not hard for them to suppress news from such faraway places as this province. When thousands die here in

floods the world never knows because the government doesn't want them to know. You can be sure
they do not want word of fighting to spread."

"How serious is it?" Che Lu asked.

Lo Fa was done rigging the blasting cap. "I
would be very quick about your business here and
be gone as fast as you can. In fact, old lady, if I
was you, I would go home now."

"I can't do that," Che Lu said.

"I should have never sent you those oracle
bones." The old man's voice lowered. "There is
something else."

"What?"

Lo Fa looked about the mountainside above
them nervously. "I've heard there are foreigners
about the area."

"Foreigners?"

"Rumors. The army was on the mountain four
days ago. There were explosions and weapons firing on the other side. I don't know what they were
doing. That is all I have heard. That is all I
know."

The cord was laid and Lo Fa put the cord from
the blasting cap into a small detonator. He waved
them all back. He looked at Che Lu. "I hope you
know what you are doing, old woman. This tomb
has not been opened since the emperor's retain-
ers sealed it. Perhaps it is best to leave it be."

"Superstitious?" Che Lu asked.

"No," Lo Fa replied in a strangely serious tone
of voice. "It is just that I do not like meddling
with things beyond me."

"This is not beyond me," Che Lu said confi-
dently, but inside she wondered. She had been
teaching too long and it had been many years

since she'd been on a dig, and never in her many long years had she been on one as potentially important as this one.

Lo Fa hesitated for the briefest of seconds, then pulled the ring on the top of the detonator. There was a flash and crack, the sound confined in the courtyard.

Che Lu winced when she saw the damage done to the doors, but there was no other way. A black line was singed into the bronze along the seam, with a small opening about chest high.

"The jack from the Jeep," Lo Fa ordered. He took the jack and, jamming it into the hole, began cranking the handle. With a groan the doors slowly swung open. A dry rush of cool air swept over the small party standing in the courtyard, causing all to shiver.

"Your tomb," Lo Fa said with a wave of his hand. "I am done here." He slung his backpack over his shoulder. "Che Lu, I would leave now."

Before she could respond, he had already disappeared out of the courtyard.

Several students turned on flashlights, and with Che Lu leading the way, they entered the tomb. Right inside the doors was a large anteroom. The light of the lanterns flickered off the walls. They were painted with many pictures of women and men in royal garb. Che Lu had seen similar pictures many times before. There was something different about these, however, something that caused her to pause, before moving on, but she couldn't put her finger on what troubled her.

A wide tunnel beckoned, leading into the heart of the mountain. With firm steps Che Lu led the students down the tunnel. It ran ten meters wide and was perfectly straight as far as the glow from the lights would penetrate the inky blackness. One of the students put his light next to the wall and they all stared at the smoothly cut stone. Che Lu tried to imagine the state of craftsmanship that could make such smooth walls with hand tools, and she felt a chill run down her bent spine. The Old Ones had certainly been masters of the stone.

There was no dust and the air was dry, the slightest odor of decay carried on it. Che Lu paused after about two hundred meters. There was writing on the walls where two smaller tunnels split off to each side at ninety-degree angles. She took a flashlight from one of her students and held it so she could see.

High runes. There was no mistaking the hieroglyphics. She pointed and the female student with the camera flicked on the power, lighting the wall, and quickly filmed it, then shut down to preserve the batteries.

As Che Lu turned to continue down the main tunnel, a dim red glow appeared about twenty meters in that direction. "Hold!" Che Lu ordered her startled students. Her mouth was dry and she ran her tongue over her chapped lips, watching. She did not believe in ghosts but she was old enough to know there was much she didn't know.

The red glow began to change shape from a circle, stretching and narrowing, touching the floor. The form of a person began to coalesce, but an oddly shaped person, legs and arms too long, body short, a large head covered with red hair like fire. The skin was pure white, looking like un-blemished ivory. The ears had long lobes that almost touched the shoulders. It was the eyes, though, that held Che Lu's attention. They were bright red under fierce red eyebrows and the pupils were elongated like a cat's.

The figure wavered in the dusty air, the corridor behind dimly visible through it. The right arm rose up, a six-fingered hand on the end, palm open toward them. A deep, guttural sound echoed up the tunnel, coming from the figure, although how the image could produce it, Che Lu had no idea. The language was singsong, almost familiar, but there wasn't a word she recognized.

The figure spoke for almost a minute, then faded out of sight, leaving the scared group of students huddled around their mother-professor, who truth be said, was more than a little frightened herself for the first time.

Chapter 10

·············

Viking II had traveled an elliptical path of over 422 million miles to Mars after being launched in 1976. In the twenty-plus years that had passed since it went into orbit, it had relayed data from its lander and used its outdated orbital sensors to gain information on the Red Planet. It should have gone off-line a decade ago, but the numerous failures in other Mars probes had forced NASA's Jet Propulsion Laboratory (JPL) to try to eke every extra day of service out of the aging probe. Days past its projected life had turned into months, months into years, and over a decade past its launch it was still functioning. It had finally been shut down the previous year when *Pathfinder* had arrived with great fanfare.

Now it was receiving the radio messages telling it to wake up; there was one more task to accomplish, a task more important than any it had done before.

As the electronic instructions were routed through a computer more antiquated than that in any high-school library, the machinery began to come alive. The maneuvering thrusters on the Viking II Orbiter fired and the satellite circling Mars slowly changed paths, its orbit disturbed for the first time in over two years.

■ ■ ■

At JPL, the place where the commands firing those engines were being generated, there was great concern about the status of the *Viking II* Orbiter. Mars was cursed, at least that was the firm opinion of Larry Kincaid, the director of all JPL Mars missions once they left the orbit of Earth. He still felt that way even after the success of *Pathfinder*. Driving around looking at a couple of rocks wasn't something he considered a great success. True, getting *Pathfinder* down in one piece had been something to feel good about for a while, but this achievement was overshadowed by the long and troubled history of Mars missions.

Kincaid had been at JPL since 1962, starting as a junior flight engineer. He'd been present in the control room for the first Mars-probe launching, *Mariner 3,* on November 5, 1964. He'd watched the reactions of the other scientists as the spacecraft's protective shroud failed to jettison after leaving Earth's atmosphere, causing complete mission failure.

Mariner 4, launched just twenty-three days later, made it close to Mars but its low-resolution camera sent back little useful information.

Kincaid also knew the history of Russian spacecraft sent in the direction of Mars. The Soviet *Mars 1* probe failed to make it out of Earth's orbit. *Mars 2* and *3* made it to the red planet, but the probes they dropped went dead immediately. *Mars 4* missed the planet entirely. *Mars 5* made it into orbit, but the pictures it sent back were even poorer than *Mariner 4*'s. *Mars 6* made it there also, but its lander sent back some very confusing data on the way down before going dead. *Mars 7* missed the planet.

All in all, a Mars mission had been the one place in JPL new engineers did not want to be assigned. Even with all the hubbub over *Pathfinder's* Rover running around, the cursed history of Mars exploration affected even the rational scientific types who came to work at JPL.

Of course, that had all changed with the message from the Guardian Two computer at Cydonia. Now everybody wanted to know everything there was to know about Mars, and that region in particular, and there really wasn't anything to tell or show them other than the distant images taken from orbit and from the Hubble.

Unfortunately, the Hubble couldn't see much. Even at the best refraction possible the Hubble could show Mars only as a four-inch sphere. Not exactly enough to show details, particularly about the Cydonia region. And *Pathfinder* and its Rover were stuck where they had landed, much too far away to do any good. Thus the fallback to the only current orbiter around the planet: *Viking II*.

Kincaid oversaw the action as his crew began moving *Viking II* so it could take a look at Cydonia, but his mind wasn't on it. He was wondering how much these aliens having a base at Cydonia had to do with all the disasters that had plagued the American and Russian Mars missions. As an engineer he was not a big believer in coincidences, particularly when it came to mechanical objects. The various malfunctions and failures that had plagued the American and Russian Mars probes went far beyond statistical possibility due to random chance.

Kincaid had known that for years, he just hadn't known *why*. He'd heard the other whispers around JPL and NASA over the years. The strange lights that had shadowed *Apollo 11*. The disturbing fact that no space shuttle was allowed to downlink a live video feed—it had to be sent through a special NSA office at NASA where it was viewed first and, perhaps, edited. The questions about the fuel tank failure on *Apollo 13*. So many inexplicable occurrences had taken place over the years in the space program. Kincaid was not a religious man who believed they were all acts of God. He was a scientist and he believed that there was always a cause that could be explained. Now it was obvious, though, that they had been missing some of the important data that was needed to formulate the explanation.

Kincaid could see the status of the *Viking II* orbiter on the large display board in the front of the room as the rockets began moving it. He could also see the status of the other current Mars mission besides *Pathfinder: Mars Global Surveyor*. It had been launched in November of 1996 and reached Mars in September of 1997. The only problem was that *Surveyor* had been hit by the same gremlin as the other missions. A solar array had never completely deployed and because of that, the aerobrakes had not worked properly when it arrived at Mars, the craft thus failing to attain a stable orbit around the planet. It was up there and they had been doing the best they could over the last several months to achieve a working orbit, but they were still several months away from accomplishing that. So far they had been satisfied with not completely losing the craft either by having it shoot off away from Mars or really screwing up and putting it into Mars's gravity well and having it impact with the planet.

No one had looked past *Viking* yet, but Kincaid knew they eventually would, and when they did, he had no doubt that *Surveyor*'s mission profile would be changed and the powers-that-be would want *Surveyor* sent over Cydonia, even if it meant losing the orbiter completely on a one-shot deal. And it would be Kincaid's job to make the change.

Surveyor had a payload of six scientific instruments designed to check out the planet's surface. It also carried a powerful camera that would be able to photograph the surface in greater detail than ever before. And it held more than that. Kincaid glanced over at a mirror that lined the left side of the control center. He knew there was someone behind it watching what was happening, and not just someone from JPL. There had been a stranger there for every major launch and mission since Kincaid had been at JPL, and he had no doubt the current situation had brought the stranger back again.

"All right, people," he called out, catching the attention of the duty crew. "Let's get our heads out of our asses and think. Let's get beyond *Viking II*. I want a projected TCMs for *Surveyor* that will put it over Cydonia, initiating correction one hour from now through next week." Kincaid could see the grimaces on the faces of his crew. A TCM was a trajectory correction maneuver, and it required considerable math to figure out how long and what kind of burn would be needed to change the craft's current path to the desired one, especially difficult with *Surveyor* because of its current erratic orbit.

He knew that if his last order bothered them, the next one was going to burst some blood vessels, but it had come straight from the NSA and he was under strict orders from NASA to comply. Once more Kincaid glanced at the mirrors on the wall and wondered who was behind them and who had made this strange request.

"I want the IMS extended, turned on, and focused on Cydonia. At the range the probe currently is at, we should get some good shots back every so often when it comes close. Not as good as what *Viking* will get directly overhead, but it will give us an idea what's going on, plus be a backup for *Viking*."

His senior payload specialist's mouth had dropped open at the first sentence, and the man had remained speechless while he assimilated what he was being told to do. IMS stood for Imager Mars Surveyor. It was a stereo imaging system that was loaded into the orbiter. It consisted of three subassemblies: a camera head, an extendable mast designed to rise up once the craft was in stable orbit, and two electric cards, one of which controlled the camera and arm motors and the other that processed the images.

"Jesus, Kincaid," the man finally blurted, "you can't open the payload with the probe still spinning like it is!"

"Why not?" Kincaid asked.

"It's not designed to work that way."

"I know how it's designed," Kincaid said. "I know as well as you do. And I don't see any real problem with extending and turning the camera on early and taking a look-see. Just because it wasn't designed to work that way doesn't mean we can't do it."

"But we'd have to extend the able mast," the payload specialist continued. "I don't think we can do that with rotation like it is."

Sometimes Kincaid wondered about the new breed of engineer they were getting here. He had severe doubts as to whether they would have been able to improvise and gotten *Apollo 13* home, as those whom Kincaid had worked with three decades ago had.

"You don't *think*?" Kincaid repeated. He turned to a mock-up of the probe on his desk. "I think you can. If you open this panel the camera will extend. Right?"

"Right, but—"

"But the centrifugal force multiplies as the mast extends," Kincaid finished the sentence. "We do have control over the mast, don't we? We don't have to extend all the way. Just enough to clear the door panel."

Kincaid didn't wait for any more argument. "Get working on it. You all seem confused by something. I'm not asking you to do this. I'm telling you to do it. I want a picture from *Surveyor* of Cydonia within two hours."

■ ■ ■

Area 51 was the unclassified designation on military maps for a training area on the Nellis Air Force Base. At least that's what the military had maintained for years. In actuality Area 51 had housed a top-secret installation burrowed into Groom Mountain featuring the longest runway in the world along the bed of adjacent Groom Lake.

While a few of the facilities were aboveground, the majority were built into and below the side of the mountain next to the runway. The location had been chosen by the original Majestic-12 committee after the mothership had been found hidden in a nearby cavern. More hangars had been hollowed out over the years to house the bouncers, small atmospheric craft, two of which had been discovered with the mothership, the other seven recovered from a cache in Antarctica.

Over the years Majestic-12 had trained select Air Force pilots in the art of flying the bouncers. The secret of entry into the mothership had eluded MJ-12 until earlier in the year when members of the committee had been mentally taken over by the rebel guardian computer uncovered at a dig in Temiltepec and brought back to MJ-12's other secret site at Dulce, New Mexico.

When MJ-12's secrets were finally exposed, Area 51's shroud had been torn asunder. The media had now descended upon the site, gobbling up images of the massive black mothership resting in its newly dug-out cavern and the bouncers being put through their paces by Air Force pilots. What had once been the most secret place in America was now the most photographed and visited.

Major Quinn had been operations officer at Area 51, but he had survived the purge of MJ-12 personnel because he had not been on the inner circle taken over by the guardian. He was the one man left who knew all the inner workings of the Area 51 facility and the Cube, the acronym for C3, Command and Control Central.

The underground room housing the Cube measured eighty by a hundred feet and could only be reached from the massive bouncer hangar cut into the side of Groom Mountain via a large freight elevator.

Quinn was of medium height and build. He had thinning blond hair and wore tortoiseshell glasses with oversized lenses to accommodate the split glass he needed for both distance and close-up viewing.

He sat in the seat in the back of the room that gave him a full view of every operation now in process. In front of him, sloping down toward the front, were three rows of consoles manned by military personnel. On the forward wall was a twenty-foot-wide by ten-high screen. It was capable of displaying any information that could be channeled through the computers.

Directly behind Quinn a door led to a corridor off of which branched a conference room, his office and sleeping quarters, rest rooms, and a small galley. The freight elevator opened on the right side of the main gallery. There was the quiet hum of machinery in the room, along with the slight hiss of filtered air being pushed by large fans in the hangar above. Quinn had been down here for four straight days, dealing with the unfamiliar responsibility of opening the facility to the world's media and integrating members of UNAOC onto the staff.

Now that the bouncers fell under UNAOC control, as did all pieces of Airlia artifact, every foreign country that boasted an air force had sent its best pilots to be trained on flying the bouncers. The U.S. Air Force was quickly putting in place courses at Area 51 to do just that. Quinn also had to schedule in the hordes of scientists demanding access to all the scientific data the computers in the Cube held, along with giving them direct access to the mothership.

All in all Quinn was one busy man, in what had suddenly become a very sensitive position. It was a long way from just two weeks ago when his major concerns had been doing General Gullick's bidding and maintaining security of the facility from those who continually tried to pierce its former veil of secrecy.

Quinn looked down at the small laptop screen in front of him and did a status check. The mainframe quickly informed him that five bouncers were being test-flown at the current moment; Bouncer 6 was overseas, visiting Moscow as part of UNAOC's program to spread the wealth around; Bouncer 7 was traveling around the United States; Bouncers 8 and 9 were in Europe; and a mixed group of Russian and NATO scientists were exploring the mothership.

"Sir, we've got an inbound chopper clearing perimeter," one of the men in the room called out.

Quinn frowned at the unnecessary disturbance. They had dozens of aircraft flying in and out every day now. The airspace was no longer restricted and the base was open. "And?" Quinn asked.

"It's coming in under an ST-8 classified authorization code."

"What the hell is that?" Quinn had had the highest possible classified clearance while working for Majestic and he had never heard of ST-8.

"I don't know, sir. I can't access it from my position."

Quinn quickly cleared his screen and entered his code word. He typed in the classification. His screen cleared and a message appeared:

```
RENDER ALL ASSISTANCE ASKED TO BEARER
OF ST-8 TOP SECRET CLEARANCE.
    THIS CLASSIFICATION BY ORDER OF THE
NATIONAL COMMAND AUTHORITY.
    YOU ARE TO RENDER ALL ASSISTANCE RE-
QUESTED AS TOP PRIORITY
    ALL ACTIVITY IS TOP SECRET ST-8 LEVEL
AND NOT TO BE DISCLOSED IN ANY MANNER.
    NO RECORDS OF ACTIVITY TO BE MAIN-
TAINED.
    ST-8 TOP SECRET
```

"Shit," Quinn muttered. What that told him was that he couldn't even inform his own chain of command and he had to do whatever those on the helicopter told him to. "Put the chopper on-screen."

A black UH-60 helicopter appeared over the runway. It landed and rolled forward. The side doors opened and a woman got out. Quinn unconsciously leaned forward. She was tall, over six feet, and slender, but what he noticed most was her shockingly white hair, cut tight to her skull. Her eyes were hidden by wrap-around sunglasses. She carried a metal briefcase in her left hand and wore black pants, and a black jacket with a black shirt with no collar underneath.

"Bring her to conference room," Quinn ordered, standing up and going out the rear door. He walked into the room and sat at then end of the table. He didn't have long to wait before the door opened. The woman walked in, coming around to the left of the large table. Quinn stood to greet her.

"I am Oleisa," the woman said. She put her briefcase on the table.

"Major Quinn," he said, extending his hand, but the woman ignored it, taking her seat. Quinn hurriedly followed suit. "I looked up your clearance and it said—"

"To do whatever I tell you to do," Oleisa smoothly cut him off. "I require you to detail a bouncer with your top pilot to be at my disposal from this moment until further notice. That craft is not to be used for any other purpose."

Quinn inwardly groaned. He saw a carefully prepared schedule crumble. "Who do you work for?"

"That is not a concern of yours," Oleisa said.

"I'm in charge here and—"

"You are a caretaker," she said. "You are not in charge. You are to do what you are told. A bouncer with pilot at my disposal. I also require a secure satellite communications link dedicated to my use."

■ ■ ■

On Easter Island, Mike Turcotte and Lisa Duncan were greeted by Kelly Reynolds and Peter Nabinger as they entered Reynolds's tent. The other members of the media were at the UNAOC Operations Center, waiting to see if there was to be another message from Guardian one in reply to Guardian two latest.

Turcotte and Duncan had landed several hours earlier and been briefed on everything that had occurred. Their report on the find in Ethiopia had been relayed to UNAOC during their flight back, but it seemed to have been submerged in the excitement over the second message from Mars.

Duncan's guess as to the ruby sphere's purpose had been savaged by UNAOC scientists who were trying to pick up the work that had been started by the Terra-Lel scientists. Turcotte didn't think UNAOC would have much more success than Terra-Lel, considering that the latter had had over sixteen years to work in the cavern. The initial consensus of the scientists was that the ruby sphere was some sort of mining device. Turcotte thought that was simply wishful thinking on the part of men and women who weren't used to dealing with things that were beyond their level of education and experience. For all they knew, Turcotte figured the ruby sphere could be some sort of religious object, much like a crucifix in a church. He hoped it was something like that and not what Duncan had guessed.

A storm was passing by, and the patter of rain on canvas drowned out the sound of the surf. Turcotte could feel a thin line of water running down his back. He'd enjoyed the walk in the rain from UNAOC operations to the tent. He glanced at Lisa Duncan. Her khaki clothes were dark with water, her hair plastered against her head. She caught his glance and raised an eyebrow in inquiry. Turcotte quickly turned his attention back to the others.

"What do you think?" he asked Nabinger, who was looking at photos of the cavern and the ruby sphere spread out on one of the cots.

"I have no idea," Nabinger replied. He focused on a picture of the Airlia console. "I can't read the high rune writing like this. It looks like what's down in our cavern here on the island, and you can't read all the high runes on the control console until it's powered up and backlit."

Turcotte grabbed the pictures and shuffled through them until he came upon the one that showed the black stone. "What about that?"

Nabinger looked at it for a moment, then took out his notebook. He pulled a pencil out of his pocket. "Give me a minute," he said.

The others in the tent waited for five minutes, listening to the sound of the rain and the water running down the outside of the tent, before he looked up. "Some of this isn't high rune."

"What language is it?" Kelly Reynolds asked.

"The nearest I can make out," he said, "is that some of this is in Chinese."

"Chinese?" Turcotte was surprised. "How the hell did Chinese writing get in a cavern in Africa with Airlia artifacts?"

"I don't know," Nabinger said. "The high rune part is, as usual, hard to make out, but as best I can figure it says something like:

```
THE CHIEF SHIP NEGATIVE FLY
ENGINE POWER
DANGER
ALL THINGS CONSUMED
```

"This," Nabinger said, "is very similar to what I got off the pictures of the high rune stones left with the mothership and the *rongo-rongo* tablets from here."

"I don't get it," Duncan said. "What does this cavern in the Rift Valley and the ruby sphere have to do with the mothership?"

"And with China?" Nabinger added, looking at the photo of the black stone.

"I don't like that all-things-consumed part," Turcotte said. He looked at Duncan. "Sounds too much like your doomsday-device idea."

"Curiouser and curiouser," Nabinger said, staring at the photo. He turned to Kelly Reynolds. "Do you have that satellite phone the network gave you?"

She handed it over, but not without comment. "I wouldn't worry too much about the ruby sphere. We'll have all the answers soon."

"Why do you think that?" Turcotte asked.

"Aspasia's coming."

"What, he's rising from the dead?" Turcotte said.

Kelly ignored him and addressed Duncan. "Do you think Aspasia and the other Airlia with him have been in suspended animation?"

"It's a possibility, but we can't be sure of anything right now," Duncan said. She turned to Nabinger. "You're the language expert. How do you read the message sent from Mars?"

Nabinger looked up from dialing. "The same as you. After all, it's not in high rune but English encoded in binary. I don't think it was Aspasia who sent the message, but rather the Guardian II computer, and now I think it's implementing a program to bring Aspasia back to consciousness from whatever state he's been in."

"Do you think they can do that?" Duncan asked.

"That's the way I read the message," Nabinger said with a shrug. "Hell, they built the mothership and the bouncers. I'm sure suspended animation is not beyond their technical capabilities. I'm amazed that no one thought of it before as being what happened to the Airlia."

"No one thought of it," Turcotte said, "because we never found any sign of the actual aliens here on Earth."

"Now you know why," Nabinger said. "They're on Mars."

"How'd they learn English?" Turcotte asked.

"Probably from intercepted radio and TV transmissions," Nabinger said. "It wouldn't take a computer like the guardian long to decipher our language."

"It's fantastic," Kelly said. "Imagine, not only will we soon meet our first extraterrestrial life, but life that was present on Earth over five thousand years ago! How do you think they got to Mars?" Kelly asked. "Another mothership? Or some other craft?"

"If they fly a mothership back here from Mars," Turcotte said, "wouldn't that bring the Kortad?"

"Maybe they have contact with their home planet," Nabinger said. "The war is probably over. It's been five thousand years." He put the phone to his ear and turned his back to the conversation for the moment.

"There's a lot we don't know," Turcotte said.

"But we're going to find out!" Kelly was pacing

about the tent. "It's just fantastic. Here we were, hoping that at best we could access the guardian computer. Now we have the people who built the thing coming!"

"That was our best hope," Turcotte acknowledged. "What about our worst fears?"

"Oh, you're always so pessimistic," Kelly said, thumping a fist into his shoulder.

"Didn't your dad teach to always worst-case things?" Turcotte asked. He knew that her father had been a member of the Office of Strategic Services (OSS), the forerunner to the CIA, during World War II.

"Oh, give me a break," Kelly said. "Aspasia saved mankind by defeating the rebel Airlia five thousand years ago and leaving us alone to develop. The facts speak for themselves."

"Then why's he coming back now?" Turcotte wanted to know. "Isn't that interference?"

"Because we're ready now. We weren't five thousand years ago. He tells us that in the message."

"Don't you think . . ." Turcotte began, but he could see the enthusiasm in Kelly's eyes and he just couldn't bring up the negative strength to fight it. He had vague feeling of unease, not the thrill of anticipation of first live contact with an alien race like she did.

He noticed that Nabinger had gotten off the phone and was looking at a pad on which he had made some notes. "What's up?" Nabinger seemed quite preoccupied.

Nabinger looked up. "I got a contact I can fax the Chinese writing to and get a translation. I also

had a message on my answering service. Someone's found a place with more high runes."

"Where?" Turcotte asked.

Nabinger smiled. "China."

"China?" Turcotte repeated. "Well, isn't that
nice. What a coincidence."

"Yep," Nabinger said. "It's not surprising that
the Airlia were there too. Remember, they did
have the bouncers to fly. They could go anywhere
on the face of this planet in a matter of minutes."

"How come we haven't heard anything from
China before now?" Kelly asked.

"Same reason the Russians just offered up their
crashed Airlia craft," Nabinger said. "Probably
keeping it secret for their own reasons. Or, even
more likely, the Chinese don't know they have
Airlia artifacts. Traditionally, the Chinese are very
reluctant to do any sort of archaeological work."

"Remember the third foo fighter did a flyby
over China," Turcotte said. "You can be sure the
guardian knows something we don't."

"The guardian knows a lot of things we don't,"
Nabinger said.

Turcotte looked at him. "There something you
aren't telling us?"

The professor shrugged. "Hell, I got hit with so
much when I was in contact with the guardian,
there's a lot that I don't know I know."

Turcotte wasn't satisfied with that answer, but
he didn't think now was a time to push Nabinger,
especially with the way Kelly was acting. He went
back to thinking about China. "One of those foo
fighters overflew the Great Pyramid, where the
rebel Airlia left an atomic weapon. Another overflew Temiltepec, where the rebels left their guard-

ian computer. What do you think could be in China? Who left you the message?" Turcotte asked.

"An archaeologist named Che Lu. I know of her. She's head of archaeology at Beijing University."

"Well, whatever she has can't be that important now," Kelly said. "Hell, we'll have the man himself here soon to speak for himself."

"The man?" Turcotte asked.

"Aspasia."

"Why do you call him a man?" Turcotte didn't wait for an answer. "He, if we can call it a he, is an alien. Not a human. Not a man."

The tent went silent for a few seconds, Kelly staring at Turcotte in surprise, her face turning red with anger.

Before she could retort, Lisa Duncan spoke. "How would high runes in China fit into all this? I think we need to back up and take a hard look at things with a new perspective. Especially now that we have what appears to be Chinese writing in Africa next to high runes near the ruby sphere. What's the connection?"

"The high rune language"—Nabinger laughed —"well, we call it a language now, but actually no one knew it was until just a month ago. I'd been studying hieroglyphics, the earliest known form of writing, for many years, particularly that in the three pyramids at Giza, and I noticed that there were some markings that didn't fit traditional hieroglyphics.

"I expanded my search and found examples of that writing at other places on the face of the planet, although I didn't have access to data from

China. But all the examples I did find seemed to come from the same root language. And the dating of the various sites indicated a written language that predated the oldest recorded language that is generally accepted by historians.

"The problem back then was trying to answer the question: How could the same written language be in places so distant from one another in an age when man was frightened of sailing out of sight of shore? Because it made no sense, no one bothered to pull together all the various high rune artifacts and sites to build a working base for deciphering the writing. Of course, now that we know the Airlia were here, it makes perfect sense."

"Sort of like this Face on Mars thing made no sense to NASA," Turcotte asked, "but now it does?"

"Right," Nabinger said. "It was a question of accepting the data and ignoring the limitations of man at the time. Anthropologists have always argued how civilization began in such remote places as Egypt, China, and Central America, all at roughly the same time period. The popular theory was the isolationist theory of civilization. Isolationists believe that the ancient civilizations all developed independent of one another. They all crossed a threshold into civilization about the third or fourth century before the birth of Christ. Isolationists explained the timing by arguing natural evolution.

"Of course, now we know this most likely isn't true. The Airlia did have some effect, and that is most likely why civilization prospered in those distant places at the same time." Nabinger's eyes became unfocused as he retreated inside his own thoughts. "From what I saw in the guardian, I believe that there were humans on Atlantis where the Airlia had their home base and that some of those humans escaped when Aspasia destroyed Atlantis to stop the rebels. These humans dispersed and were the ones who began civilization at various places and gave us the myth of that island."

"Then the Airlia did interfere with our development as a species," Turcotte said.

"They certainly must have had some effect." Nabinger opened his eyes. "After all, they were here for over five thousand years. Atlantis had to be the place where their effect was the greatest. This one-starting-point theory is called 'diffusion.' Basically it means that all those civilizations were started by people from a single earlier civilization."

Turcotte leaned forward. "Let me ask something. How did the rebel computer get into that temple in Temiltepec? And the atomic bomb inside the Great Pyramid? Wasn't that the work of the rebel Airlia, not humans fleeing Atlantis?"

"I don't know," Nabinger answered. "It would seem likely."

"Well, if Aspasia went to Mars to snooze for a couple of millennia, then where did the rebel Airlia go?"

"I assume they died out," Nabinger said, but it was clear he had not really considered it.

"Maybe they're snoozing somewhere too?" Turcotte said. "Maybe they're snoozing in China?"

"Oh, give me a break," Kelly said.

"Maybe the guardian is worried about that and

that's why it sent out the foo fighters," Turcotte said. Something else occurred to Turcotte. He turned to Duncan. "Or maybe that was what was on that lower level in Dulce. Maybe they recovered the bodies of rebel Airlia in the temple at Temiltepec along with the rebel computer? Maybe that's why Guardian I had the foo fighters take the lab out. Maybe Majestic was trying to thaw the aliens out or jump-start them or whatever?"

"Maybe, maybe, maybe," Kelly repeated. She was pacing back and forth, the plywood floor squeaking under her boots. "Why don't we stick with the facts?"

"Which ones?" Turcotte asked. "If any of the rebel Airlia are still around somewhere, what if they're coming awake also? What if these two sides pick up where they left off five centuries ago? What if this Che Lu professor has stumbled onto something significant and dangerous? Based on this marker we found in the Rift Valley, there's a good chance whatever she's onto is linked to the ruby sphere we found, which seems to be linked to the mothership, according to what Peter just translated."

"I don't know what is in China," Nabinger said. "But it could help me decipher the Airlia Earth coordinate system if I can pinpoint the location." He had an atlas in his hand and was searching through it. "All Che Lu said was she found some high runes and she was going into the ancient Chinese tomb of Qian-Ling to investigate further. I've heard of Qian-Ling." He proceeded to briefly fill them in on the mountain tomb's background.

"The runes she found could be a whole lot of nothing or just copied religious text, as is much of

what is in the Great Pyramid. They could . . ."
He paused, his finger moving over the glossy page
that showed a map of China. "Holy shit!" he exclaimed. He spun around on the stool and
reached into his battered leather backpack and
pulled out the spiral notepad with his high rune
notes.

"What is it?" Turcotte asked.

Nabinger was thumbing through the pages of
his notebook, the paper filled with hand-drawn
high rune symbols. "You aren't going to believe it.
I don't believe it myself."

"What?" Lisa Duncan and the others crowded
around.

Nabinger stopped turning pages. He looked
from the map to the paper several times, then up
at the others. "It's been right there all this time
and I never saw it. Hell, I never looked. And even
if I had looked I probably would—"

"What was right there?" Turcotte was losing
patience.

"The word," Nabinger said.

"Word?" Duncan repeated.

"The symbol." Nabinger tapped the map. "It's
been there for centuries." His eyes were focused
on something outside of the tent in his mind's eye.
"It makes sense, though. We would have been
able to see it only in the last fifty years or so since
we went into space. And then no one would have
thought to look because we didn't know about the
high rune language. Brilliant! Simply brilliant."

Turcotte looked at the others in the room, then
back at the archaeologist. "What is so brilliant?
What symbol?"

"This." Nabinger's finger was resting on a section of the map.

The others peered. "I don't get it," Turcotte said. "China? That town near your finger? What?"

"No," Nabinger said. "The Wall. The Great Wall. Look at this section here in Western China, north of the city of Lanzhou." He looked at the others. "The Great Wall is the only manmade structure that can currently be seen from space with the naked eye."

"What about it?" Turcotte asked, although he was beginning to get the idea and the magnitude of it stunned him.

Keeping his finger in place, Nabinger used his free hand to pull his notebook next to the map. "Look at the Wall here and look at that symbol."

They all saw it right away. The two were identical.

"It can't be. . . ." Turcotte began, but his voice trailed off. There was no denying it. A three-hundred-mile section of the Great Wall of China had been built in the form of a high rune symbol to be seen from space.

"What does the symbol mean?" Turcotte asked.

"As near as I have been able to translate," Nabinger said, "that is the Airlia high rune symbol for HELP."

Chapter 11

∎∎∎∎∎∎∎∎∎∎∎

After much discussion Che Lu decided to continue along the corridor past where the image had appeared. One of the students, more eager than the rest, took the lead. The young man was ten meters farther down the tunnel when suddenly there was a bright flash of light. Che Lu stopped, her eyes momentarily blinded. When she opened them and could see again by the dim glows of wavering flashlights, she gasped. The student had been neatly cut in half, the top half of his body lying just behind his legs, blood still gushing forth from a heart that had just a few more beats left in it, the eyes in the head blinking, then going dull and dead.

As one of the girls screamed, Che Lu held up her hand. "No one move!" Edging forward, she approached the body. Now she could see the tiniest of protuberances from the wall at waist height. She reached down and pulled the dead student's hat off. She tossed it by the bump and another beam of fierce light flashed, cutting the hat as it flew through.

"Ah," Che Lu said. Even as she pondered the problem, there was a deep, dull, thud reverberating down the tunnel from behind.

"The doors!" Ki cried out. He turned and ran back the way they had come. In a minute he was back, fear playing across his young features. "The doors are shut. I can hear soldiers on the other side. We are trapped!"

Chapter 12

"Help?" Lisa Duncan had Nabinger's notebook in her hand. "I don't get it."

Everyone looked up as a distant peal of thunder rumbled through the tent. The storm wasn't showing any signs of abating soon.

"I don't either," Nabinger said, "but that's what it says. It makes sense that the Airlia would use the Wall if they were in China. They did the same thing in Egypt with the Sphinx and the pyramids."

"Wait a second," Turcotte said. "What are you talking about there? I didn't know there was any *message* in the way the pyramids were built. You told me that the flat surface of the pyramids, when they were covered with their original layer of white limestone, could send out an immense radar image to outer space, but not that there was a message in that image."

Nabinger shook his head. "No, not in the radar image, it's in the ground image when you're near them. Maybe it was sort of like a secret symbol, known only to the Airlia. But archaeologists have long known, even before we knew about the lower chamber and the high runes, that the way the two largest pyramids are positioned, if you stand to the right of the Sphinx and line all three objects up, you get a hieroglyphic symbol with the Sphinx's head between the two pyramids." He sketched on his pad, drawing two pyramids and a rough outline of the Sphinx's head between them, with the ground a flat line at the bottom.

Turcotte was more interested in the map of China and getting the big picture before he tried to figure out pieces and parts. "Jesus, look at this thing. How long did it take to build this Wall?"

Kelly had her laptop open and was accessing a CD-ROM she had put in. "I've got it here. Let's see. The Great Wall is over twenty-four hundred kilometers long. That's about fifteen hundred miles. It officially became the Great Wall in the third century B.C. when Emperor Shi Huangdi of the Ch'in dynasty linked together separate walls that had been built earlier. Shi was the first emperor to unite China."

Kelly looked from the computer to the map. "This section that makes the symbol, it's mostly part of those first walls, so it was built at a much earlier time."

"So it could have been done back when the rebels and Aspasia's people were fighting?" Turcotte asked.

"Yes."

"But such a thing would take hundreds of years to build, wouldn't it?" Turcotte asked.

Kelly shook her head. "No. According to what I have here, the greater part of the Wall was built in less than ten years. Millions of peasants were used to build it and the bodies of those who died in the labor were made part of the Wall. So based on that, this section could have been built in a relatively short period of time if there was a strong leader who wanted it done. Remember, China has never lacked for bodies to do manual labor such as this."

Turcotte leaned forward to look at the map more closely, and in doing so brushed against Lisa Duncan. She didn't move away, but leaned forward with him to check the map.

"You know," Turcotte said, "this part of the Wall doesn't really seem to follow a natural defensive line. You have this river here, which would have supplemented the Wall's defenses, yet the Wall doesn't follow it. You're right. This was built to make that high rune symbol visible from space, not to form the best defensive perimeter possible given the terrain. How the hell did the rebel Airlia get the Chinese to build it?"

"How'd they get the Egyptians to build the pyramids?" Nabinger asked in turn.

"Aspasia can give us the answers," Kelly Reynolds said from her location on the other side of the tent, seated on the edge of a cot.

"You know," Turcotte said, "for all his great effort to keep our development from being influenced by their presence, Aspasia did a pretty crappy job." Something occurred to him. "Maybe they got those people to build those things the same way they got General Gullick and Majestic-12 to attempt to fly the mothership. By taking over their minds using guardians!"

Turcotte tapped his finger on the map. "That

would mean there's another guardian here in Qian-Ling."

There was a momentary silence in the tent.

"What I want to know," Lisa Duncan finally said, "is why the rebels would want to transmit HELP in such a manner to someone coming in from space."

"That goes with something that's been bugging me for a while," Nabinger said. "We determined after learning that the Airlia had hidden the nuclear weapon in the Great Pyramid that the Pyramid itself must have been built as a space beacon. The thing that bothered me about that was *why* would the rebels want to signal into space? Who were they signaling to with the Great Pyramid?"

"And *who*," Duncan said, "were they asking for help from with the Great Wall?" She walked over to the coffeepot set on a field table and poured herself a cup. She held up an empty cup to Turcotte and he nodded.

"Let's take it logically," Turcotte said. "The Pyramid was to get attention. The symbol in the Great Wall was to send a message after they got attention. That's the way I would have done it," he said.

"Done what?" Duncan asked as she handed him the coffee.

"Sent a message to outer space with the technology and manpower present on the Earth at the time if I'd lost my primary means of communication," Turcotte said. "In Special Forces one of the first things we learn in training is that you always have to have a way to communicate back to home base. A primary, a backup, an emergency, and a pull-it-out-your-ass way. I think this symbol built into the Great Wall was a pull-it-out-your-ass."

"Hold on here," Duncan said. "These aliens were rebels, outlaws. Aspasia defeated them, destroyed their base at Atlantis, and scattered them across the face of the planet. I get back to my question of who were they trying to signal to? You'd think rebels would want to lay low."

"The Kortad?" Nabinger suggested. "Maybe they just weren't rebels. Maybe they were traitors too."

"And were the people who built this part of the Great Wall the same ones who put the Ruby Sphere in the Great Rift Valley?" Turcotte asked. "Is that the China connection?"

"I'd say so," Duncan said. "It makes sense."

"You people are shooting in the dark," Reynolds called out, but the others ignored her.

"You know," Nabinger said hesitatingly, "I got some confusing stuff out of the guardian just before it cut contact. I didn't tell UNAOC because I didn't know if what I saw was a recording of reality or something the computer was making up."

"What did you see?" Turcotte asked.

Nabinger rubbed his temples. "I think it might have been the destruction of Atlantis by the mothership. It was very confusing."

"Aspasia can clear all this up when he wakes up and comes back to Earth," Kelly said. "We'll just have to wait."

"Waiting gives away initiative," Turcotte said in a low voice.

"What?" Kelly snapped at him.

"I said waiting gives away the initiative," Turcotte said so that everyone in the tent could hear. "It's a maxim of combat. Victory usually goes to the side that maintains the initiative."

"Oh, God!" Kelly exclaimed. "We're not at war."

"I don't know what the situation is," Turcotte said. "I don't know what's going on. All I know is we've gotten two messages from some damn machine on Mars and everyone's getting ready like it's the second coming of Christ. Well, I for one would like to find out a bit more about what the truth is while we're waiting for Aspasia to awaken or thaw out or whatever the hell he's doing up there."

"I would too," Lisa Duncan said. She held up her hands as Reynolds angrily stood up. "Let's slow down a second here. What else did you see about Atlantis, Professor?"

Nabinger grimaced. "People dying. Ships sailing away, trying to escape. That's why I think the diffusionist theory is. . . ." He paused as he suddenly remembered. "Ships. Spaceships. Seven of them. Not bouncers, but bigger. They flew away just before the mothership arrived."

"Flew where?" Turcotte asked.

"Straight up."

"The rebels escaping," Duncan summarized.

"Yes. That must be so," Nabinger agreed.

"So they did get away!" Turcotte was looking at the map of China again. He stabbed his finger down on the map. "I bet they went here." He looked up. "And if Aspasia and his people are awakening, who's to say the rebels aren't also?

"And," Turcotte continued, "I think the only way we're gonna find out more is to go to China, get inside this damn tomb, and take a look at what's written there. Find the guardian computer, if there is one there. If it was the rebels who did this part of the Wall, then maybe we need to know about it as soon as possible and not wait on Aspasia. After all, his guardian computer here on Earth seemed concerned enough about this to send out a foo fighter recon."

"Going there is easier said than done," Duncan replied. "China's in a lot of turmoil right now. From what I understand, Taiwan is doing considerable covert pushing in the midst of all this to try and overthrow the regime in Beijing.

"China has pulled out of the UN to protest UNAOC's actions. I think the leadership in Beijing is at a complete loss as to how to deal with this situation of alien contact, and they're doing what China has done repeatedly over the years: retreat inside of itself. All borders have been closed and communication cut off with the outside world.

"Not only that," she continued, "but I don't think UNAOC is going to be too thrilled about throwing any sort of monkey wrench into the anticipation of Aspasia's return."

Turcotte crossed his arms and stared at Lisa Duncan. "You're the ranking person here. It's your call. Remember, you work for the U.S. Government also. I say let's skip UNAOC and bounce this up our chain of command."

"I've already decided to do that," Duncan said.

Chapter 13

The Guardian II computer was a golden pyramid twenty feet high by twenty across at the base. It was four hundred meters under the surface of Mars, in a cavern hollowed out of solid rock. The route back to the surface had been sealed five thousand years ago with only links to the sensors secreted on the planet's surface left in place.

For the past several hours Guardian II had been running a self-diagnostic of itself and all the systems under its control. The priority was power. The cold fusion reactor also buried under the Martian soil was down to fourteen percent output. That was not enough to implement the other programs that had to be run.

The decision was made with simple logical computation. The majority of that fourteen percent was routed to the surface to run the alternate power program.

· · ·

At the JPL control center, a large red digital clock gave the time remaining until *Viking* would complete its orbital pattern shift and then go over the Cydonia region. There were less than three hours on it.

In the meanwhile Kincaid's people had accomplished what they said they couldn't do: extend *Surveyor*'s able mast with the IMS on the end of it and orient it toward Mars—at least it was oriented twelve percent of the time, as *Surveyor* tumbled around in space in its erratic orbit. That percentage was slowly increasing as the engineers worked their programs to rotate the IMS in conjunction with the spin of the craft. With some luck and some time they might even be able to keep the IMS oriented on Mars full-time.

One of the large screens in the front of the room showed a slowly moving image from the IMS. The Face stared back at *Surveyor,* with the large pyramid just off to the side, the entire thing moving across the screen as the camera rolled. It was a very distant shot at a hard angle, but there was no denying that the image very clearly looked like an elongated face.

Every time Larry Kincaid looked up and saw that image, he felt a shiver run through him. To know that somewhere among those apparent ruins, aliens were coming out of their long hibernation—aliens that had traveled among the stars while man was still living in grass huts and caves—made him feel very small in the universe.

Kincaid was checking some of the new data his flight engineers had come up with for *Surveyor* when a sudden explosion of commotion in the front of the room drew his attention up.

He immediately saw the cause for the excitement. The massive pyramid in the midst of the Cydonia ruins was opening. The four sides were separating, like a flower blossoming for the sun. A dark center appeared in the center as the sides slowly split.

Kincaid knew the dimensions of that pyramid and the sheer magnitude of the engineering required to do that staggered him. He leaned forward, waiting. After five minutes of slow movement the sides reached vertical, revealing a perfect black square. Kincaid's eyes, and those of people all over the world whose TV shows were interrupted with the live feed, were straining to see what was inside.

Suddenly there was a sharp glistening of light all around the upper edge. The light grew stronger as the sides started over toward the planet's surface, the inner sides reflecting the distant sun. After fifteen minutes, and twelve rotations of the IMS, the four panels finally reached the ground. The bright light they reflected was almost blinding the IMS's image.

"What the hell is that?" One of the flight engineers asked the question people all over the planet glued to their TVs were asking.

Kincaid knew what it was, but the sheer size was unbelievable. "Solar panels," he said. Solar panels were used on most of the probes and orbiters to supply power, so Kincaid had more than a passing knowledge on the subject. He pulled a calculator out of his pocket and began punching in numbers.

"Jesus," he muttered when the last figure came up on his screen. Human solar panels that big would produce enough power to run New York City, and Kincaid suspected that the Airlia probably had better-engineered panels. "What the hell is going to need that much power?" he asked out loud, but no one in the control room had an answer.

He looked up at the four large, shiny triangles that now lay where the pyramid they had formed once stood. Squinting he could just make out something in the center, underneath where the apex of the pyramid would formerly have been.

"Is this the best resolution the IMS can get?" he asked.

"Yes," one of the technicians answered him.

"Any idea what's that dark thing in the center of the panels?" Kincaid asked.

"Not yet. It's hard to make out, given the light contrast from the panels and *Surveyor*'s distance. We should know when *Viking* goes over."

■ ■ ■

Duncan held a piece of paper she'd just received from a runner from the Navy communications center on the island. "We've got authorization to go into China and find out what Che Lu is uncovering in the tomb."

"From who?" Turcotte asked.

She read the paper. "The National Command Authority under an ST-8 security clearance."

"I've never heard of that clearance," Turcotte said.

"We are instructed to get in and out without causing any international incident," Duncan noted.

"Easier said than done," Turcotte said.

The others were all gathered around the small TV, taking in the spectacle of the Airlia solar panels.

Duncan was thinking about the problem. "We know that China is not going to let us come in. We aren't even going to bother to ask. We're going to have to go in on the sly and get out without being noticed." She looked at Turcotte. "And that, Mike, I believe, is your department. According to this we'll be met at Osan Air Force Base in South Korea by a CIA liaison who can help us get to the tomb and link up with Che Lu."

Turcotte stood. "Let's get moving."

"No," Kelly Reynolds said, standing in their way, her feet planted wide apart. "I don't think we should do this."

"Kelly—" Nabinger began, but she cut him off.

"It will only cause trouble. Aspasia will be here soon. Why can't we wait? If this tomb holds Airlia artifacts, then they belong to him. If it's where the rebels are, then we shouldn't disturb it. Again, that's his problem."

"Like the fight between the rebels and Aspasia wasn't the problem of the people of Atlantis?" Nabinger asked.

"Peter's right," Turcotte said. "We can't sit around and be spectators. We're involved."

"Don't you see?" Kelly asked, grabbing the front of Turcotte's camouflage shirt. "Don't you see that you're doing the same thing you did in Germany? People are going to get hurt for no reason."

Turcotte's face went hard. He grabbed her hands and held them inside his. "This is different."

"Stay here with me and wait," Kelly pleaded, looking from Turcotte to Nabinger to Duncan.

"We can't," Lisa Duncan said. "We have to do our jobs just like you have to do yours."

"If I had done mine after we got Johnny out of Dulce," Reynolds said, "he wouldn't be dead. Instead I went along with you while you did your jobs, as you put it. I'm not doing that again."

"We're not asking you to," Duncan said. "This will be a classified military operation. All I ask is that you not report anything about it."

"I can't do that," Reynolds said.

"Kelly"—Turcotte slowly removed her hands from his shirt and let go of them—"if you report this, the Chinese will know we're coming and people *will* die. Namely us."

"If it's the only way to stop you, I will report it," Reynolds threatened.

"You're not going to stop us," Turcotte said. "We're going in no matter what you do."

"Damn it!" Reynolds exclaimed. "Why? Why does it have to be the U.S. against China? The Russians and the ship they hid? The South African corporation and what they hid? Why do we fight and lie among ourselves? We won't be ready, like Aspasia thinks we are, if we keep doing this. Human against human."

"It isn't about human against human," Turcotte said. He stepped around her. "It's about finding out the truth on our own." He walked out of the tent, the others following, leaving Kelly Reynolds alone and listening to the sound of the storm batter the tent.

■ ■ ■

Inside Qian-Ling, Che Lu and the remaining students had backtracked their way to the doors they had come in. In the dim glow of the flashlight she could see that the doors were indeed shut, and even with everyone pushing they couldn't budge the metal.

A quick check of the meager supplies they had brought in revealed they had enough water to last perhaps four or five days at best if they were very conservative.

Light was perhaps the biggest problem. Among the seven of them they had eight flashlights. Che Lu estimated even using only one at a time, they had less than sixty hours of light left.

"All right," she said to the frightened students who were huddled together around the one lit flashlight like moths around a fire. "We cannot get back out this way. Perhaps Lo Fa will come back, but I do not think so. We are on our own."

"Who would do this to us?" one of the young girls, Funing, wailed.

Che Lu had considered that and accepted the obvious answer. "The army."

"But why?" Funing asked.

"Because someone ordered them to," Che Lu said. "Someone in Beijing must have realized that they shouldn't have issued us the permission to go in, and this is the easiest solution." She kept to herself the disturbing news Lo Fa had passed to her.

"We're going to die!" Funing cried out.

"We're not dead yet," Che Lu snapped, "so quit your crying. I've been in worse situations than this." She pointed down the main tunnel. "There were two side tunnels. They have to go somewhere. From the ancient records there are supposed to be miles of tunnels in this tomb. We can find another way out."

"But what about what happened to Taizho?" Funing cried. "We could walk into the same thing!"

"We will be careful." Che Lu took a bamboo pole that one of the students used as a walking stick. "Tie a cloth to this. Then we hold the pole out in front of the first person like this," she demonstrated, "with the cloth hanging down. That will trip any beam like that which killed Taizho."

"And if there are beams in both side tunnels?" Funing asked.

Che Lu was growing weary of the girl. "Then we truly are trapped and then we will die," she said. "But we don't know that right now and we won't until we act. So get to your feet!"

"I will take the pole," Ki said, surprising Che Lu.

"Thank you," she said.

"Let's go," Ki said, and headed down the tunnel toward the intersection, one of the other students slightly behind him, holding the flashlight. The rest of them followed, single file, like blind ducks in a row.

■ ■ ■

"Look at this," Nabinger said, holding a piece of paper the driver had given him. They were in a HUMMV, being driven to the airstrip where a plane Duncan had requisitioned waited for them. The squeak of the windshield wipers added to the unhappy mood inside. Nabinger was in the front seat next to the driver, while Turcotte and Duncan were in back.

"What is it?" Turcotte asked.

"The translation of the Chinese characters on the stone that my friend just faxed back to the Naval Operations Center." Nabinger read it to the others. "It reads: *Cing Ho reached this place as directed. He did his duty as ordered.*"

"Who the hell was Cing Ho?" Turcotte asked.

"I'll have to look it up once we get airborne," Nabinger said, turning back to the front.

Turcotte felt a nudge in his side. He turned to Duncan, who leaned close so she could speak to him without being overheard. "I'm sorry about what Kelly said. About Germany. She said that to get to you. To stop you from doing the right thing."

"You know about Germany?"

"It's why I chose you to infiltrate Area 51," Duncan said.

"Because I was part of a fucked-up operation that got a bunch of innocent civilians killed?" Turcotte asked.

"Don't be an asshole," Duncan gently said. "You didn't kill any of them. And you stopped the man who did as quickly as you could."

"I was there."

"Give me a break, Mike," she said. "More importantly, give yourself a break. I picked you because you refused the medal they offered you for the 'fucked-up operation,' as you called it. Because you took personal responsibility."

The brakes squealed as they pulled up to the stairs leading up to their plane. As Turcotte started to get out, he felt Duncan's hand on his shoulder, causing him to pause.

"And remember," she said, "the facts show I chose the right man."

. . .

Major Quinn had been working on his laptop for the past three hours, weaving his way through the various codes and numbers that made up the Department of Defense satellite communications system. He had finally found what he was looking for, but the information did more to confuse the situation than clarify it.

The strange woman, Oleisa, was making satellite communications back to a ground station located somewhere in Antarctica. A station that, other than having a routing number, did not exist in any government records, classified or not, that he could find, other than a reference to an organization named STAAR.

Quinn leaned back in his chair and thought for a moment. Then he typed some new commands into his control console, accessing the security camera that was in the part of the hangar Oleisa had taken over. He wasn't surprised when the screen came back blank and the computer informed him that that camera had been taken offline.

"All right," Quinn said to himself, enjoying the challenge. "There's *got* to be a mention of STAAR somewhere. And I'm going to find it." He turned back to his laptop and began typing. Then, suddenly, he paused. Antarctica. There was a connection between that continent and Majestic-12. And there was someone who knew about that connection: the only surviving member of the original twelve members of the committee.

Quinn knew where he had to go now: the base hospital at Nellis Air Force Base where that man, Werner Von Seeckt, former Nazi and SS scientist, was being kept alive by machines.

Chapter 14

. . . .

"**W**ill Kelly report our mission?" Duncan asked.

The three of them were in the forward part of the 707, left alone by the Air Force crew. The takeoff from Easter Island had gone smoothly, and now they were heading toward Osan Air Force Base in South Korea as quickly as possible.

"No," Nabinger said, "she won't."

"What makes you so sure?" Duncan asked.

"She wouldn't put us in harm's way."

"Seemed to me," Duncan said, "that her take on it was that we were putting ourselves in harm's way." She looked at Turcotte, who hadn't said a word since they'd boarded. "What do you think?"

"I don't know. I don't think she will."

"I can give the order to shut her off from the outside world," Duncan said. "To have her put into custody."

"Then what's the difference between us and Majestic?" Turcotte asked.

"Point made," Duncan said. "I'm just a little worried, is that all right?"

"I'm worried too," Turcotte said. He didn't want to dwell on Kelly Reynolds and the way she had been acting. "When is *Viking* going to be over Cydonia?"

Duncan looked at her watch. "Five minutes." She pointed to the rear of the plane. "We can access the secure link to *Viking* and get the images it sends back. At least we'll be up to speed on that."

Turcotte and Nabinger followed her down the aisle and through the door into the communications section. Rows of computer consoles filled the space between the bulkheads, and the light was turned down low, emphasizing the glow from the screens. Turcotte recognized the plane as a command-and-control version that the Air Force kept deployed around the world.

"Over here," Duncan said, leading him to a particular computer. A young Air Force lieutenant was seated there, her screen empty except for a cursor.

"Hook us in to the NASA downlink from *Viking,* Lieutenant Wheeler," Duncan ordered.

"Yes, ma'am." Wheeler quickly typed in several code words. Her screen cleared, then a dire warning came across the screen telling anyone who had gotten this far that they were violating federal law if they were looking at this screen without proper access and to stop now.

Then the warning was gone.

```
>JPL: REPOSITIONING NEAR COMPLETE. T-5
MINUTES
```

"Is that our time or Mars time?" Turcotte asked.

Duncan was confused, but Lieutenant Wheeler figured out what he was asking. "Our time, five minutes," she said. She looked up at Duncan. "It takes two and a half minutes for a radio or data transmission to make it from Mars to Earth. Five minutes for us is two and half minutes for *Viking* plus two and a half minutes for the transmission to reach."

```
>JPL: T-3 MINUTES. IMAGING SYSTEMS
CHECK COMING.
>UNAOC: ALL STATIONS ON LINE. WAITING
TO RECEIVE DOWNLINK.
>JPL: SUPERSEDING VIKING LINK TO ALL
STATIONS.
>VIKING: IMAGING SYSTEMS ALL GREEN.
```

"You ever wonder why NASA never checked out Cydonia before," Turcotte asked Duncan, "if they could move *Viking* so easily over it?"

"I looked into that," she replied. "From what I've found out, there wasn't that much fuel to move it around. I think this shift has burned all they have left. They used up the fuel that would have kept its orbit from decaying for a few more years."

"Going over the same route, year after year?" Turcotte asked. "Maybe Majestic-12 had something to do with that," he suggested. "Maybe they knew more than they let on."

"That's very possible," Duncan said. "But we're looking now."

```
>VIKING: ORBIT ESTABLISHED AT DESIG-
NATED COORDINATES.
```

There was a pause.

```
>VIKING: ALL SYSTEMS ON. INITIATING
IMAGING.
```

The screen cleared and then both Duncan and Turcotte leaned closer as the Face on the surface of Mars came into view, the image twice as large as the one they had seen from *Surveyor*.

"Jesus," Turcotte muttered. "How could they say that's a natural formation?"

There was no mistaking the image.

"Look at the ears," Nabinger said. "The lobes are long, just like the megaliths on Easter Island."

"Well, at least we know what they look like," Duncan said.

"There." Turcotte put his finger on a rectangular object on the screen. "That's the Fort."

"What's that in the center of the panels?" Lisa Duncan asked.

"I can't quite make it out yet," Turcotte said.

```
>VIKING: SCANNING IN.
```

The image began to get larger when suddenly there was a bright light in the center of the solar panels. The light grew larger. At first Turcotte assumed it was consuming the panels, but then he realized it was getting larger because it was coming toward the camera.

The light expanded until it was the entire image, then suddenly there was nothing but static running across the screen, like the beginning of *The Twilight Zone*.

```
>JPL: LINK IS DOWN
>JPL: LINK IS DOWN
>JPL: ATTEMPTING TO REGAIN LINK
>JPL: LINK IS DOWN
>JPL: ATTEMPTING TO REGAIN LINK
>JPL: LINK CANNOT BE REESTABLISHED.
ZERO CONTACT WITH VIKING.
```

"It's gone," Turcotte said.

"This wasn't being fed live to the media?" Lisa Duncan asked.

"No, ma'am, NASA was letting it out on a five-minute delay." Wheeler shut off her computer.

"So what do you think happened?" Turcotte asked the others, but there was no reply.

As they headed back to the front of the plane, Nabinger stopped at one of the computer stations. He rejoined them in a few minutes with information. "Cing Ho was a Chinese admiral in 656 B.C. He was commissioned by the emperor to lead an expedition to the Mideast. They traveled into the Arabian Sea and the Persian Gulf. According to historians, the expedition mysteriously turned back and the Chinese never again mounted any sort of naval exploration."

"So Cing Ho carried the ruby sphere to the Rift Valley, then went home" was Turcotte's take on that information.

"Looks like it."

"I wonder why," Duncan said. "This was thousands of years *after* the rebellion among the Airlia was supposedly over. What happened in 656 B.C. to make the Chinese undertake such an expedition?"

"Hopefully we'll find out in the tomb," Turcotte

said. "And after what just happened to *Viking,* I think it's all the more important we do this."

■ ■ ■

At JPL they were focused on *Viking* and asking the same questions everyone else was about what had happened to it. Larry Kincaid knew the answer to the what: *Viking II* was gone. The how and why were two other questions altogether, with the latter predicated upon there being a deliberate act involved in the former.

He had watched the backup view from the IMS and seen the bolt of light come off the surface of Mars and envelop *Viking.* When the light was gone, there simply wasn't anything there, as far as the IMS could see.

He sat in the back of the conference room as the JPL bigwigs were still working over what had happened. The most immediate problem was what to do with the tape of the incident. It had not been made public yet, and the networks were screaming bloody murder as they'd had to extend their programming preempt waiting for the first pictures of the Airlia Cydonia compound from *Viking II.* So far the only decision made had been to hold the tape and issue a statement saying there had been equipment malfunction and that they would have to wait until *Viking II* completed another orbit and was over the site again in three hours. The networks weren't happy with that, but at least they could put their shows back on.

It took the top JPL people another fifteen minutes of arguing before they did what they usually did and turned to Kincaid. He'd spent that time pondering the other aspects of the incident that preyed upon his mind.

"*Viking II* is gone, gentlemen," Kincaid said when finally asked. "Whether it has suffered a severe malfunction or no longer exists doesn't matter, as we have lost all telemetry with the probe. Even if it is still up there in orbit and does go over Cydonia, it won't do us any good.

"Our instruments from Earth and in space, including the *Surveyor* IMS, recorded a bright flash of light from the center of the solar panel array at Cydonia just as Viking passed overhead."

"What was the light?" someone asked.

"I don't know," Kincaid said.

"Your best guess?" the head of JPL asked.

"My best guess is that it was some sort of power discharge," Kincaid said. "The key question is whether it was incidental or intentional."

The JPL head frowned. "What?"

"It could have just been a release of excess energy from the panel's processor, which logically would be in the center of the array. Such a burst would be like that which comes off the sun occasionally, although on a much smaller scale. The electromagnetic pulse would have been more than enough to fry every circuit on *Viking*. If it was a very strong pulse, then it could have physically destroyed the probe. If this is the case, then it was simply bad luck that *Viking* was passing overhead when that occurred."

"And if it wasn't?" a new voice asked from Kincaid's right. He turned. A man with white hair stood there. His face was unlined, making his age indeterminate. He wore sunglasses despite being indoors and he was dressed in black pants, shirt, sport coat with no tie, and the collar buttoned at his neck. He had an access badge clipped to his coat, the color of which told Kincaid the man had the highest clearance available.

Kincaid chose his words very carefully. "If it wasn't coincidence, then the destruction of *Viking* was deliberate."

The room burst out in pandemonium at that statement.

"Hold on!" The head of JPL finally got everyone's attention. "Let's not go off half cocked here. It was most likely just coincidence. But even if it wasn't—even if it wasn't," he repeated over the low roar that produced, "we have to remember that the message we received from Mars was from a guardian *computer,* not from Aspasia himself. The message said that Aspasia would be waking up, not that he was already conscious.

"And what does a guardian computer do? It guards. Perhaps there was some sort of defensive system that was brought automatically on-line when the pyramid opened and the solar panels were exposed? And what if *Viking* flying overhead triggered that system? I do not believe this was a deliberate act, and that is the position I will take with the President.

"As far as the media are concerned, we will continue to tell them we have an equipment malfunction, which is basically the truth. We'll tell them the malfunction was caused by moving *Viking*'s orbit."

Which is a lie, Kincaid thought but he kept his tongue still. He'd worked at JPL too long to say anything out loud. Besides, the strange white-haired man who was standing in the back of the room bothered Kincaid. The man was looking at Kincaid's boss with just the slightest trace of a smile on his pale lips.

"We will also tell the media that the malfunction was so severe," continued the head of JPL, "that we will not be able to receive any incoming transmissions from *Viking*." The man broke off and looked at Kincaid. "Is there anything we can do?"

"We have *Mars Surveyor*," Kincaid reluctantly said.

"I thought you had no control over *Surveyor*."

"We're working the problem," Kincaid said. "As you know, we've been using the IMS as backup to *Viking*."

"How long until *Surveyor* achieves stable orbit?"

"It will take us a few days," Kincaid answered. He glanced to his right, feeling the intense pressure of the white-haired man's gaze burning into him. The man turned and walked out of the room as abruptly as he had come in.

"That is all, gentlemen."

As the other administrative and bureaucratic members of JPL's hierarchy walked out of the room, Kincaid remained seated. He had a feeling the white-haired man might be waiting in the hallway, and Kincaid had no desire to get any closer to the man. Plus he didn't want to run into any of the press, some of whom he passingly knew, who were also waiting outside, and be forced to lie to them.

So instead, he simply sat there and thought, and the more he thought the unhappier he became.

Chapter 15

The going was very slow, but Che Lu couldn't blame Ki for taking his time. The image of Taizho being cut in half was ingrained on everyone's mind. They had turned left at the four-way intersection. They could have just as easily turned right, but Che Lu had acted on instinct and also the fact that right went deeper into the mountain. If she was hunting for the emperor and empress's tombs, she would have gone that way, but the priority now was to get to daylight.

The tunnel had gone level for almost a quarter mile, as near as she could tell, then it had begun going up and very slowly turning to the right. Che Lu had a feeling they were following the outer contour of the mountain tomb, but at least they were going up. They had encountered no beam like the one that had killed Taizho, nor any holographic alien images.

Ki suddenly stopped, drawing Che Lu out of her thoughts. "What is wrong?" she asked.

"I must rest for a little bit," he said. The stress

of being point man in the dark tunnel was getting to him. Che Lu looked over the other students, then took the bamboo pole from Ki's hands.

"We will rest," she said. "Then I will lead."

■ ■ ■

"The word *arctic* comes from *arktos,* which is the Greek word for 'bear,' referring to the northern constellation Ursus Major, the great bear, more commonly known as the Big Dipper." The old man paused, regaining his breath with the aid of an oxygen mask his withered hand pressed down over his face.

Major Quinn kept his face passive, not allowing his feelings about Werner Von Seeckt to surface. Quinn knew all about the German from the classified files in the Cube and from working with him ever since Quinn had been assigned to MJ-12.

Von Seeckt had been born in southwest Germany in 1918. He'd grown up in the turbulent years after the First World War. Von Seeckt had been studying physics in a university in Munich when the Second World War started and he'd been recruited by the SS to be part of an elite scientific cadre, studying better and more efficient ways to make war and kill people.

Quinn knew that Von Seeckt had been working at the rocket base in Peenemünde when he'd been recruited to go on a special mission to Egypt: the mission that had uncovered the Airlia atomic weapon under the Great Pyramid. Unfortunately for Von Seeckt, but fortunately for the Allies, Von Seeckt and the bomb had been captured by a British patrol. The scientist and his strange box had made their way to America and fallen under the jurisdiction of a classified program called Operation Paperclip.

Quinn also knew much about Paperclip; it was a program set up by the U.S. Government to bring what were considered valuable Axis scientists to the United States to "give" their expertise to America. The program was illegal, but that didn't bother those who implemented it. In this manner rocket scientists from the Third Reich, chemical and biological experts, including some of the men who invented the gases used in the concentration camps, all were given safe passage to the United States and spent the rest of their years working for that government.

But Quinn knew Von Seeckt had been one of the very first brought in under Paperclip, captured while the war was still going strong. When the casing surrounding the atomic weapon had finally been breached, Von Seeckt had been assigned to work with the Manhattan Project, which was given a large boost by being able to examine the Airlia bomb. He was then assigned to the newly formed Majestic-12 and had been with it ever since.

Quinn knew Von Seeckt should be in Washington with the other surviving members of MJ-12, standing trial, but in the last few weeks Von Seeckt's physical condition had weakened to the point where his permanent residence was the intensive care ward at Nellis Air Force Base. On the old man's side there was also the fact that Von Seeckt had aided Lisa Duncan and those with her in thwarting General Gullick.

The reason Quinn was here was because he knew that some of the bouncers had been found in the fifties in Antarctica and he also knew that

Von Seeckt had actually been there for the recovery. When Quinn had asked the scientist about Antarctica, the old man had launched into his etymological explanation of how the continent got its name. Quinn patiently waited, letting Von Seeckt work his way into useful information.

Von Seeckt pushed aside the oxygen mask. "On Earth, the region surrounding the north pole is called the arctic region on all maps. When the prefix *ant,* meaning 'opposite' or 'balance,' is added to *arctic,* the word becomes *Antarctica,* which means 'opposite the arctic,' or literally 'opposite the bear.' "

Von Seeckt closed his eyes in thought. "I have studied this subject at great length. After all, I traveled there in the search for the bouncers. Even more than the wilds of the Nevada desert and the remoteness of Easter Island, Antarctica is isolated from the visitations of humans. No one goes there unless they have a specific purpose, and survival is difficult.

"Based on Airlia information we found in the mothership cavern during World War II, Majestic was the instigating force behind Operation High Jump, which ran from 1946 through 1947, looking for the Airlia artifacts we knew were hidden in Antarctica. We managed to locate the site but it took over eight years, until 1955, before an expedition could be mounted to try and recover the cache.

"That was when we had Operation Deep Freeze mounted. It was led by explorer Admiral Byrd. While the press release touted the eight bases built and the explorations made on the icy continent, a ninth, secret base, code-named Scorpion Base, was established over the site of the Airlia cache.

"In 1956, after four months of drilling, the men at Scorpion were able to reach the cache buried under a mile and a half of ice. They found a chamber hollowed out of the ice and seven bouncers inside."

Von Seeckt's body twitched under the white sheets. "With the bouncers recovered, Majestic ordered the closure of Scorpion Base and the entire operation was classified at the highest levels. I have heard no more of any operations in Antarctica."

Quinn shook his head. "Someone's down there now. The only clue I have is the word *STAAR*, with two *A*'s."

Von Seeckt's head twitched on the pillow. "STAAR?" He muttered something in German.

"What was that?" Quinn asked.

"I have heard rumors in the many years I was with Majestic," Von Seeckt said. "Rumors of another organization. I have heard it called STAAR."

"What is it?" Quinn asked.

"I don't know. We knew at Majestic that someone was monitoring us. We also were under strict guidelines not to interfere. It was part of our founding charter."

Quinn frowned. "Then why didn't this STAAR step in when General Gullick was taken over by the rebel computer?"

"I can't answer that," Von Seeckt said, "because I don't know if STAAR really exists."

Quinn backtracked. "But they could be using Scorpion Station, couldn't they?"

"Perhaps," Von Seeckt acknowledged. "It would be a good place to put an organization you wanted no one to find. Certainly much better than we did at Area 51."

"Who would know about STAAR?" Quinn asked.

Von Seeckt's frail shoulders moved in a shrug. "I don't know. Majestic was hooked in to all the intelligence agencies and none of them had any hard data on it. Just rumors and bits and pieces."

Von Seeckt coughed and took another drag of oxygen. "The interesting thing is," he continued, "that this STAAR, if it does exist, must not have been doing much, since it's never come into conflict with Majestic, the CIA, or any of the other various government agencies that are constantly bickering with each other."

"Then what is its purpose?" Quinn wondered out loud.

"Maybe it is just to wait and watch," Von Seeckt said.

"For what?"

Von Seeckt lifted his hand at the TV mounted on a wall bracket in his room. It was turned to CNN, the sound muted. The screen showed a picture of Mars. "Maybe for that. You say STAAR is taking action now?"

"STAAR's got someone in Area 51 in charge of one of the bouncers," Quinn told him.

"So STAAR is coming awake," Von Seeckt said.

"But who could they be?" Quinn asked. "A branch of the CIA? NSA?"

"Why do you think they are American?" Von Seeckt asked.

"Because Scorpion was built by Majestic and Majestic was American."

Von Seeckt cackled a laugh. "Ahh, let me back up, young man. What makes you think they, whoever they are in Scorpion Base, are human?"

Chapter 16

Kelly Reynolds felt a bead of sweat work its way down her back. She was standing on the hot tarmac of the Nellis Air Force Base runway arguing with a young lieutenant who did not want to let her board a helicopter that the display board in operations had indicated was flying to Area 51. She'd flown here on a departing military hop as soon as the 707 with the others had taken off. She knew the only way to stop them was to uncover more information, and the best place to do that was here, where Majestic had operated for half a century.

They both turned as a car pulled up and a blue-suited figure emerged with gold oak leaves on his shoulders.

"Major Quinn," Kelly Reynolds said by way of greeting. She still distrusted the Air Force, despite the openness of the last two weeks. Her early experience with an Air Force UFO disinformation campaign, when her budding career in film documentaries had been destroyed in the process, had left her wary of men in blue uniforms.

"Miss Reynolds," Quinn replied.

"Is that your helicopter?" Reynolds asked.

"Yes."

"Can I get a ride?" The lieutenant started to say something, but his mouth snapped shut as Quinn waved for her to accompany him to the craft. Reynolds knew Quinn was doing everything he could to stay on the good side of the media. All the other members of Majestic were dead, having killed themselves like Gullick, or were being held in prison. Quinn was riding a thin line, and she also knew from Lisa Duncan that he had been ordered by the President to cooperate fully with the press.

"I just left Professor Von Seeckt," Quinn said as they entered the side door and buckled in.

"How is he?" Von Seeckt was another person Reynolds felt little affinity for. The former Nazi had worked at Peenemünde and despite his claims of ignorance, Reynolds knew he had to have known about the Dora concentration camp, where slave labor for the missile facility had been housed. Reynolds's father had been one of the first who entered the camp and experienced the death and misery firsthand. He'd told his daughter about it and the desire to never again let such atrocities go unnoticed or unpunished had been the driving force in Kelly's path into a career in the media.

"Not well," Quinn said. "The doctors give him less than a week."

Kelly snorted. "They gave him that last week.

He's a tough old bastard." She glanced over as the chopper lifted. "Why'd you see him?"

Quinn met her eyes. "There's something weird going on." He related the story of the strange person, Oleisa, showing up and commandeering a bouncer, and the messages being sent to Antarctica. He left off Von Seeckt's last disturbing question, even though it had been the only thought rattling about his brain since leaving the old man.

"You really think Scorpion Base is being used by this STAAR?" Kelly asked.

"It's the only thing that makes sense."

"Could it really be kept secret?"

Quinn nodded. "Yes. There's no set satellite coverage of the land down there, and since the base was under the snowcap anyway, it wouldn't be hard at all to keep it hidden. Also, remember that international treaty bars any weapons from being deployed on the continent, so it's the least militarized place on the planet.

"Overflights are also virtually unknown because Scorpion Base is totally off any flight route to any of the other international bases. The vicious weather that's common most of the time down there also discourages visitors."

"I've never heard of a government agency that was able to keep a total veil of secrecy around itself," Kelly said, realizing the contradiction built into her words as soon as she said them. "I want to know more about this."

The helicopter was landing now, just outside the main hangar at Area 51. "I'll show you everything I've managed to uncover," Quinn said as they disembarked.

As they rode the elevator down to the Cube,

Kelly reflected on the fact that just a few weeks ago Johnny Simmons had been captured trying to gain access to the very facility she was now being escorted into. If there was another secret government agency still at work, she promised herself that she would uncover it no matter what the cost.

The doors to the Cube slid open and Quinn led her to the raised desk at the back of the room. There was a subdued hum of activity from the rest of the room.

"I've had all our intelligence data links cued to pick up anything relating to STAAR," Quinn said as he sat down. "I've also done an exhaustive search of the classified archives. There's not much."

"What do you have?" Kelly asked, the reporter part of her intrigued.

Quinn looked at his computer. "After the bouncers were removed, Scorpion Base remained empty for several years. Then in 1959, unknown even to Majestic at the time, someone moved in, taking over the deep chamber. I've got a report here from an engineering unit that put prefab structures deep under the ice, using the wide tunnel they'd dug to bring up the bouncers. I've checked and there's no sign of the base on the surface. Aircraft going there are guided by a transmitter on a constantly changing frequency."

"Who set it up?" Kelly asked.

"Scorpion was reestablished in 1959 by President Eisenhower. I've found a copy of the order and it's very unusual. The presidential directive authorizing the base also stipulates that none of his successors were to be briefed on the existence of the station or the organization that ran it, known only by the acronym STAAR."

"Jesus," Kelly exclaimed. "How could they keep this secret all these years?"

"The appropriation for STAAR is hidden inside the sixty-seven-billion-dollar-a-year black budget," Quinn explained. This was an area he was very familiar with from his work with Majestic. "By the same presidential directive that established it, STAAR took a specified percentage every year, no questions asked, and wired to a Swiss bank account. I bet you there's a good chance no one in present-day Washington knows that STAAR exists."

"Can that be?" Kelly wanted to know.

Quinn nodded. "As far as I can tell, STAAR appears to do nothing, which means it doesn't attract any attention. The operating budget is hidden inside the highly classified budget of the National Reconnaissance Organization."

He tapped his computer screen. "Actually, the most interesting thing about STAAR that I could find isn't the budget but something that's missing: there's no personnel records for the people who make up STAAR." He leaned back in his seat. "As far as the personnel paperwork trail that any organization affiliated with the U.S. Government has to have, no matter how secret, STAAR is an organization with no people. Hell, even the CIA has some paperwork on assassins it hires."

Kelly stared at him. "What—" she began, but paused as Quinn suddenly leaned forward and began rapidly typing into his keyboard.

"Well, this is interesting. There's a live link being picked up by the NSA involving STAAR," he said.

"From where?" Kelly asked.

He pointed up at the screen at the front of the room. "From Aurora." An electronic map of China appeared. A small flashing light on the wall screen sped across the overlay of the western edge of China, heading toward the safety of the ocean with surprising speed.

Kelly knew that Aurora was the top-of-the-line spy plane that the Air Force had, the successor to the SR-71.

"Data is being downlinked from Aurora to Scorpion Station," Quinn added. "I'm intercepting a copy. Maybe we'll learn something."

■ ■ ■

Inside the STAAR command center deep under the ice, the woman who had run the organization for the past twenty-two years sat in a deep leather chair, looking at the various display screens that ran across the length of the front of the center. When she had to make contact with those in Washington or elsewhere, she had the ST-8 clearance that could get her whatever she wanted, no questions asked, and she was known only by her code name: Lexina.

She'd been picked by her predecessor for her intelligence, her loyalty, and above all her willingness to exile herself to Scorpion Station and never leave. She considered herself a soldier. A soldier who, like all soldiers, wished always for peace in her time but constantly prepared for the alternative and was willing to give her all if that alternative did occur.

"What is the status of Dr. Duncan?" Lexina asked.

"Airborne," Elek, her chief of staff, answered. In STAAR the code name was the only way one identified oneself or addressed another. "Should be landing in Korea in less than an hour."

"Who is on the ground waiting for them?" she asked. STAAR kept an active network of only twenty agents around the world. Add in the five members who ran Scorpion Base and they were an extremely small organization, which further added to their ability to maintain a veil of secrecy.

"Zandra is ready to meet the plane and brief them. Her cover is CIA," Elek said. "Turcotte knows her as CIA from the Rift Valley mission, so that works best."

The last was standard. STAAR used whichever government agency it saw fit as cover. Maintaining such covers had never caused trouble, due to their lack of intrusive activity over the years. Now Lexina saw trouble coming, but complaints from the CIA or NSA or any of the other alphabet-soup agencies were the least of her worries. She also knew it was just a matter of time before their initial veil of secrecy was pierced, but that didn't concern her either. They had a plan in place for that.

"What about intelligence?" she asked.

"We haven't heard anything out of China for—" Elek began, but Lexina cut him off.

"I know what we haven't heard. That's why we've authorized Duncan and her people to go in. How does it look for *their* mission?"

"We've got Aurora taking a look and gathering imagery," Elek said. He typed into his keyboard and one of the screens cleared. An electronic map of China appeared.

■ ■ ■

Shaped like a black manta ray, Aurora was cruising at forty thousand feet over China, at a speed of Mach 5. As it approached the target area, it slowed down to less than 2.5, still over two thousand miles an hours, but slow enough so that the reconnaissance probe could be deployed.

In the backseat the RSO, reconnaissance systems officer, made sure all the systems were ready, then he activated them as they passed the target area.

"Anything on the HF or SATCOM frequencies we were told to monitor?" the pilot asked.

"Negative."

"I wonder who the hell is down there," the pilot said. "You couldn't pay me to be on the ground in China these days."

The RSO noted a red light flash on the left of his console.

"We've got missile launches," he told the pilot. "I have what we came for. Pod's coming in. Get us out of here."

"Roger." The pilot kicked in the afterburners. Both men were slammed back against their specially designed seats as the plane more than doubled its speed in less than fifteen seconds, leaving the missiles fired by the Chinese military well behind, the guidance systems electronically wondering where the target they had locked on to had gone.

"Downloading data," the RSO said as the red

light went out and the Pacific Ocean rapidly approached.

The data went through a scrambler and the garbled transmission was recorded onto a digital disk. The disk then played forward at two thousand times normal speed, bursting the message to an orbiting satellite. That satellite bounced the message to a sister satellite farther west and down to South Korea, where Zandra waited, the data also forwarded to Scorpion Base and intercepted by the NSA and sent to Major Quinn in the Cube.

■ ■ ■

"I've got a copy of the data," Quinn announced.

"Is it going anywhere else other than Antarctica?" Kelly Reynolds asked.

"A copy is being forwarded to Osan Air Force Base in South Korea," Quinn said. "Looking through it, there seems to be mainly imagery of western China."

"Osan is where Turcotte and Nabinger are being briefed," Kelly said.

"I don't get it," Quinn said. "Who's handling their operation? I thought it was CIA."

"If you don't know," Kelly said, "I for one don't know. But this may mean that whoever is in Osan waiting for them isn't CIA but connected to STAAR."

"It's a possibility," Quinn agreed. "But whoever's there, they're obviously getting the best possible intelligence for the mission."

"What's the political situation in China?" Kelly asked. She felt very uneasy in the closed confines of the Cube, so far underground. Everything here represented what she hated, and this intrigue about the mission into China was causing her to teeter on the verge of despair.

"CNN has the best coverage," Quinn said as he turned one of the front screens to the news network. A reporter was standing in front of a modern building in Hong Kong as people hurried in the streets behind him. Ever since Hong Kong had been turned over to the Chinese government it had existed as a strange netherworld between the rest of the world and the government in Beijing. Any news that managed to get out of China came out of the small former colony like this reporter's best guesses as to what was happening on the mainland:

''There have been unconfirmed reports that elements of the Twenty-sixth Army have moved into positions around the city of Beijing. Whether these reports are true is not known, nor is it known whether the government will use these troops in an attempt to abort this movement that has been going on for the past week.

''So far things in the capital have been calm, but there are vague reports of fighting in the countryside, especially in the Western Provinces, where ethnic and religious groups have long chafed under the heavy hand of the Chinese government.

''There have even been unconfirmed reports that commandos from the Taiwanese army have been operating on the mainland, helping to foment the unrest.

''We have also been informed that we
have twelve hours to leave the country
or face arrest. Xenophobia is sweeping
the Revolutionary Council and China is
closing its borders to the outside
world.
    ''This will be our last broadcast
as-''

"Nothing from the CIA or NSA?" Kelly asked
as Quinn turned the volume down.

"Some troop movements. The Twenty-sixth
Army is indeed being moved in near the capitol.
The PLA is doing a shell game, moving units away
from where they were conscripted and putting
them where they'll be more likely to shoot at the
locale populace if ordered to do so."

"And the Taiwanese?" Kelly asked.

"According to the CIA the Recce Commandos,
part of the Taiwanese special forces, have infil-
trated several teams into mainland China to do
exactly as the reporter said. And China is closing
off from the rest of the world." Quinn looked up
from his computer screen. "Do you think this site
in China is important?"

"I don't know," Kelly said. "Turcotte and
Nabinger did, and obviously whoever is pulling
strings from Antarctica thinks it is. I just wonder
who is who here and what their motives are."

"Well, whoever this STAAR is, they sure have a
lot of power," Quinn noted.

"We need to keep an eye on things in case
Turcotte and the others need help." Kelly knew
that Quinn would give her information, but he
would not help her try to stop the mission.

"Already on top of that."

"What about the person from STAAR who took over your bouncer?" Kelly asked.

Quinn shrugged. "She seems to be waiting."

"For what?"

"Your guess is as good as mine."

■ ■ ■

The duty officer for the 1st Special Operations Squadron (1st SOS), home-based out of Okinawa, looked up as the secure SATCOM terminal machine nestled in the corner hummed with an incoming message. He put down his book and went over to the machine. After five seconds the humming stopped and the message was spit out. The man's eyes widened as he read the message.

```
CLASSIFIED: TOP SECRET ST-8
ROUTING: FLASH
TO: CDR 1ST SOS/ 1ST SOW/ MSG 01
FROM: NATIONAL COMMAND AUTHORITY VIA
CIA
SUBJ: ALERT/TANGO SIERRA/AUTH CODE:
ST-8
REQ: ONE MC-130
DEST: OSAN AFB/ROK
TIME: ASAP
POINT OF CONTACT: CODE NAME ZANDRA, CIA
END: TBD
CLASSIFIED: TOP SECRET ST-8
```

The duty officer grabbed the phone and punched in the number for the commander's quarters.

■ ■ ■

"That's Qian-Ling," Nabinger said, tapping a satellite photo that showed a large mountain. He was looking at the satellite and thermal imagery tacked to hastily erected plywood bulletin boards. The others followed him. They had landed at Osan less than ten minutes ago and an Air Force major had immediately escorted them into this hangar, past the armed guards standing next to the door, and then left them alone.

Turcotte peered at it. "Big target area. How do we find Che Lu and get into it?"

They all turned as the door slid slightly open and a figure stepped in. "Fancy meeting you here," Turcotte said as he recognized the tall, slender form.

"Captain Turcotte, Dr. Duncan, we've met," the woman said. She turned to the other person. "Professor Nabinger, my name, as far as you are concerned, is Zandra."

Nabinger raised a bushy eyebrow. "Greek?"

"It's just a code name," Zandra said, a bit taken aback. She gestured around the room. "We have all the information we can gather about Qian-Ling here for your use, including imagery from Aurora."

"What's the plan?" Turcotte asked.

"This is the launch site, and I will be your FOB commander," Zandra began, only to be interrupted by Duncan.

"You are going to have to speak English here. Launch site for who and what is an FOB?"

"An FOB is a forward operating base," Turcotte explained. "In Special Forces it's the headquarters with operational control of deployed elements." He indicated his two comrades. "Are we to be the deployed element?"

Zandra shook her head. "You will have a Special Forces split A-team accompanying you, Captain. And only you are going."

"Split A-team?" Duncan asked.

"An A-team has twelve men on it," Turcotte said. "A split team is six men, with each specialty: weapons, demolition, medical, and communications; represented by one man, plus a commander and intelligence expert."

"I'm going too." Nabinger stepped forward.

Zandra shook her head. "Captain Turcotte can relay back via digital video any information they find in Qian-Ling or get from Professor Che Lu. You're too valuable to—"

"I'm going or you're not getting my assistance."

Zandra stared at him for a few seconds. "It's the tomb, isn't it? Can't pass up the opportunity?" She didn't wait for a reply. "Fine. You can go."

"And I'm staying here with you," Duncan said, earning herself a sidelong look from Zandra.

"Where's the split team?" Turcotte asked, feeling more comfortable knowing that he would have six men with him who were part of his Green Beret brotherhood.

"Already isolated next door. They've been planning since they were alerted," Zandra said. "They don't know the actual objective, just where you are going and that they are to get you in and out in one piece."

"Does that mean alive?" Nabinger asked.

"That would be beneficial to mission accomplishment," Zandra said without the slightest crack of a smile.

"How are we getting there?" Turcotte asked.

"MC-130. The plane is en route from Okinawa," Zandra said. "It's the quickest and safest way in."

Turcotte turned to Nabinger. "Have you ever parachuted?"

Nabinger's eyes got wide. "Wait a second! Parachuting?"

For the first time there was some amusement in Zandra's eyes. "You want to see the tomb, you jump. Don't worry, at five hundred feet it's just falling off the back ramp of the plane. The static line will open the chute and then you land."

Turcotte looked at the woman more closely. "This doesn't give us much time. We'll be going in tonight."

"That should not be a problem. The team has been doing your mission planning for you. They'll be briefing back shortly. You just go for the ride and to discover whatever Airlia artifacts, if any, are in Qian-Ling. You try to make contact with Che Lu and find out what she knows. Then you come home." Zandra turned toward the satellite imagery. "By the way, we believe that Che Lu and her party have been sealed inside the tomb by the PLA, so you can kill two birds with one stone, so to speak."

• • •

"Stop," Che Lu ordered, although the command was unnecessary, for once she stopped her slow and careful steps along the tunnel, the students all froze behind her.

"Turn off the light," she ordered, and Ki complied.

They were bathed in blackness. Che Lu blinked, and peered down the tunnel. "There," she said, pointing. There was the faintest of glows ahead, just the tiniest smudge of something in the inky darkness.

"Come on," she said. Ki turned the light back on and Che Lu held the bamboo pole in front of her, the cloth hanging down to the ground. Slowly they made their way toward the light.

As they got closer, Che Lu could see that it was a small beam of light crossing the tunnel from upper left to lower right. She wondered if it was another one of the killing beams until she got even closer and could tell it was daylight. She felt a lightening of her heart as she stepped up close to the shaft. It came in from a hole in the upper left of the corridor about six inches square. The beam crossed and disappeared into another hole the same size in the lower right.

"What is the purpose of that?" Ki asked as they all gathered around, comforted by the warm ray of sunlight.

Che Lu put her face up to the hole, which she could reach if she stood on her toes. All she could see was a very faint blue square, far up the shaft. She estimated it was about a hundred meters to the outside and no one was going to be crawling up this tunnel. Still, it gave her hope that there might be a larger one farther on.

"It is like the Great Pyramid," she said, a subject she had brushed up on once she had discovered the oracle bones with high rune writing on them. "There are small shafts in it just like this that go from the king's chamber to the surface. They point to specific constellations in the sky." She turned to the lower hole. "The emperor's tomb must lie in that direction," she added.

"Was there a back door in the Great Pyramid, where you could get out?" asked Ki, ever the practical one.

"No," Che Lu said. "Only one entrance and that had been sealed up to discourage grave robbers." She sat down on the floor. "We will rest here, then continue on."

■ ■ ■

"Why don't we simply ask this Oleisa person?" Kelly Reynolds suggested.

"I don't think she's going to talk to us," Quinn said. He stood up. "But it's worth a shot."

Quinn and Reynolds left the Cube and took the elevator up to Hangar 1. As the doors opened, they entered a large room carved out of the rock of Groom Mountain. The hangar was over three quarters of a mile long and a quarter mile wide. Three of the walls, the floor, and roof—one hundred feet above their heads—were rock. The last side was a series of camouflaged sliding doors that opened up onto the runway.

They passed by one of the bouncers as they walked. Kelly knew that one could easily imagine how the rumors of flying saucers had started in the fifties if someone had seen a bouncer. The official designation by the scientists for them was MDAC or magnetic drive atmospheric craft. Each was about thirty feet in diameter, wide at the base, then sloping up to small cupola on top.

They were called bouncers because of their unique manner of flight, able to alter course instantly, which had the effect of throwing the occupants around.

Quinn and Reynolds approached the door to

the part of the hangar where the bouncer had been isolated. They pounded on it in vain for a couple of minutes, but it didn't open.

"Goddamn!" Quinn exclaimed.

"Let's take a look at the mothership," Reynolds suggested. They walked back into the main part of the hangar, past the bouncers to a door in the rear. Inside was an eight-passenger train on an electric monorail. Quinn stepped into the car, Reynolds at his side, and pressed the controls. It immediately started up and they were whisked along a brightly lit tunnel.

Kelly now knew the history of Area 51, but for over fifty years it had been one of the most closely held secrets in America. For years the primary focus of Majestic-12 had been the bouncers in Hangar One, but it was what was in Hangar Two that had helped decide the location of Area 51 when it was uncovered in the dark years of World War II. The tunnel the train was going through had been bored out years ago to connect Hangar One and Hangar Two.

The train came out of the tunnel and entered the large hole holding the mothership. Kelly knew it had been a cavern, but she'd been outside when Captain Turcotte had fired charges out of sequence trying to stop General Gullick from flying the mothership, tearing the roof down on top of the craft. Getting off the train, she could see that after extensive digging by the Army Corps of Engineers for the past several days, the rubble had been removed, enough to clear the mothership, which had not suffered any obvious damage.

Kelly looked up. The ship was now open to the sky, and the early-morning light filtered over the lip of the hole in the roof onto the glistening black skin. Despite having seen it before, Kelly Reynolds was staggered by the sheer physical size of the mothership: cigar shaped, over a mile long and a quarter mile in width at the center, it was nestled in a large black cradle made of the same black metal that composed the skin of the craft.

There was scaffolding near the front of the ship where an entrance had been opened, allowing access to the inside. With the aid of the rebel guardian computer, Gullick and the others on Majestic-12 had been able to get into the ship and fathom some of the controls, enough that they had even gotten the ship to lift off its cradle a short distance and figure out some of the drive mechanisms.

But that was it, Reynolds knew, as she walked with Quinn along the side of the ship. Majestic had been stopped from flying the ship, and up to the message coming from Mars, what should be done with the ship had been a hot topic of conversation not only at UNAOC, but around the world. Now, as evidenced by the small number of people in the cavern, there were more important things happening.

Kelly stopped walking and looked up at the black wall curving up and over her head. She had a feeling that not long after the Airlia came, someone would be coming here for a visit, because she had an inkling that the mothership might be the real reason Aspasia was coming back to Earth.

Chapter 17

The East Pacific Ridge runs from the underwater Amundsen Plain off the coast of Antarctica, north, to finally rise out of the ocean at Baja, California. Between those two points the only place the ridge crests the surface of the ocean is Easter Island. North of Easter Island, along the ridge, was the area that the foo fighters controlled by the Guardian I computer had been tracked going into the ocean.

For the past four days the United States Navy had been intensively searching the entire area under a veil of secrecy. The secrecy had been approved by the Pentagon because of the very uncomfortable fact that the foo fighters, despite being only three feet in diameter, obviously were capable of great devastation, as shown by the destruction of the lab at Dulce, New Mexico. UNAOC, and the United States Government, had downplayed the incident and the loss of fourteen security and lab personnel due both to the illegal work that had been going on there and the fact that the destruction didn't show the Airlia computer in the best light.

The flight the previous day of the three foo fighters had heightened anxiety and the pressure to find the strange crafts' home base. The three had exited and entered the ocean over three hundred miles to the west, but the Navy still believed they were in the right place. The feeling was that the fighters must have traversed the intervening distance underwater.

Up until the previous day the work had consisted of searching and scanning. The searching was conducted by several submersibles, manned and unmanned. The scanning was done by sonar and the LLS, laser-line scanner. The LLS was the most efficient piece of machinery the Navy had for the job of finding where the foo fighters were hiding. It worked by projecting a blue-green laser, capable of penetrating the ocean, in seventy-degree arcs, "painting" a picture of the bottom. The LLS was so accurate, it could show rivets on a sunken ship's hull.

The previous evening, just after sunset, the LLS had discovered an anomaly in the side of a outcropping along the East Pacific Ridge, at a depth of five thousand meters or over three miles down. The picture the laser painted showed a cylindrical tube sticking out of the side of the outcropping, extending about twenty feet, with a boxlike structure sitting on top. It most definitely was not naturally occurring.

The Navy spent the entire night moving their classified deep-sea submersible, the USS *Greywolf,* into position. The *Greywolf* was tethered to a surface support ship, the *Yellowstone,* that towed it to a spot directly over the anomaly. As dawn was breaking on the horizon, the *Greywolf* slipped its mooring underneath the *Yellowstone* and began its descent into the inky darkness. The head pilot was a twenty-five-year naval veteran, Lieutenant Commander Downing. His copilot and navigator was Lieutenant Tennyson. The third member of the crew was a contract civilian named Emory.

The *Greywolf* was the result of decades of trial and error with deep-sea submersibles. Prior to its construction the record for manned depth was just under seven thousand meters. The *Greywolf* shattered that record on its first dive, going down to eight thousand meters. Its design was radical, being neither the traditional sphere nor cigar shape most people associated with such vessels. It was shaped like the F-117 Stealth fighter, with composite, flat-planed sides, made of a special titanium alloy.

The three-man crew of the *Greywolf* didn't know they owed the makeup of their ship's skin to the work done on the mothership in Area 51, but that was where Majestic researchers had learned much about various alloys, the results being passed on to other military black projects such as *Greywolf*.

Commander Downing was not concerned about the dive itself as they cleared through two thousand meters. The depth was well within range, the currents in the area were minimal, and the submersible was operating well within all acceptable parameters. He, and the other two crew, were, however, concerned about their objective. No foo fighter had been spotted close up since the destruction of the lab at Dulce, but all three men had seen classified videotape of the results of that strike. They also knew about the loss of signal from *Viking II* as it closed in on Cydonia. It probably was all just automatic functioning of the Guardian computer, but they figured that wouldn't do them much good if they had an accident at five thousand meters caused by Guardian.

Because of the fear that the guardian might react to their presence near the foo fighter base, the *Greywolf* was being accompanied on the dive by *Helmet II*, a remotely piloted vehicle, or RPV. It had received its name because that was exactly what it looked like: a helmet with several mechanical arms and sensors bolted to the main body. A large propeller rested in the bottom of the *Helmet* and provided vertical thrust. Maneuvering was done by four small fanlike thrusters spaced around the rim of the base.

Helmet II was equipped with not only the arms and sensors, but a video camera on top that had an unrestricted 360-degree view and one that ran around on a track just above the lip and thrusters. There was a third bolted to the center bottom, able to look directly down. The views these cameras picked up were transmitted directly back to the *Greywolf,* where the remote control was, and from there up to the *Yellowstone.*

As it passed through four thousand meters, the *Greywolf* came to a halt and sent *Helmet II* ahead. That was Emory's job. He sat in a cramped section of the crew compartment and looked at video screens and a fourth computer screen that showed him essential data as to attitude, trim, depth, and speed of the RPV. He controlled it with a joystick that always reminded him of his kid's game controller for the computer at home.

As they slowly descended, Tennyson picked up several sonar contacts a thousand meters above them. He promptly reported them to Downing.

"Whales?" Downing asked.

"No. Submarines." Tennyson listened carefully, hearing the sound of screws churning through water decrease. "They're slowing."

"Ping with active," Downing ordered. "Let's get a fix, then I'll call *Yellowstone* and find out what's going on."

The subs were silent now, fixed in position. Tennyson sent out a ping and listened to the return. "We've got three *Los Angeles*–class attack submarines over our heads."

"Damn," Downing muttered. He clicked on the ULF radio linking him to the *Yellowstone*. "Mother, this is Wolf. Over."

The reply came back in the flat way ULF transmissions did, muted by the mass of water over their head. "This is Mother. Over."

"What's with the subs? Over." Downing had no time or inclination to be tactful or subtle at four thousand feet. The pressure of the water surrounding their ship would crush them in an eyeblink if the hull were breached in any manner.

Their commanding officer on the *Yellowstone* was also terse, for different reasons. "We have them on sonar also. We have no contact with them, but we have been informed by CINCPAC that they are here at National Command Authority directive. I don't know what their orders are, and when I asked, I was told to mind my own business. They won't interfere with your mission, so ignore them. Out."

Downing twisted in his seat and looked at Tennyson. "Prepare to ignore," he said.

Tennyson smiled. "Preparing to ignore. Aye, aye, sir."

"Implement ignore mode."

"Ignore mode it is." Tennyson laughed, but it echoed hollow off the titanium alloy walls and died quickly.

"If you gentlemen are interested," Emory said from his little corner, "I've got visual contact with the ridge."

The other two peered over his shoulder as the rock-strewn surface of the East Pacific Ridge appeared on the video screens.

"How far to the objective?" Downing asked.

"Another two hundred meters down and *Helmet* should be right on top of it," Emory reported.

A minute went by, then the view from the bottom camera showed something different. Emory's hands manipulated both the controls for the RPV and the camera.

"That's it!" Downing announced as the camera focused on a large smooth black tube sticking out of the side of the ridge. "That's where the foo fighters are based."

"And there they are!" Emory exclaimed as three glowing spheres shot out of the end of the tunnel. They raced directly at the camera, splitting off in three different directions just as they were about to collide with it.

The men in the submersible shifted their gaze to the top camera, which Emory frantically maneuvered to try and track the foo fighters. He caught glimpses of one of them turning abruptly and heading back toward the RPV.

Suddenly all the screens went blank as Emory cursed. "I've lost the link with *Helmet*." His fingers flew over the controls as he tried to reestablish contact. Downing and Tennyson jumped back into their respective seats.

"Give me sonar on those things," Downing ordered as he quickly powered up the engines.

"They're approaching." Tennyson was trying to listen and read his screen at the same time. "They're coming fast, real fast."

Downing goosed the engines, then gave full power, straight up. "How long?"

"Uh, forty seconds," Tennyson said.

"Still no contact with RPV!" Emory called out.

"Ping it," Downing ordered.

A loud ping echoed as the sound wave went out.

"Thirty seconds, no, wait, make that twenty."

"Damn," Downing cursed. They had gone up less than forty meters so far. He reached down and flipped open the cover on red switch.

"Negative on ping!" Emory was stunned. "*Helmet* is gone!" He pulled himself together. "Ten seconds. We should be seeing them any second!"

Downing threw the switch and the interior of the *Greywolf* went pitch black except for two small battery-powered emergency lights. The drumming of the engines went silent.

"What the hell did you do?" Emory demanded.

Downing pointed at the small super-Plexiglas portal above his head. A foo fighter flashed by.

"I killed all our power systems," Downing said.

"Why?" Emory asked.

"I did it before they did it," Downing said. "Every report from aircraft encountering foo fighters said that close proximity to the fighters totally drained the power systems. If they took out *Helmet,* we were next. We're four thousand meters down in the ocean. We're going to need our power to get back up."

"Well, what do we do now?" Emory asked.

"We wait."

■ ■ ■

On board the three *Los Angeles*–class attack ships, the crews were running to battle stations. Wire-guided torpedoes were armed and the captain of each submarine was glued to his sonar men, tracking the progress of the three foo fighters and the *Greywolf.*

Fingers were poised on launching buttons until it was determined that the three fighters and the submersible were all holding at four thousand meters.

As the minutes went by and nothing changed, the ranking commander on board the *Springfield,* Captain Forster, issued his orders, based on the instructions he had been given over the radio by some woman named Lexina with an ST-8 clearance.

"All weapons are to remain armed and locked. We will not instigate action unless the foo fighters act against the *Greywolf* or if they go above three thousand meters."

■ ■ ■

Lexina received the word of the foo fighters' appearance as soon as the *L.A.*-class subs had forwarded it to CINCPAC, Command in Chief, Pacific Fleet, and the message was placed into the highly classified U.S. Intelligence Dissemination Network.

"What should we do?" Elek asked.

"Nothing yet," she replied.

"But—"

"Nothing yet," Lexina repeated. "We've waited a long time and we cannot fail because we move too quickly. Timing is critical."

Chapter 18

Power from the solar panels was pouring in, a waterfall of energy that filled the guardian computer and its subsystems. It began accessing and opening other programs that had long rested dormant.

Two programs had priority, one biological, the other mechanical. Even deeper than the computer under the surface of Mars was a cavern lined with rows of black, coffinlike objects, each just over ten feet long by four in diameter. For the first time since they were sealed, the black metal protecting each pod slid back, revealing layers of silvery, magnetically charged material that peeled back one by one until finally a clear material was left, tightly wrapped around the bodies that had been preserved.

They were all tall, male and female, between six and seven feet, with short torsos and inversely long arms and legs. The heads were half again as big as a human's, with red hair covering the scalp. The skin was white and unmarked.

The air around each body began to crackle with electric static as the fields that had preserved them for so long were slowly reduced; all except for twenty of the eighty. Twelve of those twenty had failed and the bodies inside were mummified. The other eight were to remain asleep as a security measure.

Mechanically, power was diverted into the chamber closest to the surface, just under the object known as the Fort. Lights went on and a half-dozen ships were illuminated in their glow. Neither bouncer nor mothership, these lay in between. Each rested on the smooth rock floor, like an upright bear's claw, tapering up and curving slightly to one side until it reached a razor-sharp point. Each craft was over two hundred meters high and forty around at the base. They all pointed slightly inward, the grouping making an image like the paw of a very dangerous animal. The skin of each ship was flat black, so black that it absorbed all light and reflected nothing back.

A bolt of golden light arced from cables crisscrossing the roof of the chamber down to each ship and they began to power up.

■ ■ ■

Turcotte, Nabinger, and Duncan walked into the A-team's isolation area and were immediately challenged by one of the men, who demanded to see their identification cards. As Turcotte was pulling it out his wallet, Zandra stepped in front.

"Captain Turcotte, Professor Nabinger, and Dr. Duncan are all on your access roster," Zandra said. "As a matter of fact, Captain Turcotte is the mission commander."

A short, muscular soldier with graying hair walked over, looking none too happy. "I'm Chief Harker. I wasn't told that someone would be taking over my team." Harker had a deep gravelly voice that had smoked too many cigarettes and drunk too much whiskey. His leathery face was crisscrossed with wrinkles and lines, but his gray eyes were sharp and focused on Zandra.

"You were told to follow any orders I gave, right?" Zandra asked.

"That's correct."

"Then Captain Turcotte is in command." Zandra turned. "I leave you all to get acquainted, but don't waste time. You depart in less than two hours." She walked out the door, leaving Turcotte and the others under the gaze of the six Special Forces soldiers.

"Are all of you going on the mission?" Harker asked.

"Myself and Professor Nabinger," Turcotte answered.

"Professor of what?" Harker demanded.

"Archaeology," Nabinger said.

"Archaeology," Harker repeated. "Then maybe you can tell me then why we're infiltrating Communist China to get into a tomb."

"I'm sorry—" Nabinger began, but Turcotte stepped forward.

"There's information in the tomb about the Airlia," Turcotte said.

"I thought—" Nabinger started to speak, but Turcotte interrupted him once more.

"These men are risking their lives to help us," he told Nabinger. "The least we can do is give them the truth."

"Sure, no problem with me, but the ice queen in the other room might not like it," Nabinger said.

"The professor here," Turcotte continued, "is the world's foremost expert on both the high rune language and the Airlia."

"Hey," one of the younger soldiers said, "you're the guy who made contact with that guardian computer, aren't you?"

"Yes, he is," Turcotte said. "But right now you need to get us up to speed on how you plan on getting us to the tomb."

Harker turned and walked over to one of the plywood boards. "This is the operational area," he said.

Turcotte was impressed with the quality of the Aurora imagery. It looked as if the pictures had been taken with a zoom lens out of an aircraft at three hundred feet. Not for the first time Turcotte wondered who was behind all this. Zandra claimed to be CIA, but every contact Turcotte had ever had with that agency had demonstrated nothing like the efficiency being shown by Zandra.

"My intelligence man, Sergeant Brooks, is working on the enemy situation in the vicinity of the target," Harker said, drawing him out of his reverie. "We got a lot of information that we've been trying to process into intelligence."

Harker glanced at the closed door, then back at Turcotte and Nabinger. Instinctively, Turcotte knew what was bothering the warrant officer; it was what would be disturbing him if he were in the other man's shoes.

"Listen, we're all in this together," Turcotte said. "I'm in command, but all that means is that this mission is my responsibility, Chief. You still command your team and I'll follow whatever plan you've come up with to get us in there and out."

Chief Harker seemed to relax ever so slightly. He pointed about the room. "Chase there is our commo man. He's coordinated with Zandra or whatever the hell her name is on times, message formats, codes to be used, and equipment. We'll be using SATCOM and we have unlimited access. We'll be carrying two sets. Chase will have one, I'll have the other."

Chase had short, sandy hair and a red face. He was slightly overweight with large muscular arms. He was carefully coiling up a set of cables, taking all the care the mother of a newborn would over her infant.

"We got FM rigs for each person to wear for interteam commo," Harker continued. "Throat mikes, voice activated, earplug. See Chase to get yours rigged."

Harker moved to another table. "Pressler is our medic. He's done a medical profile on the area of operations, but we don't plan on being there long enough for native flora or fauna or diseases to be a problem. We're more concerned about man-made medical problems like bullets. He's got a cut-down M-3 aid bag he'll be carrying. Also, I'd like for you two to be rigged with two IVs on a vest inside your shirt like we all wear. One's blood expander, the other's glucose. They can save your ass from going under if you're in shock."

Turcotte nodded. He could tell Nabinger and Duncan weren't following half of what the burly Green Beret was telling them, but Turcotte planned on sticking close by the professor throughout the mission and Duncan had only to be concerned about what happened back here.

For the first time in a long, long time, Turcotte felt at home. Even when he'd been inbriefed into the Nightscape security force working at Area 51, he'd felt like an outsider. But he understood these men and how they operated.

"What's the threat?" Turcotte asked.

"It don't look good," Harker said. "The PLA, People's Liberation Army, got several units deployed in our area of operation. Looks like there's some real shooting going on between the PLA and Muslim factions. Also, that Zandra lady said that the people we're supposed to link up with are locked inside the tomb, so that means things are stirred up a bit in our AO."

Harker pointed at a spot on the side of the mountain tomb. "This is the only entrance we know of. As you can see, the PLA got a couple of vehicles parked in the courtyard and a machine position set up here, on the side of the mountain right above the door."

"How do you plan on getting in?" Turcotte asked.

"Two stages," Harker said. "First, my snipers reach out and touch someone, taking out the machine-gun position. They'll keep firing until we get noticed. Then the rest of us go in and clear out the guys left alive on the doorstep. Then my engineer, Howes, has got charges prerigged that he says can blow the doors and get us in."

"What weapons are you carrying?" Turcotte asked.

"Two Haskins .50-caliber sniper rifles with MP5-SD3 as personal weapons. Two Squad Automatic Weapons for firepower, and two M-203's for some indirect fire. You can ask your lady friend for whatever you want to carry. Whatever we've asked for, she's gotten, including some demo stuff my engineer has only read about."

"Okay," Turcotte said. "How are we infiltrating?"

"Ass end of an MC-130 at four hundred feet," Harker said.

"Four hundred!" Nabinger spoke for the first time. "I thought it was going to be five hundred."

Harker laughed, a rough sound like pebbles grating together. "Four hundred, five hundred, hell, that's only talk. For the real deal we'll be lucky if that crew goes up above three hundred feet to drop us. They're going to be staying as low as they can to keep their butts from being seen on Chinese radar."

Seeing Nabinger turn pale, Harker slapped him on the shoulder. "Don't sweat it, Prof, we came up with something that'll make your landing nice and soft." He led them over to another photo of the tomb and the surrounding terrain. He tapped on the photo. "That's where you're going to jump."

His finger rested on a small lake about two kilometers from the tomb, on the same side as the entrance. Turcotte knew what Harker meant about a soft landing, although he also knew there was a downside to parachuting into a body of water at night.

"The MC-130 navigates by reflected radar images," Turcotte explained to Duncan and Nabinger. "The smooth surface of the lake gives a very large signature that the plane can easily find, so that's good. Plus we can look out the back and double-check we're in the right place before we jump."

"Fucking-A on that," Harker said.

Turcotte knew what the other man meant—anyone with any time in Special Forces had been on drops from MC-130's where they landed miles from the intended drop zone.

Turcotte slapped Nabinger on the back. "You don't have to worry about having to learn how to do a parachute landing fall or breaking your leg."

"No, just drowning," Nabinger muttered.

Turcotte thought it best to avoid that topic right now. "What about exfiltration? Had any time to look at that?"

Harker scratched his jaw. "Well, that's another story. There are several places we can use for PZs."

"PZs?" Duncan asked.

"Pickup zones for helicopters," Turcotte explained.

"Like I said," Harker continued, "there's plenty of PZ locations. What worries me, though, is that the warning order said we were going to have two MH-60's take us out. Now, I may not be the brightest guy in the world, but I do know a little about the Black Hawk. I know that it doesn't have the range, even with external tanks, to make it from here to the target area and back. Not even close. I'm kind of curious how they think they're going to do this and who's flying the mission."

"Maybe they'll in-flight refuel," Turcotte said. "Some of the specially modified Task Force 160 Black Hawks have that capability."

"Yeah, the choppers might have the capability,"

Harker acknowledged, "but I doubt very much the Air Force is gonna put one of their tankers over Chinese airspace."

"I'll talk to Zandra about it and see if I can get more information," Lisa Duncan said.

"Well, if the Air Force gets us in the right place," Harker said, "I'll get you in the tomb."

Turcotte, Duncan, and Nabinger looked at the imagery and maps of the mountain that was Qian-Ling. "It's big," Turcotte noted. "Any idea how far it extends underground?" he asked Nabinger.

"None. As far as is known, no one's been in it since it was sealed."

"Great," Turcotte said.

A woman's voice cut in. Zandra had walked in while they were talking. "Your gear is waiting and the plane is landing, so I suggest you get moving."

As they left the room, Nabinger shook his head and spoke in a voice only Turcotte and Duncan could hear. "You know, this is kind of bizarre, don't you think?"

"What is?" Turcotte asked.

"Well, here we are, using the best technology man has, to get into an ancient tomb in China, to try and find out about the Airlia. Maybe, like Kelly said, we aren't ready like Aspasia thinks we are if we can't even agree with the Chinese government to let us take a look without having to sneak in."

"There's no doubt mankind is not united enough to join arm-in-arm with some advanced alien race," Turcotte said. "But that's not what worries me."

"What does concern you, then?" Duncan asked.

"What worries me," Turcotte said, "is whether mankind can get its shit together enough to fight an advanced alien race if we have to."

■ ■ ■

"All of you except Ki stay here," Che Lu ordered. "He and I will go back the way we came and try the right passageway."

They had taken the left passage another half mile past the light shaft, only to find it ended abruptly in a smooth stone wall. The disappointment weighed heavy on the students and Che Lu, but she knew better than to give in to the weight. She had turned them around and led them back to the shaft of light.

"If we find something, I will send Ki back." Che Lu didn't want the others shuffling behind her as she explored down deeper. She knew it was only a matter of time before one or more of the young students gave in to their fears and became a liability. At least the daylight would give them some comfort, although she knew night would be falling soon.

Taking the bamboo stick and all the flashlights but one, she and Ki headed back the way they had come, the light off to conserve it, using the stick along the wall to search for the intersection, since they had already passed this way and knew it to be safe and smooth.

■ ■ ■

"We've lost a hundred meters in the last two hours," Tennyson reported, his voice echoing through the cramped interior of the *Greywolf*.

"Keep your eye on the gauge and let me know

if we lose more." Commander Downing wasn't worried about depth right now. Condensation was forming on the interior of the submersible, adding to the chill that was seeping in from the outside. He had the battery heaters off, conserving power, and keeping the foo fighters from reacting to any indication of energy, but he knew he couldn't do it indefinitely without it getting so cold inside that they would become hypothermic.

Downing twisted his head and looked out the small portal into the dark water. There was nothing for almost five minutes; then, right on schedule, one of the foo fighters drifted past, its glow the only source of light other than the two emergency lights inside the sub.

"Damn," Tennyson muttered, looking over his shoulder. "What do you think those attack subs are doing?"

"They're waiting, just like we are."

"For what?" Emory asked from his console.

"For something to happen," Downing said. "Either the foo fighters will do something or go away."

"So we're waiting on those things," Emory said.

"Actually," Downing said, "I think we're all waiting on Aspasia to wake up and sort this all out."

Chapter 19

The members of the Special Forces team and their two straphangers finished loading their rucksacks onto the floor of the MC-130 and seated themselves along the right side of the plane on the cargo webbing seats. To Turcotte's eye the team looked like a group of seals out of water, as they all wore black dry suits over their camouflage fatigues.

In the bustle of loading onto the plane Turcotte had not had a chance to talk to Duncan alone. Just a hurried good-bye and good luck and then the back ramp had come up, sealing them off from the outside world, and the turboprop engines kicked into life. Turcotte felt a little out of sorts, and he shook his head to clear it of extraneous thoughts and focus on the task at hand.

Turcotte had coordinated several checkpoints en route to the drop zone. The loadmaster in the back of the aircraft would relay the checkpoint number from the navigator to him as they crossed each one, keeping him oriented to where they were on the route. At checkpoint one, where the aircraft dropped altitude and headed for the coast of China, Turcotte would have the team start their inflight rig to put their parachutes on. The last checkpoint was six minutes from the drop zone, where Turcotte would start his jump commands.

Turcotte glanced at Nabinger, who looked most uncomfortable in his dry suit. The professor was probably beginning to regret his enthusiasm about Qian-Ling and what might be hidden in the tomb. Turcotte knew that Nabinger would regret it even more when the plane began its low-level flight across China. Pressler, the medic, started passing out Dramamine pills to those who wanted them. Turcotte knew the Dramamine would help reduce the motion sickness that was an integral part of any MC-130 flight. He made sure that Nabinger downed one.

The wheels of the MC-130 lifted off the tarmac and the plane roared into the night sky.

■ ■ ■

Duncan watched the plane until it was no longer visible. Then she walked back to the operations center. She looked at Zandra, hunched over the communications console for a few minutes. As she walked behind her, Zandra finishing whatever she'd been doing, then turned and faced her.

"Time to work on the plan to get them out of there, don't you think?" Duncan asked.

Zandra pressed the tips of her fingers together. "Certainly. It's already being done."

"By who?"

"By a responsible agency," Zandra replied.

"Who are you?" Duncan asked.

"I told you—"

"And I know it's bullshit," Duncan said. "I've been around Washington a long time and I have some connections. You're not CIA. Hell, you've got more clout than the CIA. It would have taken the Agency a week to get that Air Force plane here to fly that mission and a ton of paperwork, but you had it here with less than twelve hours' notice and with authorization to send it into Chinese airspace."

"The authorization came from a presidential directive," Zandra said. "You can verify that if you wish."

"Not from a directive issued by *this* President," Duncan said.

"Nevertheless, I do have my authority from a presidential directive," Zandra said, "and you are required by law to support me."

"Your execution of this mission does not bear the stamp of the CIA or any other government agency I'm familiar with," Duncan said. "Nor did the Rift Valley operation."

"You question me because I am efficient?" Zandra asked.

"I question you because I want to know who you really work for," Duncan said.

"And I've told you that," Zandra said.

"What I'd really like," Duncan said, leaning close to the other woman, "is for those people you just sent to be brought back. They are not expendable, do you understand?"

Zandra didn't blink or avert her gaze. "I understand quite clearly."

■ ■ ■

Che Lu and Ki had passed the four-way inter-section twenty minutes ago and continued straight through, taking what had originally been the right-hand passage that headed deeper into the mountain tomb. At first the passageway ran straight and slightly down, but now it began to do wide turns, right, then left, then back right, going down at a steeper angle until Che Lu suspected they were below the base of the mountain and into the Earth itself.

It was slow and tense going as the fear that any second they might trip another trap weighed heavily on their psyches. Despite her fear Che Lu was amazed at the length and exact construction of the tunnel they were moving down. The walls and floor were perfectly smooth and the tunnel seemed to go on forever.

Of course, she'd had to reevaluate her entire frame of reference about the tomb since seeing the holographic alien figure in the main tunnel. Ancient Chinese workers had not carved this tunnel out of rock. She had been so concerned simply about survival that she had not taken the thought farther than that, but as her mind went in that direction she felt the very roots of her knowledge base suffer tremors of uncertainty.

What was true now? What was the real history of her people and the people of Earth, for that matter?

"There!" Ki huffed, suddenly halting.

The tunnel widened ahead, opening into a chamber, the far end, sides, or ceiling of which their weak flashlight could not reach. Ki looked over his shoulder. "What now, Mother-Professor?"

"We go in, follow the wall to the left so we don't get lost."

But that wasn't necessary, because as soon as they stepped out of the opening of the tunnel, a very dim glow appeared high above their heads. Both instinctively stepped back, afraid, but the light went dark.

"Ah," Che Lu spat out. She was tired of this tomb's games. She stepped forward several paces into the chamber. The glow came back, growing stronger with each passing second. Soon it was as if a minisun were hovering about a quarter mile above their heads.

Che Lu turned her head, taking in the scope of her surroundings. After so long limited to the confines of the small scope of light from the flashlight, she was staggered by what her senses revealed.

She was inside a massive cavern. Metal beams loomed up from the nearest wall and disappeared overhead, curving to follow the dome ceiling around to come down, she supposed, on the far side, which was hard to see because of the obstructions in the way. Obviously, the Airlia had not trusted the rock enough to hold without additional support. There were numerous large objects scattered about on the floor, the exact purpose of which was indeterminate. Most were in the form of black rectangles ranging from a few feet in size to one over a hundred meters long and sixty high. There were other shapes scattered about here and there also. As far as Che Lu could tell, the far wall was well over a mile and a half away.

To the far left was a bright green light glowing

out of the wall, brighter even than the one overhead. Unable to determine the scale of the light,
Che Lu had no idea how far away it was, but she
estimated at least a half mile.

"What is this?" Ki whispered.

Che Lu felt the same need to speak quietly,
awed by the scale of their surroundings. The place
felt old and abandoned, with a thin layer of dust
covering the floor, which was the same smoothly
cut rock as that of the tunnel.

"I do not know," Che Lu replied.

"This is not a tomb," Ki said.

"No." Che Lu realized her student hadn't yet
grasped all they had experienced yet. "It isn't of
human origin either."

"Ah!" Ki yelled and stepped back as a red circle appeared in front of them. Che Lu held her
place, recognizing the beginning of a hologram.
Soon the same figure was in front of them that
had greeted them in the corridor. It spoke for several minutes in the same musical voice, occasionally pointing over its shoulder at parts of the
room, then it disappeared.

"Let's go back," Ki suggested.

Che Lu regarded him curiously. "Back where?"

"Back to the others."

"And then?" she asked. "We wait to die?" She
pointed at a place the figure had also pointed at
several times; where the strong green light was
emanating. "We go there." She started walking,
not even waiting to see if Ki followed. She had no
fear now. The message this time was different
from the one in the tunnel, she could feel that.
The first had been a warning; this one, well, she
wasn't quite sure what it was, but it had not been

a warning. She didn't bother with the bamboo cane and pole.

She led them amid the machinery, some of which hummed with power.

"Look!" Ki cried out.

Che Lu looked in the direction he was pointing. There were three men moving between several of the large objects, about five hundred yards away, moving toward their position.

Che Lu instinctively grabbed Ki and pulled him back. The men were out of sight now, behind something. Che Lu took a deep breath.

Ki had pulled a small knife out of his belt and was gripping it with white knuckles.

"Put that away," Che Lu said sharply.

"But—"

One thing Che Lu had definitely noticed about the figures was the AK-74 weapons each held. Che Lu slowly looked around the edge of the next machine, Ki right behind her. Looking ahead, she could see one of the men about eighty yards ahead, halted and silhouetted against the green light source.

Where were the other two? Che Lu thought. Her instincts were tingling. Turning, she froze, looking into the end of two AK-74's. Che Lu looked from the muzzles to the heads; they were not Chinese, that was for sure. She combined the weapons with the camouflaged smocks they wore and made a guess as to their origin.

"Please do not shoot," Che Lu said in Russian.

The taller of the two replied in perfect Mandarin. "Who are you?"

"I am Professor Che Lu of Beijing University. And you are?"

"Colonel Kostanov of the Russian Republic. How did you get in?"

"We blew open the main doors."

Kostanov raised an eyebrow. "Are they still open?"

"No. The army shut them behind us. We are trapped."

Kostanov smiled, revealing even teeth. "Ah, then you join us and our party, eh, Professor? You are either very brave or very foolish to be here so poorly equipped. Or perhaps you know something about all this"—his weapon made a small arc—"that we do not know?"

Che Lu shrugged. "What I thought I knew about this tomb is obviously not true, so I think I know nothing you do not know. But I find it curious," Che Lu continued, "to find Russians inside one of China's most ancient archaeological sites."

"That's the least of the strangeness you have found here," Kostanov said. He shrugged. "I suppose I ought to just kill you both right now and continue on with my mission. Unfortunately, since I am unable to do the latter, I suppose I won't do the former; for the moment that is."

"Why are you here?" Che Lu said.

The muzzle of Kostanov's weapon lowered and his free hand encompassed the chamber. "You need ask?"

"How did you know this was here?"

"High runes," he answered simply. "We are not complete idiots. We can read some of them. More now that Professor Nabinger has made some of his findings public."

"How did you get in?" Che Lu asked.

"A side tunnel leading directly to this chamber." Kostanov pointed to the side of the chamber opposite where Che Lu and Ki had come in. "You came in from there?" he asked, directing his hand toward the tunnel they had come out of.

"Yes."

"That was closed yesterday," Kostanov said.

"You can't get out either?" It was a question she had to ask even though Che Lu knew the answer, and now she knew why the army had been here and why her door had been blocked so quickly.

"No. At least not the way we came in," Kostanov answered. "We went up to the door but it was sealed from the outside, as we already knew. The other tunnel led nowhere. . . ." His voice trailed off.

"And the main way down, you tried that, did you not?"

Kostanov nodded. "I lost one of my men there."

Che Lu pointed. "And the green light?"

"A control room of some sort," Kostanov answered. He smiled. "We have not been foolish enough or desperate enought to start pushing buttons whose function we do not now. Not yet," he added.

"How long have you been in here?" Che Lu asked.

"Three days now. It was dark when we came in. Nothing stirring. But two days ago the power came on in the control room and this room when you entered it. Perhaps you had something to do with that?"

"I wish I did," Che Lu answered, "because that would mean I could get us out of here."

"How long have you been in here?" Kostanov asked.

"We entered less than a day ago."

"You are not as well supplied as we were," Kostanov noted, "but we have reached your level now, as our food and water are gone."

"What is all this?" Che Lu asked.

"I don't know," Kostanov said. "We have been unable to get into any of the containers. Some seem to have machinery inside that is operating. Others are silent." His shoulder shrugged under the camouflage. "Your guess is as good as mine."

Che Lu pointed. "Let me see that control room."

Chapter 20

Inside the Mars chamber the program was running without a glitch. With a gentle sigh of air the inside of the chamber equalized with the pressure inside one of the crypts. The last of the material covering the body was gone.

Eyelids flickered, then opened. Bright red eyes peered up at the roof of the chamber. A six-fingered hand reached up and grasped the side of the container, then tightened, pulling the upper half of the body up. The alien stared about the chamber, taking in the other silent crypts. It came back to the alien then: She was the first. The program would wait on her before completely waking the others in the first echelon. She was to make sure the time was right.

■ ■ ■

In New York, a large collective sigh of relief was released by the UNAOC staff as a new message from the Guardian II computer on Mars was received and began to be transcribed on the large

screen in the front of the conference room. The
relief transformed into enthusiasm bordering on
hysteria as the latter part of the message was deciphered.

```
APOLOGY
FOR ENERGY DISCHARGE
THAT CAUSED
YOUR ORBITAL CRAFT
TO MALFUNCTION
IT WAS ACCIDENT
ALL SYSTEMS ARE
FUNCTIONING HERE
WILL DEPART THIS PLANET
FOR YOURS
SOON
WILL LAND ON YOUR PLANET
IN TWO OF YOUR ROTATIONS
PLEASE INDICATE WHERE
OUR LANDING
SHOULD BE
ASPASIA
```

Peter Sterling stood up and addressed the rest
of UNAOC. "The Earth has forty-eight hours to
prepare the reception."

■ ■ ■

At Cube operations Kelly Reynolds studied the
intelligence reports that were forwarded to her via
Quinn from many points around the globe. Much
was happening and much would happen in the
next two days.

The impression was that the excitement of
those in the UNAOC conference room mirrored
the excitement that was breaking out all over the
planet as the realization that aliens would be

landing on Earth in forty-eight hours washed over the world's peoples.

Kelly could tell that on the whole, the excitement was positive. The story of Aspasia's battle against the rebels five millennia ago, as transmitted to Peter Nabinger from the Guardian I computer, had now trickled its way into even the remotest corner of the planet. Hope had been ignited in the hearts and minds of the vast majority of Earth's population that there would soon be technological advances that would end war, famine, disease, pollution, and the other problems that ravaged the face of the planet.

The isolationists geared up to mount protests, but Kelly knew they were battling the inevitable, as there was nothing they could do to stop the wave of anticipation.

Still, Kelly knew, all was not good. Sometimes the human race made her want to tear her hair out. There were those who also saw the next forty-eight hours as critical. Reading between the lines, many humans believed that the Airlia would help the UN impose peace on the planet, and since the current state of affairs was unacceptable to certain groups, they surged forward in revolt, terrorism, and rebellion to grab as much as they could before a status quo was invoked.

It was clear to Kelly Reynolds and the intelligence analysts what some of those events would be. In the Middle East there would be massive uprisings in the Occupied Territories. According to the CIA, Iraq was preparing to launch another assault into Kuwait, one that was certain to be immediately smashed by U.S. and Allied air power flying from carriers in the Gulf and airfields in Saudi Arabia. Several ethnic regions of Russia would rise up in rebellion, and according to analysts, Moscow's weary reply would most likely be to pull its troops out of the areas and wait to see what the coming of the Airlia would bring.

In Central and South America revolution was getting ready to break out in several countries. In the United States some right-wing militia groups were preparing to conduct acts of terrorism, protesting the United States' participation in the UN and UNAOC. The FBI and ATF were already moving to preempt those acts.

Of more particular notice to Kelly, in China, the long-persecuted Muslim minority in the west had already seized several armories and, with the help of Taiwanese special operations units, had risen in revolt against the central government in Beijing as Taiwanese warships cruised close to Hong Kong harbor, raising speculation that Taiwan might attempt to attack the former colony. Kelly knew from reading the analyses that the small island state could never seize and hold Hong Kong, but agents in that part of the world reported that destruction of the strongest part of China's new economy was more the goal of the Taiwanese.

China. Kelly's gaze focused on that word. What was happening there? What was in the damn tomb? Now that there was definite time-line for the arrival of Aspasia, her anticipation was rising to an almost fevered pitch. She knew now that there was no way she could stop the mission, but she could pray, and that she did with all her heart, that the Airlia would arrive to find a united world to greet them and that her friends would make it out of China alive.

■ ■ ■

Turcotte felt the aircraft bank and experienced a slight change in air pressure as the plane descended rapidly. He unbuckled his seat belt and walked down the plane. Leaning over Harker, he signaled and then yelled in the team leader's ear, "Time to rig."

While Harker started rousing the team members, Turcotte tapped Nabinger on the shoulder and pointed to the rear of the plane. Turcotte undid the cargo straps holding down the parachutes and rucksacks. He and Harker passed the chutes out, a main and reserve to each man.

Turcotte and Nabinger buddy-rigged each other. Turcotte went first, slipping the harness of the main over his shoulders and settling it on his back. He then reached down between his legs as he directed Nabinger to pass a leg strap through to him.

Turcotte hooked the snaps and made sure it was properly seated. He then crouched and tightened both leg straps down as far as they would go. The submachine gun Turcotte had gotten from Zandra was slung upside down on his left shoulder using the sling and tied down with some eighty-pound test cord. Turcotte rigged the reserve over his belly, attaching it to D-rings on the front of the harness. He passed the waistband to Nabinger and directed him to run it over the sub and through both straps on the back of the reserve. Turcotte then cinched it tight on the right side, insuring it had a quick release fold in the buckle.

Turcotte put his small rucksack on the web seats and pressed his reserve down on top of it while he reached in and hooked the two eighteen-inch attaching straps up to the same D-rings the reserve was attached to. Turcotte liked having the ruck attached as tightly as possible to prevent it from swinging up and hitting him in the face when he went off the ramp. Turcotte then attached the fifteen-foot lowering line for the rucksack to the left D-ring.

Turcotte signaled to Harker, and swaying in the aircraft, the Special Forces warrant officer quickly ran his hands over Turcotte's equipment, starting from his head, working down the front, and then going to the back, again working top to bottom. He never let his hands get in front of his eyes as he methodically worked his way around the equipment.

Harker released the static-line snap hook from its location on the pack closing tie on the back of the parachute and ran the static line over Turcotte's left shoulder. He hooked the snap hook onto the handle of the reserve, where Turcotte could get at it to hook up to the static-line cable when the time for that came.

Finished, Harker tapped Turcotte on the rear and gave him a thumbs-up, signaling he was good to go. Turcotte then helped Nabinger rig and the jumpmaster inspected the increasingly nervous professor. He got the chute on Nabinger, then tucked swim fins in the waistband of his parachute and attached to the jumper with cord.

"You're good to go," Turcotte told Nabinger.

"Oh, that's reassuring," Nabinger said.

"Seconds thoughts?" Turcotte said. "You can stay on board and fly back if you want to."

"No. I'm going. I've got to see this. I just wish we could have picked a more comfortable mode of transportation."

"Hey," Turcotte said, "this is the most fun you can have with your pants on."

"I very much disagree with that assessment," Nabinger said, slumping down onto the web seat.

■ ■ ■

Che Lu looked about the room, her eyes adjusting to the green glow given off by the numerous control panels. They were slightly taller than waist high, black, with green glowing surfaces covered with high rune writing.

"As I told you," Kostanov said as he walked beside her, "this room was completely dark when we came in here, but it powered up forty-eight hours ago."

"You haven't tried any of these controls?" Che Lu asked.

"Not yet," Kostanov said. "We have no idea what they are for."

Che Lu stopped at a console at the front of the room, a long curving black affair that faced the smooth rock wall. She pointed. "There seems to be a door there."

Kostanov nodded. He'd seen the faint trace in the rock face.

"Perhaps something on this panel opens it," Che Lu continued.

"Perhaps," Kostanov said. "But there are a lot of places to push and perhaps if you push the wrong one, we end up like my man who was cut in half."

"If only I could talk to Nabinger," Che Lu muttered as she ran hands just above the glowing high runes.

"My radioman can't transmit through rock," Kostanov said. "We've tried even knowing that, but we get nothing."

Che Lu turned to him. "What if you had an open shaft to the sky above?"

Kostanov stepped close to her. "You know where there is an open shaft?"

Chapter 21

The loadmaster leaned over and yelled in Turcotte's ear.

"The pilot wants to talk to you," he screamed above the plane's roar. He passed his headset to Turcotte.

The pilot's voice came back through the wires from the cockpit. "We've just picked up some SATCOM traffic from UNAOC. Aspasia sent a message saying he'll be landing here on Earth in two days."

Turcotte acknowledged. He leaned over and informed Nabinger.

"Jesus," Nabinger exclaimed. "Two days? That's not much time."

"We'll be out of here before then," Turcotte reassured him.

"I hope so."

Turcotte looked around the cargo bay. Everyone was awake now and fidgeting. The ride was getting extremely bumpy as the pilots used their sophisticated electronics to keep the aircraft down in the radar cluster of the terrain.

Turcotte was sweating under his dry suit. He hated waiting and having his destiny in someone else's hands. He'd feel a lot better once they were on the ground. He turned back to Nabinger and gave the professor a smile. The older man was white under his dark beard, beads of sweat trickling down the side of his face.

"It'll be all right," Turcotte reassured him.

"Just get me in the tomb," Nabinger said through clenched teeth.

■ ■ ■

Duncan threw her cigarette to the concrete floor of the hangar and ground it out with the toe of her shoe. She went over to the commo terminal and restlessly looked through the message logs. She stiffened as she noted one of the messages.

"Find something interesting?" a voice behind her asked.

Duncan turned to find Zandra towering over her. "What's STAAR?"

"STAAR?"

Duncan held up the message log. "You received a message two hours ago from someone or something with that code name."

"And you never heard of it and you have the highest security clearance possible in the United States," Zandra said, her eyes hidden behind her sunglasses. "Correct?"

"Correct," Duncan said, her jaw clenched tight.

"Well, Doctor, you don't have a need to know."

"Goddammit—" Duncan began, but Zandra raised a hand, cutting her off with clipped words.

"Don't! Not only don't you have a need to know, this is bigger than you, bigger than the United States."

"We'll see about that," Duncan said, turning for the door.

"Wait!" Zandra called out. There was a beeping sound coming out of the radio.

"What is it?" Duncan asked as the other woman sat down in front of the device and typed into the keyboard.

"We've intercepted a message from China," Zandra said.

Duncan looked at her watch. "They can't have jumped yet."

"They haven't," Zandra said. "This is from someone else."

"Where?"

Zandra was looking at the information being relayed to her. "It appears that whoever is transmitting is inside Qian-Ling."

"What the hell—" Duncan began, but again she was cut off by Zandra.

"Shut up for a minute and let me decipher this."

```
TO: SECTION FOUR
FROM: GRUEV
TRAPPED INSIDE
PLA HAS SEALED EXITS
SUPPLIES LOW
LINKED UP WITH PROFESSOR CHE LU
BEIJING UNIVERSITY
MANY AIRLIA ARTIFACTS
NEED HIGH RUNE TRANSLATIONS
PLEASE ADVISE
```

"Who is Gruev and what is Section Four?" Duncan asked, having patiently waited while the words came up on the screen line by line.

"Section Four is the Russian equivalent of Majestic-12. Gruev is the code name of one of their operatives."

"You seem to know a lot about this."

"I do. Our intelligence sources tell me he led a small team into the tomb several days ago. The Russians didn't hear a word from them after they entered and assumed they were lost."

"Why didn't you tell us that someone from the Russians had already gone inside?"

"You didn't have a need to know."

Duncan gritted her teeth.

"Listen," Zandra said, "you'll find out all you need to in due time. In the meanwhile we need to get word to Turcotte and his team to link up with Gruev. They can work together."

"Well, at least now we know why the PLA is sitting on top of the tomb," Duncan said, her own tone heavy with sarcasm.

■ ■ ■

Turcotte held six fingers aloft. "Six minutes!"

He extended both hands, palms out. "Get ready!"

The team members unbuckled their safety straps.

With both arms Turcotte pointed at the team seated along the outside of the aircraft. He pointed up. "Outboard personnel stand up."

The members of Team 3 staggered to their feet in the wildly swaying aircraft, using the static-line cable and side of the aircraft for support. Turcotte reached out and gave Nabinger a hand.

Curling his index fingers over his head, representing hooks, Turcotte pumped his arms up and down. "Hook up!"

Turcotte watched as each man hooked into the static-line cable. As jumpmaster, Turcotte was already hooked up and facing the team as he screamed the jumpmaster commands. The loadmaster was holding on to Turcotte's static line and trying to keep him from falling over as Turcotte used both hands to pantomime the jump commands.

"Check static lines!"

Turcotte checked his snap link and traced the static line from the snap link to where it disappeared over his shoulder. He then checked Nabinger's.

"Check equipment!"

Turcotte made sure one last time that all his and Nabinger's equipment was secured and the connections made fast on their parachute harnesses.

Turcotte cupped his hands over his ears. "Sound off for equipment check!"

The last man in line, Chief Harker, slapped the man in front on the rear and yelled, "Okay." The yell and slap was passed from man to man until Nabinger. Turcotte gave him a big thumbs-up and yelled, "All, okay!"

"Yeah, right," Nabinger muttered, leaning against the side of the plane.

With all the jump commands, except the final "GO," done, Turcotte gained control of his static line from the loadmaster and turned toward the rear of the aircraft. He waited for the ramp to open. He swayed to the front as the aircraft slowed down from 250 knots to 125 knots.

The loadmaster leaned over Turcotte's shoulder and stuck an index finger in his face. Turcotte looked at the team and screamed: "One minute!"

"Hang tough," Turcotte yelled in Nabinger's ear. "We're almost there."

Ten seconds later Turcotte felt his knees buckle as the plane rapidly climbed the two hundred and fifty feet up to the minimum safe drop altitude. The noise level increased abruptly as a crack appeared in the ramp and grew larger as the gaping mouth drew wide open. As the ramp leveled off open, Turcotte stared out into the dark night. The wind was swirling through the back of the plane, the sound layered on top of the roar of the engines.

Turcotte got to his knees. Grabbing the hydraulic arm on the left side of the ramp, he peered around the edge of the aircraft looking forward, blinking in the fierce wind. It took a few seconds to get oriented, but there it was in the moonlight. Only about twenty seconds away a lake loomed. It had the right shape. He could see a large mountain, it had to be the Qian-Ling, to the left of the lake. Despite himself Turcotte was impressed. Over four hours of low-level flying and they were right on target.

Turcotte stood up and yelled over his shoulder as he shuffled out to within three feet of the edge of the ramp. "Stand by!" He made sure Nabinger was right behind him. He could see that the professor's eyes were wide open.

Turcotte stared at the red light burning above

the top of the ramp. Now that he knew that they were on track for the right drop zone, as soon as the light turned green they'd go.

Turcotte edged a few inches closer to the edge. Looking down he could see the leading shore of the lake below.

The green light flashed.

Turcotte yelled "GO!" over his shoulder and was gone.

The team moved forward. Nabinger hesitated but the pressure of the six men behind him tumbled him off the edge into the swirling air.

Jumping at five hundred feet left little time for anything other than landing. Turcotte was only two hundred and fifty feet above the water of the lake when his main parachute finished deploying. He checked for Nabinger but the impact of the water quickly regained his attention as he went under. The natural buoyancy of the air trapped under his dry suit popped him back to the surface after a brief dunking.

The parachute settled into the water away from him where the wind had blown it. As the pull of his two weight belts tried to draw him back under, Turcotte quickly pulled his fins out from under his waistband and put them on to tread water. Rapidly he worked on getting out of the parachute harness. Unhooking his leg straps, he then pulled the quick release on his waistband. He pulled out the parachute kit bag that had been folded flat under those straps and held on to it while he shrugged out of the shoulder straps.

With the harness off Turcotte pulled in on the lines to his parachute. Holding one handle of the kit bag with his teeth, he used his hands to stuff

large bellows of wet parachute into the bag. After
a minute of struggling Turcotte succeeded in getting the chute inside and the kit bag snapped shut.
Turcotte took off the second weight belt he wore
and, attaching it to the handles of the kit bag, let
it go. The water-logged chute and kit bag disappeared into the dark depths.

Allowing his rucksack to drag behind him on a
short five-foot line, Turcotte turned to swim in the
direction he believed the aircraft had been heading, where Nabinger should be. As he lay on his
back and started finning, he checked his wrist
compass to confirm the direction, straight along
the azimuth the aircraft had flown over the DZ.
Soon he heard muffled splashing ahead, which
verified that he was heading in the right direction.

■ ■ ■

When Nabinger popped to the surface after
landing, he found his parachute descending on
top of him and covering him in the water. The
two weight belts he wore gave him an almost neu-
tral buoyancy, and without his fins on, he found it
difficult to keep his head above water as the nylon
of his parachute descended around him. When
Nabinger reached up with his arms to push the
nylon away so he could breathe, the movement
caused his head to slip underwater. With the
chute bearing down on him, Nabinger quickly
panicked.

Two feet below the surface of the water he was
momentarily trapped. In his fear Nabinger started
struggling that much harder and got himself more
entangled. He stroked vigorously and broke surface underneath the canopy. Taking a gulp of air,

Nabinger sank back underwater and wrestled with his parachute, which was becoming waterlogged. Nabinger remembered Turcotte had told him that a parachute would stay afloat for only about ten minutes before becoming completely soaked and sinking. He estimated he had been in the water over five minutes now, using only his one free leg to get him to the surface to grab quick breaths.

Nabinger was tiring and the chute was starting to press down on him like a cold, wet blanket.

■ ■ ■

Turcotte saw the blue chem light come on ahead. It was then that he came across Nabinger desperately treading water in the middle of a half-submerged parachute. Turcotte grabbed the apex of the chute and pulled it off the professor.

Nabinger spit a mouthful of water out. "I'm *never* doing that again!"

"Can you make it to shore?" Turcotte asked.

"Hell, yes," Nabinger said.

"Drop your weight belts and hang on to me. Don't worry, I'm not gonna leave you. We got plenty of time."

Turcotte hooked himself to Nabinger with his buddy line. Together they swam toward the blue chem light.

When Turcotte arrived at Harker's position he found the entire team accounted for. They quickly swam for the nearby shore, the bulk of Qian-Ling rising up in the sky ahead of them, a darker form against the night sky. After only a minute of swimming the team got to where the bottom came up to meet them. They quickly discovered that the shore was not solid, as the lake melted into a bamboo swamp. They stood up and trudged through the swamp for two hundred meters until they hit a patch of firm ground. The men then formed a circular perimeter. One man started taking his dry suit off while the other readied his weapon and provided security. Turcotte helped Nabinger with his gear, peeling off the dry suit, knowing that time was of the essence.

"Let's go." Harker gave hand and arm signals and the team fanned out, moving forward, sliding night vision goggles over their eyes. Turcotte slid his own pair down and turned them on. The night gave way to a bright green field of vision. He helped Nabinger adjust his set and then they quickly followed the team.

"Stay right with me," he whispered to the professor.

Chapter 22

Che Lu could see nothing. It was pitch black, even right next to the shaft to the outside world. She could hear a few snores and the nervous fidgeting of others who were too wound up to sleep. She could feel the hard stone floor under her as she lay on her side, her eyes open to the darkness. She'd slept under worse conditions but she'd been younger then. Now it was just uncomfortable and irritating.

The Russians had pointed their small satellite dish directly up the shaft and sent out a message earlier. Kostanov had explained to her that they could send, but they would not get a reply for a while according to some sort of schedule he had, and he wasn't even sure if they could pick up a reply through the narrow opening.

She didn't know how much good that would do. She doubted that the Russians would be so flagrant as to send in a force to rescue Kostanov and his men now that the PLA knew they were in here and were waiting outside. She also wasn't thrilled with the idea of having Russians inside the tomb or even outside of it.

She wondered what was going on in the outside world. Were the Airlia coming? If so, then this tomb certainly had to play some part in their plans. From the news stories she had seen, the guardian cavern underneath Easter Island was a small complex compared to the machinery that was in the main chamber.

She also wondered what was deeper in the tomb, through the wall on the far side of what they had dubbed the control room. And what was down the corridor protected by the powerful beam? Perhaps the same thing, approached from a different direction? Or were there other, deeper chambers in the tomb? Where did the light shaft go?

Too many questions with no answers. Che Lu sighed. Maybe with the morning there would be some answers.

■ ■ ■

Kelly Reynolds watched the midmorning news conference beamed live from the UN in New York as anxiously as billions of others the world over. The decision had been made as to where Aspasia and the rest of the Airlia would land: right in the center of New York City in Central Park. There had been surprisingly little opposition to the decision from the Russian delegate.

Reynolds was thrilled that her own country would be the site of first contact between humans and an alien race. She considered trying to catch a commercial flight from Nevada to New York, but she decided to stay where she was, as New York would be saturated by the media. After all, she surmised, the Airlia would have to send *someone* here to check on the mothership.

■ ■ ■

At JPL, Larry Kincaid had driven in before the sun was up and was sitting at his desk eating from a box of doughnuts, drinking his fourth cup of coffee. He'd watched the same telecast as Reynolds, but his take was different.

"They don't even know what the hell they're going to have landing," he muttered. He'd seen pictures of the mothership. If something like that was coming, the clearing in Central Park, big as it was, wouldn't be able to handle it. Of course, the aliens could have some sort of landing craft to shuttle down in.

He was just biting into a doughnut when the screen of the front of the room showed a change in the Cydonia region as seen by the *Surveyor* imager. The rectangle in the center of the Fort was changing color on one side.

Kincaid was at first puzzled, then he realized what was happening: a cover was opening. The bright rectangle grew larger until it encompassed the entire square.

Suddenly the entire square flashed bright white, the IMS's computer trying to compensate. Once the light level was settled, a half-dozen lean black vessels were revealed to be sitting inside the Fort.

Kincaid knew the stats for the Fort. His engineering mind quickly calculated. Each vessel was big, not anywhere near as large as the mothership, but impressive nonetheless. And they looked dangerous to Kincaid. He couldn't articulate the feeling, but that rapier shape and black color told him that there was more to these ships than met the eye, and they were nothing like either the mothership or the bouncers.

"Well, we know how they're coming," he said to no one in particular. He looked at his own computer and checked on the status of *Surveyor*. Not much longer now until they would have to think about retracting the IMS and reorienting the craft for orbit over Cydonia.

■ ■ ■

Harker raised his fist, halting the team in a small streambed that headed up to the mountain grave, now less than a half mile away. They could see lights on the side of the mountain where the PLA unit guarded the entrance to the tomb.

Turcotte sank down to one knee, giving a hand to Nabinger. Chase pulled out the radio to send the initial entry report. He set the antenna dish up and oriented it. He hooked a digital message data group (DMDG) device to the radio. The DMDG took whatever was typed into it, transcribed it into Morse code, and then placed it on a spool of tape. When the message was sent, the tape was run at many times normal speed, transmitting the message in a short burst that greatly reduced the opportunity for interception. Even satellite transmissions could be intercepted if they were too long or were sent in the vicinity of an unfriendly satellite.

Turcotte knew the FOB, in this case Zandra, would receive the burst and copy it on tape. The tape would be slowed down and run across the screen of the FOB's own DMDG.

"All yours," Harker whispered to Turcotte, indicating the radio.

Turcotte knelt next to the machine, and in the dim glow given off by the screen, he typed in their initial entry report, telling Zandra they were on the ground in the right place and ready to proceed with the next phase of the operation.

He pushed the send key and the encoded message was burst-transmitted in less than one second.

He waited, then blinked as a reply came across the screen:

```
LINK UP WITH CHE LU AND RUSSIAN OPERA-
TIVE, CODE NAME GRUEV, INSIDE TOMB.
THEY ARE ALL SEALED IN.
```

"Goddamn," Turcotte muttered. He typed in a new message, asking about exfiltration.

```
PICKUP ZONE AT GRID 294837 AT 2000
HOURS LOCAL.
```

"I wish they'd tell us what the ride's gonna be," Harker whispered.

"Where's that grid?" Turcotte asked as he broke down the DMDG and handed the gear to Chase.

Harker had a red-lens flashlight shining on his map, the two of them hidden under a poncho liner. "Right here. Small field among the trees north of the tomb about four klicks."

"Got to be a chopper."

"Chopper can't reach here on a tank of gas from friendly territory and get us back out."

"Well, we have to trust that they figured something out."

"I don't trust that bitch Zandra," Harker said.

"Dr. Duncan will be there for us," Turcotte said. He saw the look Harker gave him. "I trust her."

Harker shrugged. "She don't come through, we're history."

"She'll come through. Your guys ready?" Turcotte asked.

"We'll be ready in ten minutes."

Turcotte looked to the east. The sun would be up soon. "Let's get in while it's still dark."

■ ■ ■

On the bridge of the USS *O'Bannion* Commander Rakes uneasily looked over the shoulder of his chief radar operator. His ship was threading the eye of a needle and Rakes didn't like the eye hole. To the north the radar blipped the outline of the southern tip of Liadon Peninsula, only fourteen miles away. To the south, roughly the same narrow distance away, was the image of the north end of Shantung Peninsula. Those two pieces of land on either side squarely placed the *O'Bannion* in the entrance to the Gulf of Chihli, at the northeast end of the Yellow Sea, a veritable Chinese lake with only one way in and one way out.

The *O'Bannion* was a *Spruance*-class destroyer. Its primary armaments were Tomahawk cruise missiles and Harpoon ship-to-ship missiles. It had a flight deck to the rear large enough to handle two helicopters. Despite the armament and flight capability, the *O'Bannion* was designed to operate as part of a battle group, not on its own.

Rakes was uncomfortable with the whole situation. No U.S. warship that he knew of had ever gone this far toward Beijing. Technically he was still in international waters as long as he kept Chinese land twelve miles from his ship, but he knew the Chinese were not big on such technicalities.

While the rest of the *O'Bannion*'s battle group was sailing southwest toward Hong Kong to participate in a show of force regarding the recent unrest between Taiwan and mainland China, he'd been ordered to break off on this course less than twelve hours ago. Following his orders he had gone in the opposite direction, straight toward the Chinese capital.

For his destination all he had been given was a set of coordinates, 119 degrees longitude and 38 degrees, 30 minutes latitude. The *O'Bannion* was to stay within a one-kilometer circle of that point on the ocean.

Go to that location and be prepared to land and refuel two helicopters, the orders read. When Rakes had radioed his commander to ask for more information, he was informed there wasn't any more. When he'd protested about sitting still, surrounded on almost all sides by Chinese territorial waters, his commander had informed him that nobody had told him, either, what was going on but that these orders had come from very high.

"Yes, sir, yes, sir, three bags full," Rakes muttered to himself as he scanned the dark horizon through his binoculars.

"Excuse me, sir?" the officer of the watch asked.

"Nothing," Rakes said. "I didn't say anything."

■ ■ ■

Major O'Callaghan pulled in collective with his left hand and felt the Black Hawk's wheels leave the ground. He climbed to four hundred feet and then waited until the other Black Hawk, with Captain Putnam at the controls, slid into place to his left rear.

While his copilot updated the Black Hawk's Doppler navigating device with their present location, O'Callaghan pushed his cyclic control forward and turned on an azimuth of due west out of Camp Casey Airfield, just north of Seoul, South Korea.

O'Callaghan estimated a 3.7-hour flight to the *O'Bannion,* arriving at midmorning. That would give them some rest on board ship before having to take off to fly the rest of the mission. Just as importantly, it allowed them to fly this leg in the daylight; saving their goggle time for the actual penetration of the hostile airspace. Not that flying through the narrow gap into the Gulf of Chihli wouldn't be flirting with Chinese airspace. O'Callaghan planned on keeping the chopper as low as possible to avoid radar and thus avoid flybys by the Chinese air force checking on them.

Once he was sure everything was working fine, O'Callaghan let his copilot take the controls. He leaned back in his seat and closed his eyes, saving his energy for when he would need it.

Chapter 23

■■■■■■■■■■■

The time was right. The Airlia had scanned the data banks, quickly getting up to speed on the present situation. A long finger reached out and lightly touched various points on the master control console. The program for first-echelon resuscitation was continued.

Checking the sensors, there was one other minor detail that needed to be taken care of. The alien instructed the computer to send a message to Earth.

■ ■ ■

Larry Kincaid didn't break anything when he got the order to abort the attempt to stabilize and reorient *Surveyor,* which was a case of considerable restraint on his part. The message had come in the clear from Mars just moments ago and UNAOC had relayed the "request" from the Airlia not to have the region overflown again.

UNAOC didn't consider the probe important anymore, and there was no desire in New York or anywhere else on the planet to go against the wishes of the Airlia.

"What the hell do you want me to do with *Surveyor*?" Kincaid asked his manager.

"I don't give a shit, Larry," his boss answered. "Just keep it away from the Airlia base."

"You ever wonder why they don't want us to get a closer look?" Kincaid asked.

"No." Seeing Kincaid's look of disgust, the manager amplified his answer. "Don't you get it? We're dinosaurs here, Larry. When the Airlia get here in those ships our space program is going to look like a bunch of hand-pulled carts next to an Indy 500 car. Things are changing and this entire program is going to be out of date in another day."

"It's *our* program," Kincaid said. "What makes you think the Airlia are going to share *their* technology with us?"

"Just do what you're told. *Surveyor*'s been a disaster anyway. Let it go."

Kincaid rubbed a hand across his forehead and bit back his sarcastic reply. He walked back to the control room and sat down. He started calculating to see if he could put *Surveyor* on a stable orbit that didn't overfly Cydonia, when he sensed someone behind him. He turned in his seat. The pale, white-haired man was standing there, sunglasses looking in Kincaid's general direction. Kincaid stared at him, but it was hard to win a stare-down when the other person wore shades.

"What?" Kincaid finally snapped.

"Stabilize *Surveyor* as you planned," the man said.

"Say what?" Kincaid looked at the man's clearance tag. There was only one name written there: Coridan. The clearance level said ST-8. The tag's scarlet, almost black, clearance indicator color showed that ST-8 was higher than anything Kincaid had ever dealt with before.

Coridan held out a piece of paper. "I've calculated what you need to do to stabilize the craft's orbit immediately. Once the burn is done, shut everything down and put the on-board computer to sleep and shut down the IMS."

"And then?" Kincaid asked.

"And then wait."

"I just got ordered to stand down," Kincaid said. "Why should I do this?"

"Because I have authorization higher than your boss's." Coridan tapped his badge. "And because you don't trust the Airlia and I don't either."

■ ■ ■

Turcotte had witnessed death many times in his time in the army. He'd once been part of an elite counterterrorist force in Europe where he had done his own share of killing. But what he was about to witness bothered him because it all seemed so pointless, man against man, when there was so much more at stake.

Harker had deployed his team on the hillside above the entrance of the tomb. The snipers had bolted together their rifles and zeroed their night vision scopes on the Chinese soldiers manning the machine gun at the entrance to the small courtyard. The rest of the team was waiting, ready to slide down the mountain.

Harker turned to Turcotte, who was lying next

to him. "I don't like this," he whispered. "What's so fucking important in that tomb?"

"I don't know," Turcotte answered. He didn't have the heart, time, or energy to make Harker feel better.

"It's your call," Harker said.

"Do it." Turcotte said the words flatly.

"Fire," Harker said in a slightly louder voice.

The two sniper rifles fired at the same time, a jet of flame coming out of the end of the barrel, the only sound the working of the bolt sliding back in the breech. Each round was a hit, knocking back the two soldiers manning the machine gun.

The sniper rifles continued firing as the rest of the team slid down the mountainside, weapons at the ready. By the time they got to the entrance level, all twelve Chinese soldiers were dead.

"Let's go," Turcotte said to Nabinger. He grabbed the other man's arm and helped him down the steep hillside.

Howes, the demo man, was already at the doors, looking them over. Turcotte walked over to the vehicle. A radio set was inside, the screen lit. He knew that meant that the dead operator had probably been doing regular checks in with higher headquarters and when he failed to make the next scheduled contact, they could expect PLA troops in force.

"Stand back," Howes called out.

There was a sharp crack and the door split open.

"Let's move it," Turcotte ordered.

■ ■ ■

Che Lu stood up as the rest of the group stirred at the sound of the explosion reverberating up the tunnel.

"We have company," Kostanov said. He snapped out some commands in Russian and his men prepared their weapons.

"I suggest you keep your people here," Kostanov said. "We'll see who's come knocking."

■ ■ ■

Turcotte took the lead, putting Nabinger near the rear. They left Howes and DeCamp to guard the doorway. Through the night-vision goggles Turcotte could see the tunnel clearly. He recognized the smooth stonework as being similar to what he had seen in the complex in the Great Rift Valley and at Area 51.

Even trying to move stealthily, he could hear the scraping of his boots on the floor, and his own breathing sounded unusually loud. The sound of the men right behind bothered him, disturbing his concentration.

Turcotte halted, holding his hand up, and the group froze. He could have sworn he'd heard a noise. Turcotte held his submachine gun at the ready. "Professor Che Lu?" he called out.

An accented voice came out of the dark. "She's busy. Who may I say is asking for her?"

Turcotte knew that voice and that accent. He searched in his memory for when and where. He could make out what appeared to be an intersection in the tunnel about fifty meters ahead.

"Gruev?" Turcotte asked.

A figure walked out of the side tunnel. Turcotte quickly pulled off his goggles as the man turned

on a large flashlight, bathing the tunnel in its
glow. Turcotte squinted as he walked toward the
man. He recognized him when he was ten meters
away.

"Kostanov!"

"Captain Turcotte." Kostanov gave a mock
bow. "Fancy meeting you here."

"You were Russian all along," Turcotte said.
"All that stuff you told us on the carrier was bullshit."

Kostanov shook his head. "What I told you was
mostly the truth, but we don't have time for that
now."

"Maybe we ought to make time," Turcotte said.

"We *don't* have time," Kostanov insisted. "I will
explain all later."

"What have you found in here?" Turcotte
asked.

"A control room." Kostanov was looking past
Turcotte. "Ah, Professor Nabinger, there is some-
thing you must see." He snapped something in
Russian to his right. "I am sending one of my men
to get Professor Che Lu. Then we go that way."
He pointed to his left.

■ ■ ■

Captain Rakes squinted into the wind as the
second helicopter settled down on the helipad. He
waited until the blades on both birds stopped
turning and then walked out to the lead one. He
was already disquieted by the fact that both helicopters bore no marking. He recognized the type:
Sikorsky UH60. But he'd never see a UH60 Black
Hawk with a flat black paint job and the extra fuel
tanks hung on small wings above the cargo bay.

With those extra tanks they must be flying an awfully long way, Rakes estimated. That made him feel even more uneasy. The only country in three directions was China. And those birds had come from the fourth direction. He didn't think the Navy would go through all the trouble of moving his ship here to meet two helicopters that were going to just refuel and go back to where they had started from. Of course it wasn't completely out of the realm of possibilities. He'd done stranger things in his time in the Navy.

Rakes watched warily as the pilot got out of the first chopper and walked over to him.

"Evening, sir," O'Callaghan said. "We'd appreciate it if your men could top our birds off and if you could find the four of us a quiet place to get some rest for a couple hours. We're not leaving again until just before dark."

Rakes designated one of his ensigns to show the pilots a stateroom where they could rest.

"Ours is but to do and die," Rakes muttered to himself as he turned and went back to his bridge, where at least he was in charge of something.

■ ■ ■

"Goddamn, it's cold," Emory sputtered between chattering teeth.

Downing had expected the civilian to be the first to say something about the freezing temperature inside the *Greywolf.* Condensation had formed on all the fittings, and the drip of water was the predominant sound inside the submersible. The dim glow from the control panel was the only light, other than the occasional flicker from a foo fighter passing one of the portals.

Downing looked at his depth gauge. They had lost another two hundred meters in the last hour. Still not too bad. The problem was that as the submersible got even colder, it would lose more of its buoyancy and then depth might become a problem.

"How long are we going to wait?" Emory asked for the fifth time in the last hour.

Downing didn't bother to answer. He pulled his flight suit in tighter around his body and tried to keep from shivering.

"Why doesn't UNAOC contact this Aspasia guy and ask him to call off the foo fighters?" Emory demanded, his voice on edge.

That was a new question, one that Downing had already considered and knew the answer to. "Because UNAOC doesn't know we're down here," he said.

"Then who the hell gave the order for us to go here?" Emory demanded.

"Your guess is as good as mine," Downing said. "But I would suppose it's the same person who gave the orders for those L.A.-class attack subs to be hanging around."

■ ■ ■

At the Cube, Kelly Reynolds was playing the role of spectator, and it didn't bother her in the slightest. The images that had been beamed from the *Surveyor* IMS, showing the Airlia craft on the surface of Mars, had kept her glued to the TV set in the control center. There had been activity around the ships, but the resolution on the IMS camera had not been such that they could make out what the activity was. There was no doubt, though, that the ships were being readied. *Surveyor* was now shut down and the Hubble had taken over the watch.

A series of red digits was in the upper right-hand corner of the screen and they had been there, slowly winding down, ever since the timing of the Airlia landing had been announced. In less than forty-two hours the alien craft would be touching down in Central Park.

That timing fueled speculation as to the capabilities of the ships inside the Fort. It was obvious that if they were going to cross the distance between Mars and Earth in a little over a day, then they would have to attain tremendous velocity. It was just one more technological wonder that the scientists and most Earth people hoped they would have access to shortly. There was also speculation about where those six ships had come from. There was a bay inside the mothership with cradles specifically designed to hold the bouncers. But there was no place inside the ship where these "talon ships," as the media had dubbed them, could have been carried on an interstellar journey.

The answer had been advanced by several analysts around the globe at roughly the same time, so it was hard to pinpoint who exactly should get credit for it: the talons had not been carried *inside* the mothership, but rather *outside* it. Calculating as best they could with the IMS image, scientists determined that the talon ships would fit around the curved front nose of the mothership.

That conclusion had led to further speculation

that the talons, both because they were transported in such a ready position, and because they simply looked so fierce, were warships. Concern about that had quickly been allayed by UNAOC when it was pointed out that if the Airlia had wanted to do humans harm, they could have most easily done so before they flew the talons from Earth to Mars so many millennia ago. Besides, Aspasia was the protector of the human race, UNAOC added.

Turning her gaze from the screen, Kelly wondered about her friends and how they were doing in China. Occasionally the news shifted from the pending alien contact to more immediate matters here on Earth. Saddam Hussein's attempt to invade Kuwait for a second time had been readily smashed by Allied Air Forces and his army was once again in retreat.

From China the news was also grim. There were reports of fighting on the outskirts of Beijing and in the streets of Hong Kong. PLA forces were entering the newly acquired city in large numbers and there were rumors of massacres and Taiwanese commandos fighting alongside the students.

But of the ancient tomb Qian-Ling there were no rumors or reports. And for that Kelly was grateful. She had the greatest confidence in Captain Turcotte and she was sure he would see Professor Nabinger through whatever they were doing and return safely. And hopefully in time to see the Airlia land, Kelly thought to herself as the screen once again shifted to the Fort and the Airlia spacecraft.

Kelly reached out a hand and touched the screen. "So beautiful," she whispered, her fingers running over the image of the ships. "So beautiful."

Chapter 24

∎∎∎∎∎∎∎∎∎∎∎

"**C**an you figure it out?" Turcotte asked Nabinger.

They were in the control room, along with Kostanov and his men and Che Lu and her students.

"My God, there's never been a find like this," Nabinger said, looking at the various consoles and panels. "Even the room on Easter Island was nothing compared to this."

"No guardian computer, though," Turcotte noted.

"Not here," Nabinger agreed. He pointed to the far wall. "But who knows what's in there? Plus there's the central passageway, which no one has gone down yet."

"Yeah, because you'll get cut in half if you try," Turcotte noted.

"Can you get us in there, Professor?" Kostanov asked, nodding his head toward the far wall. "We do not have much time."

"What is the rush?" Che Lu asked.

"The PLA is going to be knocking on the door

soon," Turcotte said, "and they're not going to be happy."

"Plus, as you told us," Kostanov noted, "Aspasia will be on Earth in less than forty-two hours."

"And?" Turcotte prompted. "What does this have to do with that? Isn't this Aspasia's equipment?"

"It's Airlia equipment," Kostanov said, "but I don't think it's Aspasia's."

"The rebels?" Nabinger asked.

"We believe so," Kostanov said.

"Who's we?" Turcotte demanded.

"Section Four has been tracking all of this for a very long time," Kostanov said.

"If you've been tracking this for so long, why is it so important that you uncover this base now?" Turcotte said.

"Because the Airlia are coming." He turned to Nabinger. "Professor, what can you tell us about this room?"

"It's a control center," Nabinger said. He was looking at the console.

"Controlling what?" Che Lu asked.

"This." Nabinger waved a hand absently around his head. "This entire complex. From what I can gather, this entire mountain was built to house"—he paused, his eyes running over high rune symbols—"to house the equipment in the other room that we passed getting in here—and . . ."

"And?" Kostanov prompted.

In reply Nabinger pushed his right hand down onto the panel. A red glow suffused the black top, outlining more high rune symbols.

"What are you doing?" Turcotte asked.

Nabinger ignored those around him, concentrating on what was before him. His hands hovered over the top of the console for a long minute. A group of hexagons, fitted tightly together, appeared. Nabinger pressed his hand down on the hexagon field in a certain sequence. Everyone in the control room took a step back as there was a loud humming noise. A crack appeared along the edges of the door in the far wall as it began to slide upward. Turcotte and the other Green Berets instinctively swung up the muzzles of their guns to cover the door, as did Kostanov and his men.

Nabinger walked through their line of fire and disappeared into the room. Turcotte was next through and he was half expecting what he saw as he stepped through. Sitting in the center of a small room hewn out of the rock was a six-foot-high pyramid, the surface glowing with a golden haze that extended out a few inches from the material that it was made of.

Turcotte also wasn't surprised when Nabinger walked right up to the pyramid and put his hands on the surface, the golden glow extending around the archaeologist as if he had become part of the machine.

Chapter 25
•••••••••••

Exactly on schedule O'Callaghan smoothly banked his aircraft away from the *O'Bannion* and headed for the shore. He adjusted the throttle for maximum fuel conservation and they were on their way, skimming along at fifty feet above the waves at 130 knots.

The sun was starting to settle in the sky and he knew that soon, just before they reached the shore, it would be dark, which was just the way they had it planned. Just under six hours of flying to the pickup zone.

The sound of automatic fire echoed dully into the chamber. Turcotte's head snapped up and he grabbed his MP-5 before hustling out the door, followed by the rest of his men and Kostanov. Turcotte had sent Howes and DeCamp to guard the entrance as soon as Nabinger had made contact with the pyramid.

Halfway up the side corridor they paused as a

loud explosion thundered down the rock walls, the sound multiplied by the confined space.

Farther up they met the two Special Forces men, both of them covered in dust. "We had to blow the entrance," Howes said. "The Chinese were bringing up a tank."

"What now?" Kostanov asked.

"We'll figure something out," Turcotte said. "What about where you came in?"

"It was on the other side of the large chamber but now it's blocked from the outside."

"We'll get out," Turcotte said, wishing he were as confident as he hoped he sounded.

■ ■ ■

Inside the "Fort" the cables fell away from the ships. Through tunnels hooked in to the base of each ship figures moved, crews manning vessels they had last been on board over five millennia ago. The tunnels pulled back.

Without any visible sign of energy being expended, the ships smoothly lifted off the surface of Mars. As they gained altitude their paths began to interlace in an intricate dance, six lean talons, their tips pointed toward Earth.

Chapter 26

■■■■■■■■■■■

Turcotte checked his watch for the third time in the last ten minutes. Looking up, he caught Kostanov staring at him. The Russian raised his eyebrows in inquiry and pointed at his own watch. Turcotte looked past the Russian toward Nabinger, who was now leaning against the golden pyramid, his entire body encased in the golden glow. He'd been like that for two hours.

"The Chinese are out there in force by now," Kostanov said.

"Yep," Turcotte replied shortly in his northern Maine accent.

"We can't go out the way you came in and we can't go out the way I came in." Kostanov summed the tactical situation up succinctly.

"Yep," Turcotte said. Then he added his own tidbit. "And my exfil is going to be time-on-target in four hours. If we aren't on the PZ then, well, it's a long walk home."

"How far is your pickup zone?" Kostanov asked.

"Six klicks north."

"We can make it in two hours," Kostanov estimated. "If we can get out."

"If no one shoots us," Turcotte added.

"That, too, my friend, that too."

"What about you?" Turcotte asked.

"My men and I have long since missed our exfiltration window. Perhaps if we got out and could make communications with our higher command again, we could arrange something, but I do not believe we will have the time."

"You can come with us," Turcotte said.

"I believe that is the only option," Kostanov acknowledged.

"Why did you pretend to be a freelancer working for the CIA on the carrier?" Turcotte asked.

Kostanov rubbed the stubble of his beard. "Hard as it may be to believe, we Russians support UNAOC. We thought my pretending to be what you thought I was would be the easiest way to give that information up to UNAOC and get the Terra-Lel site checked out. After all, we caught quite a bit of public grief over the revelation that we'd kept secret a crashed Airlia craft in our possession for decades, much as you Americans suffered a publicity problem over Area 51. We wished to minimize the publicity fallout."

"I don't buy it," Turcotte said. "Not all of it."

Kostanov smiled. "You are right, my friend." The Russian sat down, leaning his back against his rucksack. Turcotte followed suit. The Chinese students were gathered around their professor talking quietly among themselves. Harker had his Green Berets in the main chamber, arranged in a defensive line in case the PLA broke into the tomb, something Turcotte didn't think was likely to happen. He figured the PLA would be more than happy to let them starve in here. Kostanov's two men were with Harker.

"Let me give you some information," Kostanov said in a low voice. "Information that crosses national boundaries. Have you ever heard of an organization code-named STAAR?"

Turcotte shook his head.

Kostanov ran a finger along his upper lip, deep in thought. "Where to start? Ah, it is very confusing, so I will just start with what I know and then move to speculations. I did tell you some truths on your aircraft carrier. I was a member of Section Four of the Interior Ministry. The lie was not telling you that I still am a member of Section Four. Like your Majestic, Section Four was dedicated to investigating extraterrestrial activity and discoveries. Like Majestic we *knew* that extraterrestrial life had visited Earth because we had the remains of an Airlia craft. We searched for more artifacts, as I told you.

"But we had another mission. It is a logical one if you think of it: we were to prepare for alien contact, most specifically prepare for *hostile* alien contact. In fact, we made the assumption that any contact would be hostile simply based on the fact that they would not be human and therefore would have different objectives and thus there would inevitably be a conflict of interests. Also"—Kostanov smiled—"you have to remember, we Russians have historically always been quite paranoid, and for good reason. We've had Napoleon and Hitler knocking at the gates of Moscow. It was not much of a stretch to look to the skies and see a threat from that direction.

"We had the crashed craft. We had intelligence reports about some of what your Majestic had. We knew at the least that you were flying the bouncers. Your security at Area 51 was not as good as you would have liked.

"We were aware of the discovery of the bomb in the Great Pyramid. We knew that because at the end of the Second World War we recovered the Nazi archives from Berlin and had the after-action report of the submarine that discovered the high runes and map on the stones off Bimini that directed Von Seeckt and the SS to the pyramid. The Nazis had accepted that the high runes were a language and were working hard at deciphering it. Fortunately, we rolled over Berlin and the war ended before they got very far.

"So as you can see, we had a wealth of information. In fact, from what we captured from the Nazis"—Kostanov leaned closer to Turcotte—"we knew about Cydonia and the Face and the Great Pyramid on Mars and the Fort. We knew that it was connected to the Airlia. After all, why do you think we launched so many probes and missions toward Mars?"

Turcotte believe him. It wasn't just the logic of what he was saying, but also the bond Turcotte felt for the Russian special forces officer.

"But there is something more we did," Kostanov said. "We assumed the Airlia Base on Mars to be a mechanical outpost, run by a computer, perhaps even abandoned and dead, but we could not take the chance that it was active. Also we could not take the chance that you Americans would get to Mars first and claim whatever was there. After all, you already had the bouncers, we could not let you get that much more. So we put nuclear warheads aboard our probes that we launched toward Mars. The decision was made in the mid-sixties at the highest level of the Russian government to destroy the Cydonia site."

"But—" Turcotte began, stunned by this revelation, only to be cut off by the other man.

"As you know, we did not succeed."

Turcotte rubbed his forehead and waited, trying to assimilate what he was being told.

"This brings me back to what I first asked you," Kostanov said. "We investigated and we heard rumors, nothing substantial but the tiniest of whispers here and there, of an organization called STAAR. For a long time we thought it was an American agency. Perhaps part of Majestic. But soon we began to suspect it was something much bigger and much more frightening: STAAR seemed to transcend national boundaries and also seemed to wield power in many countries, including Russia, as we at Section Four were constantly frustrated in our quest for hard information on STAAR."

Turcotte waited, but the other man had fallen silent, his eyes hooded, deep in thought.

"And? Have you discovered who or what STAAR is?"

Kostanov grimaced. "No. Not for certain. We lost some good men, friends of mine, trying to find anything we could on it. We even captured an operative in the early nineties who we believed was a member of STAAR."

Turcotte could well imagine that person's fate.

Section Four most certainly had to have had access to the many information-gathering techniques perfected by the KGB. "What did you get from the operative?" he asked.

"Nothing directly," Kostanov said. "He died before we could extract information."

"The interrogators killed him?"

"No, he simply died. Like turning a light switch off. There was no evidence of poison or other trauma. He simply stopped living. His heart just stopped and he was dead. We could not revive him."

"You said 'nothing directly,' " Turcotte noted.

"Ah, yes," Kostanov's eyes were distant. "Naturally, we did an autopsy on the body and we found something very strange." Kostanov turned and stared at Turcotte. "The agent was a clone. Our scientists had done enough research into cloning and genetic engineering that they could tell by looking at the man's gene structure that he had been cloned."

Turcotte pondered that. "Who could be doing this?"

"I have a suspicion," Kostanov said. "One that I nurtured for many years without vocalizing for fear of ridicule and disbelief but one that has grown since hearing what he"—Kostanov pointed at Nabinger, who was still in the thralls of the golden glow—"received from the guardian computer under Easter Island."

"And?" Turcotte repeated.

"I believe STAAR might be the Airlia rebels, operating from a secret base and using human clones as their agents among us."

Turcotte stared at Kostanov. "What—" he began, but then was distracted as Nabinger staggered back from the golden pyramid and collapsed on the floor, his eyes closed and his body in the fetal position. Turcotte jumped up and ran over.

"Come on, Professor," Turcotte said, kneeling next to Nabinger, straightening his body and lifting his head. "Wake up."

Nabinger's eyes flickered open, but they were unfocused. "Oh, God," he exclaimed. "We've got to stop him."

"Stop who?" Turcotte asked as he got the other man into a sitting position.

"Aspasia."

"I thought he was the good guy," Turcotte said.

"No." Nabinger shook his head empathetically. "He's coming here to destroy us and take the mothership."

Chapter 27

####### ■■■■■■■■■■■

"I had it all backward," Nabinger said to his captive audience. "Aspasia was the rebel, the one who wanted to use humans as his slaves and exploit this planet for its natural resources. The Kortad"—he looked about at the strange mixture of Chinese, Russian, and American faces surrounding him—"the Kortad weren't different aliens. *Kortad* is the Airlia word for, for, well, as best I can make out, 'police.' And they just managed to stop Aspasia, but in doing so they were stuck here on Earth."

There was a brief silence as everyone absorbed that, before Nabinger continued. "The leader of the Kortad was an Airlia named Artad, or perhaps that is simply his title. He dispersed those loyal to him after destroying Aspasia's base at Atlantis. Aspasia retreated, using the warships they had carried on the outside of the mothership to Mars, and an uneasy truce evolved. Artad had control of the mothership, but Aspasia had control of their interstellar communication device.

"That's why Artad's followers built the Great
Pyramid as a space signal. They put the atomic
weapon in it to destroy it if the signal attracted
the wrong group. They built the high rune signal
into the Great Wall. They built this tomb to house
their equipment. They dug out the great chamber
in the Rift Valley and hung the ruby sphere over
it, threatening to destroy the sphere and the
planet if Aspasia tried to come back to Earth.
They hid the bouncers in Antarctica and the
mothership in Area 51. They hid several guardian
computers around the planet to monitor things:
one here, one at Temiltepec which Majestic uncovered last year, and there are more."

"Why is Aspasia coming back here now?"
Turcotte asked, his mind reeling from Kostanov's
suspicions that STAAR was an Airlia organization
operating on Earth and Nabinger's new revelation
that it appeared they'd had it all backward about
the Airlia.

"Because he thinks the long standoff with the
Kortad is over *and* he must think the war is over."

"What war?" Che Lu spoke for the first time.

"Beyond our solar system there *was* a war between the Airlia and another alien race, and that
was a factor. Artad couldn't fly the mothership
because of that. But since Aspasia had their communications system, he couldn't contact their
home. But . . ." Nabinger paused, confused, the
images in his brain swirling about.

"I'd love to stand here and discuss these most
interesting revelations," Kostanov said, "but I
think our first priority is to get out of here and get
to the pickup zone."

Chapter 24

■■■■■■■■■■■

"**C**an you figure it out?" Turcotte asked Nabinger.

They were in the control room, along with Kostanov and his men and Che Lu and her students.

"My God, there's never been a find like this," Nabinger said, looking at the various consoles and panels. "Even the room on Easter Island was nothing compared to this."

"No guardian computer, though," Turcotte noted.

"Not here," Nabinger agreed. He pointed to the far wall. "But who knows what's in there? Plus there's the central passageway, which no one has gone down yet."

"Yeah, because you'll get cut in half if you try," Turcotte noted.

"Can you get us in there, Professor?" Kostanov asked, nodding his head toward the far wall. "We do not have much time."

"What is the rush?" Che Lu asked.

"The PLA is going to be knocking on the door

soon," Turcotte said, "and they're not going to be happy."

"Plus, as you told us," Kostanov noted, "Aspasia will be on Earth in less than forty-two hours."

"And?" Turcotte prompted. "What does this have to do with that? Isn't this Aspasia's equipment?"

"It's Airlia equipment," Kostanov said, "but I don't think it's Aspasia's."

"The rebels?" Nabinger asked.

"We believe so," Kostanov said.

"Who's we?" Turcotte demanded.

"Section Four has been tracking all of this for a very long time," Kostanov said.

"If you've been tracking this for so long, why is it so important that you uncover this base now?" Turcotte said.

"Because the Airlia are coming." He turned to Nabinger. "Professor, what can you tell us about this room?"

"It's a control center," Nabinger said. He was looking at the console.

"Controlling what?" Che Lu asked.

"This." Nabinger waved a hand absently around his head. "This entire complex. From what I can gather, this entire mountain was built to house"—he paused, his eyes running over high rune symbols—"to house the equipment in the other room that we passed getting in here—and . . ."

"And?" Kostanov prompted.

In reply Nabinger pushed his right hand down onto the panel. A red glow suffused the black top, outlining more high rune symbols.

"What are you doing?" Turcotte asked.

"This information is critical!" Nabinger exclaimed.

"Hold up!" Turcotte's voice caused everyone to fall silent. He pointed a finger at the guardian computer, while his eyes remained fixed on Nabinger. "Why do you believe *this* guardian now? You believed the one under Easter Island until this one told you a different story. Now Aspasia's the enemy and Artad's the good guy. Before Aspasia was the good guy. It's all bullshit. There's only one fact we have to keep in mind."

"What is that, my friend?" Kostanov asked.

"That *we're* human and they aren't. We have to look after our own interests regardless of what these damn computers tell us." Turcotte took a step closer to Nabinger. "Do you know what Aspasia wants? Why he is coming back?"

"For the mothership."

"Why didn't he come sometime in the last five thousand years and take it and go home and leave us alone?" Turcotte asked.

"Because they were in a standoff all these years, each one's guardian computers monitoring the situation, waiting."

"What was the standoff?" Turcotte asked.

"Artad controlled the ruby sphere," Nabinger said. "I know what it is now! We have to go to it. It's what Aspasia needs before he can fly the mothership. It's the energy source for the interstellar engine. The mothership can fly without it, but it can't go into interstellar drive without it. I know the code to get the sphere released."

"So why is Aspasia coming now?" Turcotte repeated the question.

The words came out of Nabinger in a tumble.

"Because General Gullick and Majestic moved one of Artad's guardians that was linked to the Rift Valley and the ruby sphere. And that guardian was destroyed by the foo fighters—so now Aspasia must think he can get the sphere and the mothership."

"What about this guardian?" Turcotte asked, pointing at the golden triangle.

Nabinger put his hands to his head. "It's very confusing. As best I can tell, Artad dispersed not only his people but his assets. This guardian is responsible for different things than the one Majestic uncovered under Temiltepec."

"I don't get it," Turcotte said. "Why did the guardian Majestic uncovered try to get them to fly the mothership? Obviously that upset the standoff when the one under Easter Island reacted."

"Maybe . . . hell, I don't know," Nabinger said. "Maybe the guardian computer Majestic got thought they were Kortad. It's not really clear to me either. But what is clear is that we have to stop Aspasia from getting control of the ruby sphere."

"Then we'd best get out of here," Kostanov said, tapping his watch. "I think we need to focus on our most immediate problem."

Turcotte agreed with that, at least. "Did the computer give you another way to get out of here?"

Nabinger shut his eyes. "The information it gave me was all in images. It's hard to remember and . . ." He paused, then his eyes snapped open and he looked about the room. He walked over to the control console. "There's a shaft. It goes diagonally from the main chamber to the surface." He paused in thought, trying to sort through an over-loaded brain. "I can open this end from here, but the surface end could only be opened by a special command code. I don't have that code."

"How thick is the surface door?" Turcotte asked.

Nabinger shrugged. "Hard for me to say. A couple of feet."

"Is it the black Airlia metal?"

"No. As with most of the chamber, they used local materials."

"Open the inner door," Turcotte ordered.

Nabinger ran his tongue across his lips as he placed his hands over the console. There was a glow of green lights. Everyone turned as they heard a rumbling noise to their rear. Turcotte ran out into the massive chamber where the soldiers were looking up. A large piece of metal was moving to one side, exposing a forty-foot-wide opening on the side of the chamber, about twenty feet off the ground. The tunnel sloped up into darkness.

"Let's go!" Turcotte yelled, getting everyone moving across the floor to just below the opening. He had a reason for speed beyond the time the choppers would be at the pickup zone. If Nabinger was right and Aspasia was a threat, they had just over thirty-six hours to do something.

■ ■ ■

According to the news reports VIPs from all over the world were flowing into New York. Feeling totally out of the stream of action, Kelly Reynolds could only watch the TV in the Cube and follow as the focus of interest made its third shift in the past week: from Easter Island and the guardian computer, to Area 51 and the bouncers/mothership, and now to New York, where soon, if all went as planned, the first live contact between humans and an extraterrestrial life-form would take place.

The intricate dance of the talons could be seen by the Hubble with more clarity the closer the Airlia ships got to Earth, and the effect was mesmerizing. Scientists and crackpots alike were tossing out theories as to why the ships' flight paths made such a weave, but none of the theories had struck Kelly as quite right. As with everything else they didn't know about the Airlia, she had no doubt that question would be answered when Aspasia landed.

There was no further word from China. And Quinn had discovered nothing more about STAAR. Kelly thought all those issues less important now that there was a definite timeline to Aspasia's arrival.

■ ■ ■

Turcotte started moving up the tube even as the others were still clambering up the rope Harker's men had fastened just inside the entrance. The tube went up at a forty-degree angle, manageable, but not very comfortable, especially given that the stone his boots were on was practically polished smooth.

From the diameter Turcotte had no doubt that this entrance had been built to accommodate bouncers, allowing them access to the cavern below. It was also the way all that gear had probably been put in there.

He could hear labored breathing behind him as he climbed, but his focus was on the narrow beam of light the flashlight on top of his MP-5 cast.

After five minutes Turcotte saw the end. A smooth wall of metal closed off the path. He stopped and looked over his shoulder. A long string of flashlights indicated the scattered line behind him. "Howes!" Turcotte called out. "Everyone else, hold where you are."

The Special Forces engineer made his way forward, his bulky rucksack resting on his back. Howes dumped the ruck at Turcotte's feet, holding it in place with a boot while he surveyed the metal.

"No idea how thick?" he asked.

"The professor says maybe a couple of feet."

Howes nodded, his mind already working the problem. He opened a pocket on the outside of the ruck and pulled out a fifty-foot length of 10mm climbing rope and several pitons. He handed a hammer and two pitons to Turcotte and pointed to the right while he went left. They climbed as far as they could up the side of the tunnel, then got to work hammering the pitons into the rock.

Once both his pitons were in, Turcotte looped a length of rope through the snap link on the end of each one and brought the two ropes back to the center. Howes met him there and slowly pulled a large black cylinder, pointed on one end, out of the pack. It was almost three feet long and a foot and a half in diameter. Howes tied off the four ropes to bolts on the side of it.

Using the frame of his rucksack as a support, and the ropes to hold it in place, Howes wedged the shaped charge up so that the pointed end pointed at the metal.

"Hope this works," Howes said. "Fire in the hole!" he yelled as he pulled the fuse.

Both he and Turcotte dropped down on their butts and slid forty feet down the tube to where Kostanov waited at the head of the column. The Russian grabbed them and halted their slide. "How long is the—" he began, but he was answered by a bright flash and explosion. A wave of hot air blew down the tunnel.

The shaped charge was sixty pounds of high explosive, molded in such a way that the major force of the explosion was focused several feet in front of the point. It burrowed into the metal door, heat and shock forcing its way.

Turcotte started climbing back up. This would be the moment of truth. If the charge hadn't burned through the cap, he didn't know how they were going to get out. Turcotte paused. He could feel fresh air on his face. "Let's go!" he yelled.

He clambered his way forward, toward the jagged opening through which he could see stars shining high up above. Grabbing hold of the sides of the hole, he pulled himself out, then immediately tumbled down the side of the mountain tomb until he could arrest his fall by getting a grip on some bushes. He could hear Howes behind him, climbing through more carefully and attaching a rope in place to bring the others up.

Turcotte scanned the countryside. The opening was about two hundred meters from the crest of the tomb. Turcotte could see the lights of a town several miles to his right. Checking his wrist compass, Turcotte confirmed that he was on the eastern side. The pickup zone was to his left, several kilometers north.

Turcotte froze as he spotted a long line of small lights below him, about eight hundred meters away. A skirmish line, moving very slowly up the side of the tomb. He knew they were reacting to the explosion that had opened the shaft.

"Let's put a move on, people," Turcotte hissed over his shoulder. "We've got company."

Turcotte climbed the short distance back up to the exit. He could see that the metal had been covered by earth and bushes, well hidden for centuries. The shaped charge had ripped a narrow hole about three feet wide through the cover.

Harker had his entire team out, now helping the Chinese students through the hole. The Russians under Kostanov were bringing up the rear.

"We're going to be in the shit soon," Turcotte told Harker, pointing at the long line of small lights.

"Jesus, that's at least a battalion," Harker said, estimating the situation. The Special Forces warrant officer scanned the sky. "I don't see any Chinese helicopters. They get air on top of us, we're finished."

Turcotte pointed to the north. "We're going that way. We'll stay at this height, go around, and come down on the north. It should be clear."

"They'll come up behind us at altitude," Harker noted. "With the old lady, we can't move fast. We'll be in their sights and they'll have the high ground."

"Got any better ideas?" Turcotte asked.

"Mission accomplishment," Harker said shortly. "My assignment is to get you and the professor out of here alive, not a bunch of students and some Russians."

"Ah, most true," Kostanov said from behind them. "Mission accomplishment must come first."

"We go together," Turcotte said, not wishing to waste any more time. "Are we all up?"

"Yes." Che Lu was poised precariously on the side of the tomb, a bamboo pole in her hand dug into the earth, keeping her in place.

"We have to—" Turcotte began.

"I know what we have to do," Che Lu interrupted. "Do not worry about me. I will keep up."

"I'll cover our rear," Kostanov said.

"Let's go." Turcotte moved past the cluster of students and soldiers. It was hard going, walking along the forty-degree slope, and Turcotte knew the tactical reality was against them.

He heard the rattle of pebbles and swung up the muzzle of his MP-5, the laser aiming-dot reaching through the darkness. Turcotte centered the dot on the forehead of the lead figure in a group of five men about twenty feet ahead.

A voice cried out in Chinese from the group and Turcotte's finger curled around the trigger and began to pull it back when Che Lu called out, "Do not shoot! They are my friends." She immediately said something in Chinese as she worked her way along the group to stand at Turcotte's side.

"Lo Fa!" she exclaimed as the old man walked up, body leaning against the slope.

"I told you not to disturb things best left alone," Lo Fa said. He looked past them at the line of lights climbing up the hill, getting closer. "We have been searching for what the army searches for. I told these other idiots"—he gestured at the men with him—"that it was just a foolish old woman poking her bent nose where it shouldn't be. You must come with me if you wish to get away."

"Which way?" Turcotte asked.

Lo Fa pointed straight up the hill. "We go over the top and then west."

Turcotte shook his head. "We have to go north."

"The army is north," Lo Fa said. "You cannot go that way. We came from the west and we know a secret way to go in that direction."

"We have to go north," Turcotte said. He knew they didn't have time to make a wide sweep around the Chinese. Not only was their PZ clock ticking, there was the larger clock of Aspasia's pending arrival.

"As you wish." Lo Fa shrugged. "Old lady, bring your students with you."

Che Lu turned to Turcotte and Kostanov. "It will be easier for you without me."

Turcotte didn't have the time or inclination to discuss it. "All right."

Che Lu reached out and grasped his arm. "Bring the truth to the world. I must stay here with my people." She took Nabinger's hand and pointed down. "Besides, there is much in here we have not uncovered yet."

"Good luck," Turcotte said, but she was already scrambling away in the dark, following Lo Fa and his guerrillas.

As they disappeared upslope, Turcotte was moving, leaning into the mountain tomb, working his way to the north. The skirmish line was now less than six hundred yards away. Turcotte looked along it to its right wing. At the current rate the two groups were traveling, he knew that he would not clear the right wing before it reached his altitude.

"Harker!" he shouted, still moving.

"Yeah?" the warrant officer replied.

"Get Chase up here with the radio."

When the commo man caught up with him, Turcotte paused. "Get the SATCOM ready. I'm going to transmit in the clear to warn . . ." he began, then paused. He could hear the thump of helicopter blades.

A searchlight flashed on, lighting up Turcotte and the soldiers, overloading their night-vision goggles and blanking them out.

Overlaid on top of the blade sounds came the chatter of a heavy-caliber machine gun fired from the helicopter. Turcotte ripped off his night-vision goggles and grabbed Nabinger, covering the professor with his body. The rounds ripped by, tearing into Chase and throwing the commo man against the mountainside. The body tumbled down toward the skirmish line. Turcotte knelt and raised his weapon and fired, joined by the others.

The searchlight shattered and the chopper banked hard right and flew away to a safer distance.

"Status!" Turcotte yelled.

Harker's voice came from his right. "Chase and Brooks are dead and the radio's destroyed."

"I've got a man wounded," Kostanov answered.

"Let's go!" Turcotte ordered.

"No," Kostanov said, scrambling across to come to his side. "My man can't move. All of us will never make it without someone slowing them." He pointed down at the gaggle of lights that were now coming straight toward their position, less than four hundred yards away and steadily climbing. "I will give you cover. You go with your men. We will make our stand here." Kostanov held up a hand covered in blood as Turcotte started to say something. "This is more important than our lives."

Turcotte reached out and grasped the hand, then he let go. "Come on," he ordered the four surviving Special Forces men and Professor Nabinger.

■ ■ ■

Kostanov went back to his men. He checked the stomach wound on the one man, pressing the bandage down tighter to try and stop the flow of blood.

"Fire some rounds, Dmitri," he ordered the other. "Let the pigs know we are here."

Dmitri put the stock of his weapon to his shoulder and fired a long, sustained burst, emptying his magazine in the direction of the Chinese soldiers, causing confusion and consternation in their lines, gaining a few seconds for Turcotte and his men and also focusing the direction of the attack toward the Russians.

Bullets cracked by overhead as the Chinese fired back. The flashlights went out and Kostanov could well imagine the soldiers crawling their way up the hillside toward his position.

Kostanov reached into his combat vest and pulled out all his magazines, stacking them next to him. He reached into another pocket and pulled

out a battered blue beret. It had been issued to
him over twenty-five years ago when he'd first
joined the Soviet Airborne. Much had changed
since then for both his country and himself, but
Kostanov wanted the Chinese to know who had
made this stand.

Dmitri noted Kostanov putting the beret on.
"For Mother Russia," he said.

"For Mother Earth," Kostanov corrected as he
put his weapon to his shoulder and pulled the
trigger.

■ ■ ■

Turcotte could hear the firing. It spurred him to
move even quicker, to not waste the valiant sacri-
fice made by the Russians. After five minutes the
furious sound of the firefight behind them faded
to a few scattered shots, then silence.

Turcotte checked his compass. They had made
it around the tomb. Due north beckoned downslope. Turcotte started sliding down the slope,
knowing the PZ was only four kilometers away.

Chapter 28
■■■■■■■■■■■

Kelly Reynolds looked at the computer print-outs in frustration. She could make as much sense of them as the UNAOC decryption experts, which was to say she could make no sense of the garbled letters and numbers transmitted in one continuous stream.

The Guardian I computer under Easter Island was bursting information to the incoming Talon fleet almost nonstop, and in turn getting messages from the ships transmitted back to it. Kelly had to assume, as UNAOC did, that Aspasia was updating his information base. After all, Kelly reasoned, a lot had happened on Earth since Aspasia had gone into his self-imposed exile on Mars. Five thousand years of human history would require such extensive communications to get caught up on.

There had been no further messages from Aspasia to UNAOC, other than to acknowledge the landing site in Central Park. The clock was now under thirty-six hours to live contact, as the media had dubbed the moment Aspasia's ship was scheduled to land.

Kelly hoped her friends would be back from China in time to see the landing and the beginning of a bold new chapter in the history of the human race.

■ ■ ■

Three more kilometers, Turcotte knew, and they'd be at the pickup zone. The going downhill was much easier. The terrain had also become less steep. Looking to the east Turcotte could see the first hint of dawn on the horizon, a light smudge in the amplified imaging of the night-vision goggles. Looking back to the north, he could see movement. The PLA had gotten smarter and wasn't running around with flash-lights on anymore, but he could hear the distant rumble of vehicles and voices. The chopper was still hanging back, several kilometers to the east.

As the elevation dropped, the vegetation grew thicker, which provided them with more cover.

"How you doing, Professor?" Turcotte asked.

"I'll make it," Nabinger said. "How much farther?"

"Under three klicks."

"Keep going."

Harker whispered out of the dark, "Hold up." The warrant officer grabbed Turcotte's arm. "We got trouble."

Turcotte could see that Harker was holding a bulky scope in his hands, looking through it in their direction of travel. "What do you see?" Turcotte knew the thermal site could penetrate the vegetation and highlight the heat of living creatures and working machinery.

"We've got a picket line about six hundred meters ahead at the base of hill," Harker said. "They're holding still, just waiting. Looks like there's a large stream down there, and the Chinese are along the northern bank. The line coming up the hill behind us must have been the hammer to drive us; they're the anvil up ahead."

Turcotte checked his watch. They had less than two hours before the choppers showed up. There was no time to go in any other direction, plus there would most likely be Chinese forces waiting whichever way they went.

"Suggestion?" Turcotte asked.

"We're going to have to split," Harker said. "I'll take DeCamp with me. We'll have the sniper's rifles with the thermals." He pointed over his left shoulder to a ridgeline coming off the mountain tomb. "We'll go up there and start firing. That should cause some confusion as they react. There should be a hole for you to get across the stream, through their lines, and get to the PZ."

"And what about you?" Nabinger asked.

"Once you get on the choppers, send one to pick us up," Harker answered.

Turcotte knew the odds of Harker and DeCamp still being alive by that time were slim, but he didn't have time to stand and discuss it. He also knew Harker was aware of the dire reality of the situation.

"All right," Turcotte said. "How long do you need?"

"Give me fifteen minutes to get in position. You'll hear us when we start shooting."

"Let's go," Turcotte said. He grasped Harker's hand briefly, feeling the dried blood that had come off Kostanov's hand grit between their flesh.

■ ■ ■

"Is everything good to go?" Lisa Duncan asked.

Zandra was listening to radio reports. "Yes. The helicopters are on time and in the clear so far."

"The Chinese aren't onto them?"

"I can't tell that from here," Zandra said. "Their air defense units haven't been alerted."

"How do you know that?" Duncan demanded.

"I have an AWACS on station off the coast of China monitoring the situation."

"And if the helicopters do get spotted?"

"Then I will do what is necessary," Zandra said.

"That's rather vague," Duncan said.

"I'm sorry you feel that way, but I don't have to explain myself to you," Zandra said in a calm voice.

"*Who* do you answer to?" Duncan wanted to know.

"We've already gone over that," Zandra said.

"I want to know what you have done to protect those people on their way out," Duncan insisted.

Zandra flipped a switch on the radio set in front of her. "Here. You can listen in to what's going on as relayed from the AWACS. You'll hear what I have done."

■ ■ ■

Colonel Mike Zycki was the commander of the Airborne Warning and Control System (AWACS) plane that Zandra had ordered into the air using

her ST-8 clearance. As the modified Boeing 707-
320B leveled off at thirty-five thousand feet, Zycki
ordered the thirty-foot dome radar dish, riding on
top of the fuselage, to be activated. The advantage the AWACS had over ground-based radars
was its ability to look down. The radar signals
emitted at altitude were not blocked by the curvature of the earth or terrain. Zycki and his crew
had an accurate radar picture almost four hundred miles in diameter as the rotodome completed a revolution every ten seconds.

Unfortunately, even that coverage was insuffi-
cient to reach the area he had been ordered to
take a look at. He could paint an accurate radar
picture of the coast of China from Beijing almost
to Shanghai, but the aircraft he was supposed to
watch were over a thousand miles inland, near
Xi'an.

Still, the AWACS could function in a command-and-control role by linking with a KH-14
spy satellite that was in geosynchronous orbit
above central China and downloading the current
data the various gathering devices on the satellite
were picking up.

Quickly, Zycki's crew began the process of
identifying and coding out all known images the
KH-14 was picking up in the air. Civilian aircraft
liners were blanked off the screen. In a short
while they had a manageable screen. There were
only a few spots of activity left: some helicopter
activity in the vicinity of Qian-Ling. And two blips
moving quickly toward that spot.

The radar operator pointed. "That's our aircraft right there. They're flying right on top of the

earth. Airspeed's right for Black Hawks flying low level."

"Punch in transponder code alpha-four-romeo," Zycki ordered.

The operator did so, and four small dots appeared over eastern China, heading directly toward Qian-Ling. "Who is that?" the operator exclaimed. "They don't show up on down-looking radar or"—he paused as he hit a switch to access another asset of the KH-14 spy satellite—"thermal imaging!"

"That's our ace in the hole," Zycki said, "four F-117 Stealth fighters to provide air cover for the exfiltration."

Chapter 29

∎∎∎∎∎∎∎∎∎∎∎

On board the USS *Springfield* Captain Forster was the senior commander among the three *Los Angeles*–class attack submarines hovering above the *Greywolf*'s position. The *Springfield* and the *Asheville* were at a standstill, power down to a minimum to keep life-support systems operating on board the boats. The *Pasadena,* the third ship of the flotilla, had all systems active and was monitoring the situation for the group.

The first indication that the foo fighters were moving again was from the *Pasadena,* which reported two foo fighters coming up from the depths.

Forster didn't reply, still running silent as they had planned. The captain of the *Pasadena* had his orders.

■ ■ ■

On board the *Pasadena* the crew reacted as they'd thoroughly been trained to, rushing to battle stations. The firing crew began tracking the two targets.

■ ■ ■

On board the *Greywolf* Commander Downing watched the two foo fighters sweep by, heading up. The three that had been shadowing the submersible still remained on station. Downing turned and met Tennyson's glance.

"Your guess is as good as mine," he said.

■ ■ ■

As the foo fighters passed the *Greywolf*'s depth, the captain of the *Pasadena* gave the order to arm the Mark 48, Mod 2 torpedoes.

"Fire!" the captain of the *Pasadena* ordered as the foo fighters passed through three thousand meters.

Four torpedoes launched with a hiss of compressed air, each foo fighter double-targeted. The torpedoes raced away from the sub, a spool of wire unreeling behind each one, allowing it to be continuously targeted by the submarine. Each Mark 48 weighed over 2,750 pounds and was ten feet long by twenty-one inches in diameter. The conventional warhead consisted of over a thousand pounds of high explosive.

"Tracking," the weapon officer announced in the crowded control center. "I've got four good ones. All tracking clear, tracking two separate targets. Time to impact forty-two seconds. . . ." He paused, his eyes widening at the information his computer was giving him. "We've got inbound!"

"Inbound what?" the captain demanded.

"Our own torpedoes!" the weapons officer exclaimed. "They've been turned." His fingers were working the keyboard, trying to regain control of the weapons. "Time to impact, twenty seconds." Every eye in the control room fixed on the commanding officer.

The captain was staring over the man's shoulder, reading, interpreting.

"Fifteen seconds!"

"Abort, abort, abort!" the captain yelled.

The weapons officer flipped up a red cover and pressed down on the button underneath. All four torpedoes detonated less than two hundred meters away from their launch point.

"Prepare for impact!" the captain ordered, knowing his order had been much too late as the shock wave from the four simultaneous explosions hit the sub.

■ ■ ■

Captain Forster, on board the *Springfield,* was listening passively through a hydrophone headset. He tore the headphones off when the thunderous noise of the torpedoes going off hit them. The submarine rocked in the water. Forster yelled for a damage report as he put the headphones back on.

He heard the sounds coming from the *Pasadena* every submariner feared the most: the screech of metal giving way, water rushing in, air being blown out under pressure. He even imagined he could hear the screams of the crew of the *Pasadena* as they were crushed, but that might simply have been his imagination.

There was absolute silence throughout the

Springfield as even sailors not wearing the headphones could hear the faint sound of bulkheads giving way echo through their ship, like the sound of popcorn popping in the distance.

"Sir!" the first officer hissed. "What do we do?"

"We do nothing for now," Forster ordered, turning away from the other men in the control room. He felt his hastily eaten breakfast threatening to come back up as he imagined the fate of the crew of the *Pasadena*. "We do nothing."

■　■　■

On board the *Greywolf* they had heard the explosion and now they could also hear the sound of the *Pasadena* dying. Half a minute later they could pick up the noise of the battered hulk of the once proud submarine dropping by, heading for the ocean depths, more bulkheads shattering as the pressure increased.

Chapter 30

■■■■■■■■■■■

Turcotte was now walking slower, to allow Harker time to get in position. They were going down slightly, as the terrain sloped into the wide streambed that ran along the northern base of Qian-Ling. It made tactical sense for the Chinese picket line to be waiting on the far bank of the stream, using it as a control measure. Turcotte slowed his pace further, moving as stealthily as he could through the darker shadows. The one big advantage Turcotte knew he held over the Chinese was that the PLA did not have ready access to night-vision equipment.

Another five minutes and they reached the edge of the thicker undergrowth along the south bank. Turcotte wanted to get as close to the enemy line as they could prior to Harker initiating contact. He halted in an area of especially thick underbrush.

■ ■ ■

Harker and DeCamp were positioned slightly under six hundred meters away from the Chinese picket line. They were about a hundred meters higher than the men they would be shooting at. They crouched among jumbled rocks and stunted pines along the first crest of the ridge that marked the northern side of the draw they had been descending.

Harker looked through the thermal scope, which he now had mounted on the sniper rifle. The rifle and scope were rated effective out to twelve hundred meters, and Harker felt confident that he could hit the soldiers he could clearly see as glowing images. He also could see Turcotte's group, a small cluster of glowing dots, just south of the Chinese on the near bank.

Harker counted twenty Chinese soldiers in the immediate area of the team. Harker zeroed in on one glowing figure nearest the team. There was no wind that he would have to correct for. The hundred-meter drop required some adjustment, but Harker had done enough long-range firing to be able to account for that.

Five meters to Harker's left DeCamp was hidden. He had his sniper rifle propped between two rocks. Harker glanced at his watch again. Another minute.

Behind the two Special Forces soldiers the mass of Qian-Ling loomed, waiting for the first rays of daylight to touch it from the east.

■ ■ ■

On the other side of the world glowing figures were also being watched, but these were small dots on a massive screen in the front of a subterranean room. At the Space Command's Warning Center, deep under Cheyenne Mountain, they had the two foo fighters on-screen. They were going west over the Pacific, directly above the equator.

■ ■ ■

Harker smoothly pulled back on the trigger and the bark of the rifle echoed across the draw. A Chinese soldier, thinking he was secure in the dark, was slammed back as the 7.62mm round tore a fatal path through the man's chest. Without conscious thought Harker did as he'd been trained. He arced the muzzle of the weapon to his second target. The man had heard the first shot but didn't know what it meant. He never would, as Harker's round hit him in the center of the chest and he tumbled down in a heap.

Harker fired all ten rounds in the magazine. Nine hits for ten shots. He reloaded a fresh magazine and decided to wait a few minutes to allow the Chinese to react.

■ ■ ■

"What the hell is going on?" Kelly Reynolds asked Major Quinn. A new message from the Airlia, broadcast openly to the entire world, not in binary, but in English, had just been picked up by receivers all over the globe.

```
PLEASE
DO NOT INTERFERE
WITH
OUR PROBES
THEY ARE GATHERING
IMPORTANT INFORMATION
```

FOR OUR ARRIVAL
ASPASIA

Quinn pointed at the front screen in the Cube. "Space Command is tracking a pair of foo fighters."

"What does Aspasia mean by *don't interfere*?"

Quinn looked past her to make sure no one was close by, then leaned forward. "The Navy just lost a sub over the site of the foo fighter base. The Pentagon's going nuts."

"Lost a sub?" Kelly repeated. "You make it sound like they misplaced it. What happened?"

"I don't exactly know. I'm picking up classified reports going from CINCPAC to the Pentagon, and as near as I can tell, the foo fighters did something to the sub and it's down in deep water. No survivors."

"Jesus Christ." Kelly Reynolds shook her head in dismay. "What about China?"

Quinn bit his lip. "I'm not getting straight feedback, but I get the impression there's some trouble. I'm intercepting a lot of traffic between this Zandra person and STAAR in Antarctica."

"Are they going to get out?"

"The choppers going in to pick them up are on schedule."

Kelly Reynolds shook her head. "We're going to screw this up, aren't we? Our big chance and the human race is going to screw it up."

■ ■ ■

Turcotte could see and hear movement in the Chinese lines. There was the roar of tank and armored personnel carriers starting their engines. Orders were being yelled.

Even with the night-vision goggles it was unclear what was happening out there. For all Turcotte knew, the Chinese might be moving the whole picket line forward. He knew they had spotted Harker's position by the green tracers from the 12.7mm machine guns mounted on top of the tanks and APCs.

"When do we move?" Nabinger whispered.

"Any minute now."

■ ■ ■

From the high ground Harker could pick out the beginnings of what appeared to be a line moving forward toward his position. Harker gave a brief whistle and DeCamp whistled in response. Harker placed his weapon down and stretched his shoulders and arms out. He took several deep breaths and leaned back against a rock. He had a few moments before he had to start killing again.

■ ■ ■

Turcotte pulled on Nabinger's arm, indicating they were going to move out. Howes and Pressler rose up and followed. They slowly moved out of the bushes they had been hiding under.

Turcotte heard another brief burst of fire from Harker and DeCamp's position. Turcotte was sweeping from left to right and back with the night-vision goggles. He held the MP-5 at the ready. Off to his left he could barely discern a tank about seventy meters to north. Between the tank and the stream he could see nothing else.

Slowly they slid down into the streambed.

Turcotte felt his shoulders hunching, anticipating the bullet out of the darkness, but none came. He reached back and gave Nabinger a hand as they climbed up the far bank.

Turcotte checked his watch. Another twelve hundred meters and they should be at the pickup zone. Twenty minutes and the choppers should be there also.

■ ■ ■

The nearest troops were only five hundred meters away. It was time to be moving on, Harker thought. The Chinese were getting the range. Harker briefly considered not firing again. He decided they had to. He couldn't be sure that the others had made it through yet.

Harker fired five rounds in under three seconds, shifting rapidly from target to target even as the Chinese soldiers dived for cover. DeCamp fired just as quickly. The two pulled their weapons in and slid down the loose rock, putting the outcropping between them and the enemy. Just in time, as the return fire was extremely accurate and incoming rounds cracked by overhead.

"Let's go." Harker led the way as they scrambled to the north, keeping the outcropping between them and the Chinese for as long as they could. There was only one direction for them to run: toward the top of Qian-Ling.

■ ■ ■

The PZ was a dry rice paddy surrounded by tall trees on every side. They had run into no one on the rapid kilometer-and-a-half walk to it.

Turcotte checked his watch. Ten minutes. They

were clustered on the edge of the pickup zone. Everyone's ears were straining. Listening for the sound of rotor blades.

At eight minutes to time on target they heard blades off to the south. *Too soon,* thought Turcotte. *But maybe they're ahead of schedule.*

The blades were getting closer. Still off to the south. Then Turcotte realized what it probably was. More Chinese choppers to reinforce the first.

Turcotte leaned close to Nabinger. "You get on the first chopper that lands. I'll get on the second. There's a thing I learned in Ranger School that we have to do now. It's called disseminating the information. That way if only one chopper makes it out, the word gets out. And there's some other things I need to know, but first tell me how we can stop Aspasia."

Nabinger nodded and began speaking.

Chapter 31

∎∎∎∎∎∎∎∎∎∎

The bulk of the tomb appeared right on schedule. O'Callaghan slid the Black Hawk on a course that would take them north of the man-made mountain. Five minutes out. The kilometers flashed by beneath. Four minutes. O'Callaghan could see tracers firing to the southwest.

Two minutes. The mountain was now to the south. O'Callaghan slowed down and started scanning to the right as Spence scanned to the left, looking for the IR chem lights and strobe the team should be lighting right now.

■ ■ ■

Turcotte stood at the center of the small clearing and turned his IR strobe on. He could hear more helicopters coming from the east. His mind was buzzing with what Nabinger had told him and even more with speculation: what else might Nabinger have learned from the guardian computer that he had not had time to relate?

■ ■ ■

O'Callaghan could see the strobe. Perfect. Nine hundred and fifty kilometers from the *O'Bannion* and a perfect linkup. He slid over the pickup zone to let Putnam land first.

Putnam flared his Black Hawk and started to descend. O'Callaghan could see the figure with the strobe extinguish it. Putnam brought the bird to a halt on the ground. Two men ran out and got on board.

The first Black Hawk started to lift.

■ ■ ■

Turcotte watched the first helicopter with Nabinger and Pressler, the medic, on board, go up into the sky. He ran forward as the second bird landed, followed by Howes.

Turcotte leapt on board.

■ ■ ■

O'Callaghan did a quick scan of the area as he lifted and turned east.

"We got company," he said, seeing the navigational lights of an MI-4 helicopter, four kilometers away near the mountain.

O'Callaghan knew the Chinese helicopter couldn't see him yet, as the Black Hawk was blacked out and the Chinese pilot didn't have goggles. He wasn't about to give it a chance to find him.

O'Callaghan opened the throttle up and pushed the cyclic forward. The Black Hawk shot forward past Putnam, who immediately followed.

■ ■ ■

Harker took a quick glance over his shoulder as he climbed and saw the bright searchlights of two helicopters probing the darkness near the site he and DeCamp had occupied only minutes ago. On the ground Harker could also see the headlights of numerous trucks that were bringing more troops into the area.

Their only chance was to get over the top of Qian-Ling and then—that train of thought was broken off in Harker's mind as he watched two Chinese helicopters fly to the top of the mountain tomb and settle down. They landed about a hundred meters apart and then took off, heading back down toward the coast.

Harker turned to DeCamp. "They're putting troops in ahead of us."

DeCamp wearily rested the butt of his weapon on the ground. "What now?"

Harker weighed their options. "We keep going up the mountain. Those choppers can only carry ten troops on board. The odds are better."

■ ■ ■

Turcotte grabbed a headset off the roof of the cargo bay and put it on. They were going over the trees and the chopper was moving fast, but in the wrong direction. Turcotte keyed the intercom. "We've got to go back. We've got two more men on the mountain!"

"Jesus!" O'Callaghan exclaimed. He could see helicopters moving up there and tracers cutting through the air.

O'Callaghan pressed the button that transmitted to the other chopper. "Putnam, run for the coast. I've got more passengers to pick up."

Putnam didn't need to be told twice. "Roger that." The other Black Hawk raced off to the east as O'Callaghan brought his chopper around on a tight turn to the west.

■ ■ ■

DeCamp discerned the enemy soldiers first. He gripped Harker on the arm and pointed. Harker stopped and squinted into the darkness. There were ten of them. Two hundred meters away and heading downslope. The Chinese were spread out, weapons at the ready, with twenty meters between each man. Harker looked around quickly. In the ground between the two parties there was a small knoll of boulders rising slightly above the rest of the ground. It was about a twenty meters ahead of where he and DeCamp now stood. He pointed it out to DeCamp. "We'll make our stand there."

■ ■ ■

"We've got company," O'Callaghan yelled through the intercom as he accelerated the helicopter and jerked it hard to the left. Those in the back were tumbled on top of each other. Turcotte got on one knee and looked out as two Chinese helicopters roared by out of the southwest and started to circle east.

"The next one will be a gun run," O'Callaghan said. "They're circling to come back."

■ ■ ■

The AWACS's control room continued to track the action. They had the one Black Hawk escaping to the east, the other inexplicably turning back to the west, flying near two blips indicating Chinese helicopters.

Things got worse in a heartbeat as one of Colonel Zycki's operators called out. "We've got four fast movers lifting off out of the airbase outside Xi'an, sir."

Zycki swore. "Jesus. This thing's getting out of control. The Chinese must have picked up the Black Hawks on local radar. How long till the jets are in the area near the Black Hawk?"

The analyst next to the radar operator quickly calculated. "Twelve minutes, sir."

"How far out are the F-117's?"

"They can make intercept, sir, but we need authorization for them to go hot."

"Goddamn. Get me this Zandra person on the line."

■ ■ ■

Harker and DeCamp settled in among the boulders on the crest of the small knoll and watched the Chinese squad approach in the moonlight. They were only a hundred meters away now and moving slowly toward them. Harker whispered to DeCamp, "Another fifty meters and we start firing."

DeCamp checked his submachine gun and insured he had a round in the chamber and the magazine was seated properly. Harker laid out two more magazines for quicker reloading.

■ ■ ■

"This is Zandra. Go ahead." She was ignoring the glare of Lisa Duncan standing next to her, listening to the report from the AWACS.

"Yes, ma'am. Things are getting hairy over there. We've got one Black Hawk heading for the coast, but it's got a hell of a long way to go. The other's turned west for some reason. They've obviously been picked up on local radar as we've got two Chinese helicopters vectoring in on it. They're about a minute out from intercept. We've also got four fast movers scrambled out of Xi'an. They're nine minutes out. Our F-117's will be in range to intercept, but we need authorization for them to fire."

"I understand," Zandra said.

Zycki's voice came out of the box. "Ma'am, neither of those helicopters is going to make it out without help. Those Chinese helicopters vectoring in are probably armed."

"All right, order the flight leader of the F-117's to escort out the one Black Hawk that's heading for the coast. It must have what we want on board."

"That's abandoning the other chopper to certain death," Zycki argued.

"I don't have time to—" Zandra began, but the mike was ripped out of her hand by Lisa Duncan.

"This is Lisa Duncan. I'm the President's science adviser to UNAOC. You will order two F-117's to escort the Black Hawk heading for the coast," Duncan said, "and the other two go help the second chopper. Is that clear, Colonel?"

"Quite clear."

Zandra had made no attempt to regain the mike.

■ ■ ■

Harker took a deep breath. He let it out. "Are you ready?"

"Roger that."

Harker took a deep breath and held it. He pulled back on the trigger and the submachine gun spoke. He hit his first two targets before the rest had gotten under cover. The return fire was intense, green tracers racing by in all directions.

■ ■ ■

O'Callaghan had the Black Hawk down very low, cut short in his attempt to go straight to the mountain by the interception of the Chinese helicopters. O'Callaghan was skimming along just above the surface of the streambed Turcotte had crossed not too long before. While he was down lower than the enemy could go, he was forced to go much slower than the Chinese helicopters at a higher altitude. As he took a left-hand bend in the river he glanced back. He could see the running lights of the lead enemy helicopter only eight hundred meters back. There was no way he could go to the other two men and pick them up without getting nailed.

"Arm the Stingers," O'Callaghan ordered. He had his attention split between the course he was flying, the firefight on the mountain to his left, and the Chinese helicopters closing.

"Armed," Spence replied.

O'Callaghan pulled back on the cyclic, kicked his left pedals, and swung the Black Hawk around 180 degrees to face the two oncoming Chinese helicopters.

As the Chinese pilots started to react to this startling maneuver, O'Callaghan pressed the fire button once, then a second time. Two Stingers leapt from the side of the helicopter. The lead MI-4 Hind took the missile straight in its air intake just below the blades and blossomed into a fireball. The trail MI-4 started to turn, but the supersonic missile lanced into the side of the engine.

Turcotte keyed the intercom. "Let's get our guys and get out of here."

O'Callaghan pulled up out of the riverbed and accelerated.

■ ■ ■

Harker turned and stared to the north at the ball of fire that had been ignited in the air down there. Then there was a second one. A burst of automatic fire from ahead caused him to turn his attention back to matters closer at hand. He fired another magazine, scattering rounds all over the hillside, keeping the Chinese at a distance.

■ ■ ■

"There. Ahead and to the left. Did you see those green and red tracers?" Turcotte was leaning forward, pointing between the two pilots. "The red is our people."

"No shit I see them," O'Callaghan said. "The problem is, are they gonna see us? That's a hot landing zone."

"We've got a solution for that," Turcotte said as he turned back to the cargo bay.

■ ■ ■

Harker heard the rotor blades coming toward them. At first he didn't see anything. He quickly pulled his goggles up and turned them on.

"Get your harness buckled!" Harker yelled out. DeCamp turned in surprise. "We've got a Black Hawk inbound." Harker turned his infrared strobe on and held it up.

On board the helicopter, Turcotte slid the left door open while Howes slid the right open. Each held a 120-foot nylon rope in a deployment bag in his arms. O'Callaghan flared the Black Hawk to a halt eight feet above the tumbled ground surrounding the IR strobe. The two bags were thrown out and hurtled to the ground.

"I've got this one." DeCamp yelled as he ran forward and secured the rope. He pulled the deployment bag off and hooked the loop tied in the end through the two snap links in the shoulders of his combat vest. Twenty feet away Harker did the same. The two ran together and linked arms.

There had been no shots fired yet by the Chinese soldiers. They probably still didn't understand what was happening and assumed the helicopter was one of their own.

■ ■ ■

"We've got them," Turcotte yelled as he peered off the deck of the cargo compartment. O'Callaghan snatched in collective and quickly pulled the helicopter onto an easterly heading.

Harker and DeCamp felt their vests tighten around them as the rope became taut. Their feet came off the ground and they were savagely swung out to the west by centrifugal force. Harker

gasped for breath as he and DeCamp held on to
each other.

O'Callaghan straightened out the chopper and
turned to the east.

"Find someplace to land. We've got to get them
in." Turcotte watched tracers from the ground
make a pattern around Harker and DeCamp and
pass by the helicopter.

"We can't. There's no time. Pull them in!"
O'Callaghan yelled back.

DeCamp felt his rope jerk. He looked up and
saw someone hanging over the edge of the deck
signaling him to separate from Harker. He shook
Harker and pointed up. They both began pulling
themselves hand over hand up the ropes, even as
the ropes were being pulled in.

DeCamp was pulled into the cargo compartment. Harker was hanging less than twenty feet
below, slowly being pulled up. That was good
enough, O'Callaghan figured. He dropped down
close to the earth and raced off to the east as fast
as he could push the chopper.

Chapter 32

Twenty miles to the east, lying on the floor of the cargo bay of the first Black Hawk, Professor Nabinger had his eyes closed. His mind was absorbed with the images he'd received from the guardian inside Qian-Ling. There was much he didn't understand, but one thing was clear to him: He had to stop Aspasia!

Then he remembered something else. The central tunnel in the tomb that was guarded by the holograph and the ray! He knew where it led and what was down there. And he knew how to get in there! No matter what happened, Nabinger knew he would have to come back to Qian-Ling.

He pulled out his leather-bound notebook and began writing furiously.

■ ■ ■

At Osan Air Force Base in South Korea, Zandra and Duncan were listening to the radio traffic from the AWACS when there was a beeping noise from Zandra's laptop.

She quickly turned in her seat and entered a code. She read the message on the screen, then rapidly typed out commands.

"What's wrong?" Duncan asked.

"Foo fighters," was Zandra's succinct answer. "Two of them are heading for China."

■ ■ ■

In the Cube at Area 51 Kelly Reynolds knew nothing of the drama being played out over the skies of China, but she could follow the progress of the foo fighters. They were almost at the end of the Pacific and nearing the coast of China.

"What's going on?" she asked Quinn, who had been hooked in to the military's secure MILSTAR communications net.

"They're pissed in the Pentagon. They lost a lot of men on that sub."

"But they interfered . . ." Kelly began, stopping as she saw the look on Quinn's face. She suddenly realized that perhaps not everyone was as anxious to have Aspasia land as she was. And that those who had died on the submarine were more than just numbers to a lot of people.

"They think the foo fighters are going to intercept the choppers," Quinn added.

"Why would they do that?"

"That's a good question, isn't it?"

■ ■ ■

"Splash four," the pilot of one of the F-117's laconically reported over the radio to the AWACS, as if it were an everyday event. The F-117's had launched four air-to-air missiles from over forty miles away. The Chinese pilots had never even known they were targeted when their planes exploded.

"Roger that." Colonel Zycki dropped down into his padded command chair and relaxed for the first time in hours.

It only lasted a few seconds.

"Sir, we've got two foo fighters three minutes out from the lead Black Hawk."

"Are the F-117's out in front?"

"Yes, sir. One minute to intercept," the radar operator informed Zycki.

Zycki had received word over the secure scrambler about the fate of the *Pasadena*. "Tell them to fire as soon as the foo fighters are in range."

■ ■ ■

"Great," the pilot of the lead F-117 muttered as he received that order. He had the two foo fighters on his small radar screen, closing fast. He hit the fire button immediately, launching two air-to-air missiles at the incoming objects. His wingman did the same.

Nabinger's Black Hawk was ten miles behind them, flying low to the ground.

■ ■ ■

Colonel Zycki could see the four missiles racing toward the foo fighters. They had closed half the gap when the missiles simply disappeared.

"Oh, shit," Zycki whispered.

Then as the two foo fighters closed on their position the dots representing the four F-117 Stealth fighters blipped out. That left just the foo fighters and the two Black Hawks. The foo fighters closed on the lead one.

"Twenty seconds until intercept!"

■ ■ ■

"We've got foo fighters inbound!" the pilot yelled, startling Nabinger out of his reverie about what was secreted in the lowest level of the imperial tomb of Qian-Ling. "Our escort is down!"

The chopper shook as the pilots began evasive maneuvers. Nabinger reached forward and grabbed one of them on the shoulder. "I need a radio link!"

The pilot threw him a headset. Nabinger put it on and keyed the mike. "Hello! Hello! Is anyone listening?"

■ ■ ■

Duncan still had the mike in her hand, listening to events forwarded from the AWACS. She recognized the voice on the radio.

"Professor, this is Dr. Duncan!"

■ ■ ■

Nabinger's hand was wrapped tight around the small boom mike. He could now see the two foo fighters looping in, small glowing golden orbs in the sky.

He pushed the transmit button. "In the tomb—Qian-Ling—in the very bottom chamber—there's—" He paused as a rushing noise filled the headset, rising to an ear-piercing screech, forcing him to rip the headset off, trying to stop the agonizing pain that tore through his brain.

The Black Hawk's engines abruptly stopped

functioning along with every other piece of machinery on board the craft. The helicopter nosed over and dropped like a rock.

The last thing Nabinger saw before impact were the two foo fighters hanging overhead, like two small moons illuminating his death.

■ ■ ■

"Professor!" Duncan yelled into the microphone.

"It's down," Colonel Zycki announced over the radio.

■ ■ ■

In the back of the trail chopper Turcotte had listened to the death of the lead helicopter and Professor Nabinger in stunned silence. He'd had a run-in with foo fighters before and knew they could easily incapacitate a helicopter. There was also no way to outrun the small glowing orbs.

"Cut all your power!" he yelled into the intercom. "Set us down!"

O'Callaghan twisted his head to look at Turcotte in disbelief. "What?"

"Kill the engine and autorotate," Turcotte yelled, "or we're all going to die!"

"Shut down!" O'Callaghan ordered Spence.

O'Callaghan reached up and hit the emergency shutdown, a move that was never supposed to be done while the helicopter was in the air. At the same time Spence disengaged the transmission, freeing the blades to rotate on their own, slowing the chopper's descent. He then began running his hands down the rows of controls, flipping off every system that had been on.

O'Callaghan glanced down. He spotted a small clearing among the trees. He pushed hard on the cyclic, trying to get the chopper to it.

Two foo fighters appeared, racing past the helicopter and disappearing to the rear.

"Brace for crash!" O'Callaghan yelled as he realized they weren't quite going to make the open area. The Black Hawk hit the trees and rolled to the left.

The aircraft tore through the thick tree cover and came to a halt on the ground. The combination of the original forward speed and the sudden drop in altitude produced a collision that crumpled the left front of the helicopter. Shattered glass, twisted metal, and pieces of trees filled the front of the aircraft.

On impact all the occupants of the cargo bay had been thrown forward in a pile. Turcotte shook his head, trying to clear it. He could smell jet fuel leaking. As soon as that fuel touched part of the hot engine, Turcotte knew the helicopter would become an inferno.

Someone got the side door open. He could see Harker silhouetted against the door for a moment, then tumble out. Turcotte turned to the front to help O'Callaghan, who was trying to tear through the wreckage and free his copilot. Turcotte could see the blood seeping from under the man's helmet. Turcotte reached forward and felt the copilot's neck.

Turcotte let go and grabbed O'Callaghan, who was fumbling with the copilot's shoulder harness. "He's dead!"

O'Callaghan shook his hand off and continued to work to free the body.

"Leave him!" Turcotte yelled. "The chopper's gonna blow!"

Turcotte simply grabbed the pilot and pulled him between the seats into the cargo bay. Then he shoved O'Callaghan toward the open cargo door.

Fuel reached the hot engine exhausts and burst into flames. Instantly, the helicopter became an inferno. Turcotte staggered away from the flames, pushing O'Callaghan ahead of him.

They were thirty meters away when the helicopter exploded. The impact threw them all to the ground.

■ ■ ■

"Second Black Hawk is down." Colonel Zycki's voice was flat. "All aircraft are down."

Duncan pushed back from the control console and stared at Zandra. "There! Are you satisfied now? We have nothing!" She pointed at her watch. "Twenty-eight hours until the Airlia arrives and all we've managed to do is kill some damn good people."

Chapter 33
∎∎∎∎∎∎∎∎∎∎∎∎

The six talons were still crisscrossing each other's paths as they moved toward Earth. The large open field in Central Park had been cleared and blocked off. UNAOC was busy preparing the format for the reception of the Airlia and determining the pecking order of world leaders who would get to meet Aspasia.

It was the middle of the night, four hours before dawn, the last dawn before the Airlia arrived. The headlines of the early-morning editions currently being printed trumpeted it as the last day the human race would stand alone on the face of the Earth.

∎ ∎ ∎

Things behind the scenes in the Cube looked very different, though. Major Quinn had finally been brought fully into the loop by the Pentagon, based on the assumption that if anyone knew how to counter the foo fighters, it would be the personnel at Area 51. He also had forwarded in-

tercepts from Zandra in South Korea to STAAR
in Antarctica, and that was causing great consternation in the covert world in Washington as the
CIA was denying she worked for them and no one
could quite figure out who Zandra or her organization, STAAR, was, or how it had managed to
gain such power.

Kelly Reynolds watched all this with dismay
overlaid with grief over the news that Peter Nabinger and Mike Turcotte were dead. She was in
the Cube conference room with Quinn, listening
to the latter's video-conference call with the Joint
Chiefs of Staff and the President in the War
Room under the Pentagon.

"What about this STAAR person you have
there, Major?" General Carthart, the chairman of
the Joint Chiefs of Staff, asked.

"She's still in the hangar with the bouncer,"
Quinn answered.

"Any idea what she's up to?" Carthart asked.

"No, sir."

"The hell with that," Hunt, the director of the
CIA, snarled. "If none of us in this room know,
then something is seriously wrong."

"I don't think so," the President said. "There is
a presidential directive authorizing STAAR. It
was signed forty years ago by Eisenhower but it is
still legal and binding today. I have to believe my
predecessor had a good reason for signing it and
deliberately keeping us in the dark." The President turned to the chairman of the Joint Chiefs.
"General?"

Carthart leaned forward. "We've got twenty-
four hours until the Airlia land. I agree we ought
to proceed a bit more cautiously. Our actions

might be precipitating the aggressive actions of
the foo fighters. I suggest we hold off on taking
direct action until we know for sure what is going
on."

"What about China?" Kelly asked.

"I recommend we cut our losses there,"
Carthart said.

"And the foo fighters?" the President asked.

"The two that downed our aircraft in China are
heading southeast," Quinn said, "and are currently over the Indian Ocean."

"Their estimated destination?"

"We believe they are going to a site in the Rift
Valley where UNAOC has uncovered other Airlia
artifacts."

"What about this Antarctica business?" the
President asked.

Quinn had the answer for that. "I think that
STAAR took over a place called Scorpion Base.
It's the only logical place for these messages from
the STAAR operatives to be terminating."

"Anyone know anything about this Scorpion
Base?" the President asked those in the War
Room with him. When he got no reply, the President jabbed a finger at his camera, pointing at
Quinn and Reynolds. "I want you to forward all
information about the location of Scorpion Base
to the War Room. We'll proceed cautiously," the
President finally said, the strain of the last week
showing on his face. "General Carthart, move the
forces you need to cover the Airlia and STAAR
sites."

"I have a suggestion." Kelly Reynolds was frustrated with these people and their defensive reactions.

"Go ahead," the President said.

"Why don't we just ask the STAAR representative here at Area 51 who they are?"

"That's a good idea, Ms. Reynolds. Major Quinn, you do that. We'll do what we have to on our end."

The screen went dead and Kelly turned to Quinn. "He made the right decision about taking things slowly."

Quinn didn't look very agreeable. "What if he made the wrong decision?" He didn't wait for an answer. "He made that decision, Kelly, because there is no other decision to make. Every time humans have confronted the Airlia's equipment we've lost. Our best weapons don't do us any good, so it's easy to make a decision to keep our fingers crossed and hope for the best."

"It's all been a tragic mistake." Kelly's voice brooked no dissent. "Aspasia will clear this up when he lands."

"What about Turcotte and Nabinger?" Quinn asked.

"I told them not to go," Kelly said. "They should have listened."

"But—" Quinn began, but she cut him off, whirling on him and getting close to his chest, poking him with her finger.

"No one is listening! No one! Not the President. Not you. No one. Don't you understand? If we would only listen, it would all be all right, but we're screwing everything up!"

Reynolds stormed off toward the elevator, leaving Quinn staring at her rapidly departing back.

■ ■ ■

Turcotte took stock of the situation in the growing daylight. They were only thirty meters from where the helicopter had crashed. The explosion had scattered wreckage in a hundred-meter circle and scorched the forest.

Harker, Howes, and DeCamp were battered but ready for action. O'Callaghan, the pilot, was nursing a broken hand but other than that seemed all right. Turcotte knew it was only a matter of time before the Chinese had aircraft flying overhead, searching for them. The terrain in the immediate area was extremely hilly and unpopulated.

"We need to get a message out," Turcotte said.

Harker gave a bitter laugh. "How? We don't have any radios. We're screwed. No one knows we're down here, and I don't think anyone really gives a damn."

Turcotte was looking about the clearing the chopper had torn through the trees. "Someone gives a damn. Dr. Duncan will be looking for us."

"So?" Harker snapped. "How she gonna know we're here and alive? And then how's she's gonna get us out?"

"I don't know how she's going to get us out, but I trust her to come up with something. But I do know how to let her know we're here and alive."

■ ■ ■

"Goddamn!" Major Quinn was fuming as he reentered the Cube. He quickly dialed the War Room in the Pentagon.

"The bouncer and Oleisa are gone," he reported to the duty officer who answered.

"Gone?"

"They just took off. I guess we can't ask Oleisa who the hell she works for now." Covering the phone, he looked at one of his men. "Put Space Command's link on screen. I want to know where our bouncer is going."

Chapter 34

∎∎∎∎∎∎∎∎∎∎∎

"**N**o survivors," Zandra said, throwing down the faxed computer imagery in front of Duncan. "Nothing but wreckage at all the crash sites. The Chinese are already all over the area where one of the Stealth fighters went down."

Duncan picked up the photos taken by the KH-14 spy satellite and looked through them.

She paused at one of the photos and looked more closely. Her hand began to shake as she realized what she was seeing. "Somebody's still alive. Either Turcotte or Nabinger."

Zandra's head snapped up from her computer. "How do you know that?"

Duncan tossed the imagery onto the keyboard. "Look."

"What exactly am I looking for?"

Duncan pointed. "Someone's traced out the same Airlia high rune symbol for HELP that's written into the Great Wall, using pieces of the wreckage. We have to get them out of there. And we

have to do it without the Chinese *or* the foo fighters stopping us."

Zandra nodded. "It is time to confront our enemies."

"What the hell does that mean?" Duncan demanded.

"It means we no longer stand and watch."

"We being STAAR?" Duncan asked.

"Correct. Things have progressed past the
point of no return."

"And?" Duncan was out of her patience with
her enigmatic comrade. "Do you have a way of
getting those people out of China?

"Actually, I have just the thing," Zandra said.

■ ■ ■

Larry Kincaid was all alone in the control center. JPL was a ghost town, everyone anticipating
the arrival of the Airlia in New York the following
morning. It was as if decades of work at JPL had
faded away in just a couple of days.

He heard the door behind him open and slowly
swing shut. Kincaid was not surprised when
Coridan, still wearing sunglasses and black
clothes, took the seat next to him.

"*Surveyor* in a stable orbit?" Coridan asked.

"Yes." Kincaid didn't ask how the man had
come up with calculations that would have taken
his own scientists and computers days to figure
out.

"Is it still powered down?" Coridan asked.

Kincaid nodded.

"There's something you need to do," Coridan
said.

Kincaid waited.

"Bring up the data link for *Surveyor,* please."

Kincaid finally broke his silence. "Why?"

"Because we're going to take care of some unfinished business."

▪ ▪ ▪

In the South Atlantic a U.S. Navy carrier task force headed by the supercarrier USS *John C. Stennis* was steaming due south toward Antarctica at flank speed. They had the location of Scorpion Base plotted, and the operations officer was busy figuring when would be the earliest the ship would be in range to launch aircraft to make it to that location and back.

▪ ▪ ▪

In the other major ocean, the U.S. Navy was deploying its Pacific Fleet in two areas: half heading toward Easter Island, the other half heading for the spot in the ocean under which lay the foo fighter base.

▪ ▪ ▪

Just above the foo fighter base the crew of the *Greywolf* huddled together, trying to draw warmth from each other's bodies. They were still slowly descending, but after knowing what had happened to the *Pasadena* there were no more complaints from Emory.

Three thousand meters above the submersible, the two surviving *Los Angeles*–class submarines also waited, running silent and powered down, biding their time, the crews full of thoughts of revenge but without a clue as to how to wreak that revenge without suffering the same fate as their sister ship.

Chapter 35

∎∎∎∎∎∎∎∎∎∎∎∎

"**W**e're not going to be able to hang around here much longer," Harker muttered, looking about the countryside. They'd spotted some Chinese helicopters to the south earlier in the morning, but so far their position remained undiscovered.

Turcotte could sense the pessimism and unease in the Special Forces men he was marooned with. They wanted to start moving, get out of the area of the crash, and make for the nearest border. The fact that the nearest border was over a thousand miles away and with Mongolia didn't faze them much. They just wanted to do something, rather than wait for the Chinese to show up.

But Turcotte knew their only chance to get out in time was to hope that the high rune symbol he'd put around the nearby crash site using wreckage would be picked up by a satellite and that Lisa Duncan would figure it out. Of course, he wasn't too sure how she was going to get them out, but he figured anything was better than trying to walk out.

"What the hell?" O'Callaghan said, standing up and staring to the east.

Turcotte spotted what the chief was looking at: a bouncer coming in fast and low. The disk raced up to their position and halted. It slowly came down until it was resting on top of the wreckage of the Black Hawk. The Special Forces men raised their weapons and aimed.

"Hold your fire," Turcotte ordered.

The hatch in top opened and a woman stuck her head out. "Hurry up!" she yelled.

Turcotte didn't need a second invitation. He ran toward the bouncer, followed by Harker, O'Callaghan, and the other Special Force soldiers. He scrambled up the sloping deck and then down inside.

An Air Force pilot was strapped into one of the two depressions in the center floor, his hands on the controls. The woman who had called out to them was standing off to one side near the communications console that had been put in. She immediately reminded Turcotte of Zandra—in fact, for a second he thought it was her, but then he noted that she was a couple of inches shorter than the agent they had left behind in South Korea.

"Whoa!" O'Callaghan said as he dropped down next to Turcotte. Being inside a bouncer took a lot of getting used to. The hardest thing was the disorienting effect of the skin of the craft appearing to be transparent from the inside. Majestic had never quite figured out how the Airlia technology did that, but it was difficult to remain calm as, now that all were on board, the bouncer lifted, the ground seeming to move away under their feet.

"I am Oleisa," the woman said.

"Are you with Aspasia or Artad?" Turcotte asked.

The woman had a blank look on her face. "I'm with STAAR. I'm here to take you to Zandra in Korea."

Turcotte shook his head. "I need to get to the Rift Valley in Africa."

The pilot looked up from his seat.

"Osan Air Force Base," Oleisa said. The pilot returned his attention to flying.

"Listen—" Turcotte began, but the woman raised a hand.

"We will go to Africa after we pick up Zandra. It will not take long."

"What about the foo fighters?" Turcotte asked.

"They haven't picked us up yet," Oleisa said.

"And if they do?"

"We'll deal with that if it happens."

■ ■ ■

Lisa Duncan was surprised when Mike Turcotte wrapped her in a big hug as she climbed down inside the bouncer that was now parked on the runway at Osan Air Force Base. The entire area was surrounded by flashing lights as the air police blocked it off.

"Thank you" was all Turcotte said, before turning away for a moment to collect himself. The stress of the last couple of days—all the losses, all the emotions he had kept at bay while trying to keep his mind focused on the mission—was finally breaking through.

Zandra had also come on board, the Special Forces men and helicopter pilot debarking prior to her getting on board, leaving the pilot, Turcotte, Duncan, Zandra, and Oleisa as the only passengers.

"We have to leave now," Zandra said, sealing the hatch.

Turcotte turned back. "The Rift Valley?"

Zandra nodded. "Do you know how to release the ruby sphere?"

"Nabinger told me," Turcotte confirmed.

"Good."

"How come you don't know?" Turcotte asked as the bouncer took off and the pilot accelerated to the southwest.

"What do you mean?" Zandra asked.

"You work for the Airlia. You're part of them. How come you don't know? Hell, for all we know, you're Airlia yourself."

"I'm not Airlia nor do I work for them," Zandra said. "I work for the human race."

"I thought you worked for STAAR?" Turcotte pressed.

"Yes, I do."

"And it is?" Duncan asked.

"Strategic Tactical Advanced Alien Response team," Zandra said. "When Majestic discovered the mothership and bouncers, President Eisenhower knew that Earth had been visited by aliens. It seemed perfectly logical for the government to consider what would happen if Earth made live contact with an alien life-form.

"A committee was formed of the leading experts at that time, including psychologists, military, scientists, sociologists; anyone who might be able to contribute was invited. They sat and brainstormed for several weeks, then issued what they simply considered an academic and theoretical recommendation for a hypothetical situation: that a secret government organization be formed to be in place to deal with live first contact."

Zandra paused, those in the bouncer hanging on every word, as they flew over the South Pacific, heading south before they would turn east toward Africa.

She continued. "One of the most important stipulations of the report was that the organization, which was named STAAR, have the highest possible security clearance and have an authorization code to be able to take action when necessary without having to go through administrative channels. It was felt that time would be of the essence in case of live contact and STAAR, since it was dedicated to the mission, would be in the best position to decide on a response."

"That's circumventing the democratic process and our elected leaders," Lisa Duncan said.

"It was felt to be necessary by the elected leader at the time," Zandra replied. "The idea is quite logical if you think about it. Rather than divert a large amount of resources, and thus a large amount of scrutiny, to STAAR, Eisenhower simply gave it the authority to use resources that already existed, whether they be military or CIA or NSA or anything else, to gather intelligence and, when the time came, to take action."

"So you've been waiting all this time?" Turcotte asked.

"Yes."

"Why haven't you done something before now?"

"Our charter and authorization for action under the presidential directive is very specific. Our jurisdiction is only over live contact with alien life."

"And now?" Turcotte asked.

"Now, since live contact is pending, we must act."

"What are you going to do?"

"I'm not sure," Zandra said. "Our course of action has not been decided, because we don't have enough information. It might be to welcome Aspasia and the Airlia with open arms or it might be to oppose him with everything we can muster in a fight to the death." She turned to the communications console. "I'd like to bring my superior, Lexina, in on this."

Neither Turcotte or Duncan objected, so she flipped on a speaker. "Lexina, this is Zandra. I have Dr. Duncan and Captain Turcotte here with me."

A woman's voice came out of the speaker. "Captain, you have the information we need to make a very important decision. The foo fighters, which Aspasia controls, are certainly acting in a hostile manner, but before committing to a course of action we've been waiting to hear what you found in Qian-Ling. What did the guardian there tell Professor Nabinger?"

"Nabinger was convinced that Aspasia was coming to Earth to take the mothership and destroy the planet," Turcotte summed it up succinctly. "The Qian-Ling guardian reversed the story he got from the Easter Island one: Aspasia was the rebel and it was the Kortad, or Airlia police, under someone named Artad, that saved the human race and the planet."

"Which do you believe?" Lexina asked.

"Neither."

Zandra's eyebrows rose over her sunglasses. "You think we should do nothing?"

"I didn't say that."

Dr. Duncan spoke for the first time. "Why do you believe neither, Mike?"

"I don't have any evidence. We're getting conflicting stories, and for all we know they could both be bullshit. The bottom line is that Earth is *our* planet. These Airlia came here, set up shop, blasted Atlantis back into the ocean when they couldn't keep their act together, and have been dicking with us every once in a while for millennia.

"Everyone's made a big deal about Aspasia, saying he didn't interfere with our growth as a species, but as far as I can tell he didn't help either. None of the Airlia did. I mean, this isn't *Star Trek*—it's not like the Airlia have a prime directive not to interfere.

"Let's look at what both sides admit to: Aspasia's guardian says he blasted Atlantis and left the guardian on Easter Island, which is controlling the foo fighters right now; Artad's guardian says *he* blasted Atlantis, and left the guardian computer in Temiltepec that took over Gullick; plus, it says he left a nuke in the Great Pyramid, and I think we have to assume got the Great Pyramid built in the first place, and I'd sure say that affected a whole bunch of humans, not to mention all the poor human slobs who died building the section of the Great Wall simply to spell HELP.

"We know foo fighters accompanied the *Enola Gay* and watched the U.S. atom-bomb Japan; well, the human race could have used some help there. Or many other times in our history. They didn't leave us alone but they also didn't help us. Why should we think that's changed now? I think we can safely assume that Aspasia is going to be looking out for his own interests, not ours. So the question is, why is he coming back now? What's different?"

The room was quiet as everyone turned over the events of the past week in their minds. Lisa Duncan spoke first. "The guardian at Temiltepec was moved and then destroyed."

Turcotte nodded. "You were right in a way about the sphere being a doomsday device. According to Nabinger, that guardian was responsible for the ruby sphere in the Rift Valley.

"It could release the sphere," Turcotte said, "into the chasm and an explosion that deep would start a chain reaction that could destroy the planet. When they took the guardian out of Temiltepec, Majestic made the sphere vulnerable," Turcotte said. "*That's* what's different and that's what Aspasia wants.

"Also remember they blew *Viking* out of the sky over Mars so we couldn't see what was going on. The foo fighters destroyed the *Pasadena* and killed all those men on board. And that happened after Aspasia was awake. Taking aside what the different guardians have said, I think the Airlia haven't exactly been the friendliest and most peaceful encounter we could have for first live contact. And now they're coming here in six ships that certainly don't look like ET's ship waving a white flag of peace."

Turcotte stared at the others inside the bouncer. "We either roll over on our stomachs like a beaten dog and hope they scratch our belly and not blow our brains out or we fight them. But there's no way of absolutely knowing which is the right course until it's too late."

Lexina's voice filled the short silence that followed. "You are correct. Our charter that was signed by President Eisenhower directs us to take whatever means necessary to oppose an alien landing if there is not absolutely clear-cut evidence that the aliens are benevolent. Thus, for STAAR, our course of action is clear. We oppose Aspasia."

Turcotte rubbed the stubble on his chin. He knew Kelly Reynolds would be blowing a gasket if she could hear this conversation. He also kept unvoiced his suspicion that STAAR wasn't all it pretended to be either. Take things down in the order that they'll kill you, was the maxim he'd had beaten into him in the mud at Fort Benning and the forests of Fort Bragg.

And right now Turcotte knew that Aspasia was what had to be stopped first. He'd deal with STAAR when he could.

■ ■ ■

But Kelly Reynolds had been listening. She looked up at Major Quinn. The speaker that had played the intercepted conversation sat on the tabletop between them. Quinn had had the NSA zero in on any communications between Scorpion

Base and anywhere in the world. It had not been hard to piggyback the communications that were routed through a MILSTAR satellite. Kelly had returned to the Cube twenty minutes ago.

"They can't," Kelley said as the radio went dead. "Aspasia has said he is coming in peace. We have to believe him."

"Tell that to the men on the *Pasadena,*" Quinn said.

"They fired first!" Kelly yelled.

"Yes, they did," Major Quinn acknowledged. "But the foo fighters didn't have to destroy the sub. They could have disabled the torpedoes and gone about their business."

"That was just an automatic response!" Kelly reached out and grabbed Quinn's arm. "Please. Give me a bouncer. Let me get to Easter Island and the guardian before things go too far."

Quinn had a lot of other things on his mind at the moment, and they would be easier to accomplish without Reynolds looking over his shoulder. "Take Bouncer 6. I'll alert the pilot."

■ ■ ■

"Space Command has picked up a foo fighter heading in this direction," Lexina's voice rang out to those inside the bouncer. "We are going to have to evacuate our position here. There also seems to be some activity from the foo fighters over the Rift Valley compound. I think Aspasia is showing his hand.

"Good luck!"

■ ■ ■

Some activity was a large understatement.

Two U.S. Navy F-14's from the *George Washington* had been on station fifty miles away, shadowing the two fighters. They were the first to get destroyed, as the foo fighters raced at them, disabling their engines. The fighters then turned for the compound. They crisscrossed the skies overhead, a tightly focused beam of golden light coming out of each, destroying the helicopters that were on the ground, blasting those that tried to take off.

Colonel Spearson and his surviving SAS men were gathered by the entrance, weapons in hand, waiting for the final assault and desperately radioing for help.

■ ■ ■

The talons were less than eight hours out from Earth, their tight formation still weaving the same pattern. But there was a brief flash of golden light from each ship as it took the lead in the formation.

A human fighter pilot from World War II would have recognized what they were doing: they were testing their weapons, making sure they functioned.

Chapter 36
••••••••••

"The ruby sphere is the key," Turcotte said. "We can't let Aspasia get it."

The bouncer was racing through the sky, now heading west toward Africa, the southern tip of India passing by to the right.

"How do we stop him?" Duncan asked. "Not only does he have that fleet incoming, what about the foo fighters and the guardian computer under Easter Island? How do we destroy those?"

"We haven't simply been sitting still all these years at STAAR and doing nothing," Zandra said. "We've analyzed the data of all confrontations with the foo fighters, and it seems that they have found a way to control electromagnetic energy and use it to disable or control the attacking craft or missile."

"That's why we can escape them if we shut all power down," Turcotte noted.

"Correct."

Turcotte thought about that, and for the first time in a while, a smile crossed his face. "I have an idea how we can attack the foo fighters. It won't be easy, but it is possible. We need to coordinate. If all don't follow the same procedures, we won't have a chance."

"That's a lot to do in not much time," Duncan said, shaking her head. "It's almost impossible."

"We still have ST-8 clearance and authorization," Zandra said. "I can access MILSTAR and talk to every military force the United States has. Tell me your plan and let's make the impossible possible."

"Our first priority is to get into the Rift Valley complex and get the ruby sphere," Turcotte said. "To do that," he continued, "we're going to have to eliminate the threat of the foo fighters."

"How?" Duncan asked.

The smile came back on Turcotte's face. "We're going to have to make the Air Force and Navy become dumb again."

■ ■ ■

There were four F-14 Tomcats from the *George Washington* circling over Kenya, a hundred miles from the Rift Valley complex. They'd heard their two fellow crews go down and they were itching to get into the fight; but so far their orders had been to hold in place.

Lieutenant Commander Perkins was the flight leader, and he was more seasoned than the other seven fliers who were part of his group. He wasn't as anxious to tangle with the foo fighters as they were. It wasn't cowardice, it was experience. There was no purpose in fighting a battle that couldn't be won, and as far as he knew, dating back to World War II, no human plane had ever won an encounter with the small alien spheres.

Thus, when a man named Captain Turcotte came over his radio and briefed him on a plan to take out the two foo fighters over the Rift Valley complex, Perkins listened with a mixture of enthusiasm that someone finally had a plan and trepidation over the difficulty of executing the difficult maneuver Turcotte was suggesting.

In the end though, all he said was "Roger that," and gave the orders for his four planes to head north.

■ ■ ■

On board the *Springfield* Captain Forster and the fleet commander on the surface above the foo fighter base listened to the problem and course of action that Turcotte radioed to them with similar feelings. The situation there was compounded by the problem of the *Greywolf* being in close proximity to their target.

After a short discussion with Turcotte, Forster came up with a plan. It was half-ass, as they would say back at sub school, but still it was a plan, and that was more than they'd had.

Slowly and with minimum expenditure of power and electromagnetic signature, the *Springfield* and *Asheville* turned away from the foo fighter base. As the distance between them and the base increased, both submarines increased energy until both reactors were at full power, pushing the two geared turbines and, in turn, the one drive shaft at maximum RPM. The subs raced away from the foo fighter base at over forty miles an hour underwater.

■ ■ ■

At JPL, Larry Kincaid started awake as the door to the control room opened. Coridan walked over to his console. The rest of the room was still empty, the other workers all waiting on the arrival of the Airlia the following morning.

"Have you plotted the TCM that will put *Surveyor* over Cydonia?" Coridan asked.

"You specified such a quick burn," Kincaid said, "and then not being able to check position and trajectory after the burn . . ." Kincaid stopped, realizing he sounded like one of the whining youngsters he so despised. "It's plotted."

"Execute it for a time-on-target of four hours from now," Coridan ordered.

■ ■ ■

The foo fighter came over the Antarctic ice at five times the speed of sound. Reaching the appropriate spot, it halted. A golden beam lanced out from the small sphere, slicing down through the ice toward Scorpion Base, but the onboard sensors told it that it was already too late: there was no electromagnetic power being generated below. Whatever and whoever had been there was now gone.

The foo fighter shut off the beam and raced back to the north.

■ ■ ■

Bouncer 6 was already over southern California and flying at four thousand miles an hour. Kelly Reynolds sat in the copilot's seat and slowly rocked back and forth, her mind focused and trying to figure out what she could do to get through to the guardian and then to Aspasia to stop the oncoming disaster.

Her hands were pressed against her temples, trying to stop the pain she felt in her head.

■ ■ ■

On board the *Greywolf* Commander Downing's head jerked up as he heard the faintest of noises. He glanced over at Tennyson, who had come awake also. They listened for a minute before Downing realized what he was hearing: someone banging out Morse code, metal on metal, echoing down from the surface.

Downing grabbed a grease pencil, blew on his frozen fingers, wiped the condensation off the metal plating in front of him, and began writing the dots and dashes down. When he realized the message was repeating itself, he went back to the start and began translating the code into letters. When he had the message he stared at it for a few seconds, then nodded.

He didn't know why and he didn't know how, but it was better than sitting here freezing to death.

"All right. Time to be going."

Chapter 37

The bouncer was holding, three hundred miles off the east coast of Africa. Turcotte and the others inside were listening to the radio nets of the various forces they'd set in motion. First into action were the four F-14's to their west, attempting to clear the foo fighters out of the sky over the Rift Valley complex so they could move in and get the sphere.

· · ·

"Sixty miles and closing," Perkins's navigator and weapons officer, Lieutenant Sally Stanton, reported. "Space Command reports no movement from the foo fighters."

Perkins's hands were steady on the controls of his F-14, trying hard to keep the plane under control. They were pushing the edge of the envelope and the plane was struggling with it. The F-14 was rated with a ceiling of 56,000 feet. Perkins and his flight were already passing through 62,000, over eleven miles high, and a half mile higher than any F-14 had ever been flown.

"Fifty miles and closing," Stanton reported. "Still nothing."

"Good," Perkins muttered. "Good so far."

He had the wings of the plane in their full-out position, trying to grab as much of the thin air as possible. At this altitude he was worried about engine flameout. If either engine got too little oxygen it would quit. Restarting in flight was a tricky proposition, plus it would mean aborting the mission.

"Forty miles and closing. Still nothing."

"Flameout!" Perkins's wingman called out over the radio.

Perkins looked to his left and watched the F-14 there peel off in a steep dive. He could see that one engine was still providing thrust, so the plane should make it back to the carrier, but they were down to three now.

"Thirty miles and—" Stanton was interrupted by another pilot reporting flameout.

"Both engines down. I'm going to hang with you and try to make it," the pilot reported. Perkins looked out to his right. The third F-14 was already losing altitude. He knew it wouldn't make it to the target zone.

"Turn away and get your engines started," Perkins ordered the pilot.

Perkins felt a trickle of sweat slide down inside his oxygen mask. They were down to his plane and one other. When they reached the target, it was going to be one-on-one.

■ ■ ■

On board the bouncer Turcotte exchanged a worried look with Duncan. If they lost another F-14, they would have to abort.

■ ■ ■

"Twenty miles." Stanton's voice was calm. "We have two foo fighters heading our direction on an intercept course."

"All right," Perkins called to the one surviving plane. "Hold steady. Execute on my command. I have left and lead, you have right and trail."

"Right and trail," the other pilot acknowledged.

"They're closing fast," Stanton reported. "Fifteen miles. Intercept in thirty seconds."

"Execute!" Perkins ordered. He pulled the nose of the F-14 up. They had passed through 63,000 feet when a warning light flashed on his console. His left engine had flamed out. Perkins immediately did the opposite of what had been drummed into him throughout years of intensive flight training: he shut down his right engine. Then he continued, fighting his instincts, shutting down every electrical system he had.

In the backseat Lieutenant Stanton did the same, cutting all her navigational and targeting computers, the radio, the SATCOM up and down links, and the missiles that rested under the wings.

She couldn't even talk to her pilot through the intercom. The F-14 was now a very heavy glider, losing altitude rapidly. Perkins looked out and spotted the one remaining plane to his right, also dropping, all systems dead.

The electronic controls were out, so his eyes fastened on his attitude indicator, making sure he

kept the plane as level as possible given that the
horizon was a hazy line in the distance. He also
watched the hand on the altimeter spin around
rapidly, counting off altitude lost.

Sixty thousand feet and dropping.

Fifty-five thousand feet and still going down.
Perkins looked around. Where the hell were the
foo fighters?

He turned on the plane's radar for two seconds,
then turned it off. "Come to Papa," he whispered.
He again lit up the radar, trying to suck the foo
fighters in.

He felt a pounding on the back of his seat.
Stanton signaling. Perkins turned off the radar
and looked about. There they were! Ahead and to
the left, climbing to meet them, two small glowing
orbs, rapidly closing in.

Perkins strained with the plane's hydraulics,
turning toward the foo fighters. He had his entire
being focused on the left one, no longer able to
spare any attention to determine whether the
other plane had also spotted them.

Perkins let go with his left hand and flipped up
a small plastic aiming circle, an anachronism that
had been built into the plane simply on the incredibly small chance that the plane's computer-
driven forward targeting display, which was
projected against the Plexiglas of the cockpit,
would be down.

Perkins began struggling with the plane, trying
to get the center of the aiming circle centered on
the foo fighter. He knew he would have only one
shot before the fighter was past him. He also
knew he had to take into account his own speed
and descent ratio while also factoring in the foo

fighter's trajectory. It was a situation to make even the sharpest ace of World War II cringe as the two craft were coming to meet each other at over two thousand miles an hour, one dropping in altitude at the rate of a thousand feet every ten seconds, the other climbing just as fast.

"Come on, baby, come on," Perkins whispered to himself, his eyes focused. They would pass in less than five seconds.

The foo fighter was passing through the right bottom of the aiming circle as Perkins pushed hard right. His finger was resting lightly on the trigger built into his joystick. It was attached to the only electrical system still on, drawing such little amperage that the foo fighter couldn't pick it up.

Perkins's finger pulled back. The M16-A1 20mm cannon was on the left side, just below the cockpit. Perkins could feel the plane shudder as the milk-bottle-sized projectiles roared out of the mouth of the Gatling gun. He'd never fired it before with the engines off. He could hear the gun firing, the whine of the barrels spinning, the explosion of the rounds going off.

His eyes, though, were focused on the line of tracers reaching out from his plane toward the foo fighter. The tracers were high and right, then descended down as the foo fighter came up, right into the path!

Twenty-millimeter rounds smashed into the side of the foo fighter. It was built to project power, not armored to take such an unexpected attack. The uranium-cored rounds tore through, destroying the small Airlia computer on board and ripping apart the magnetic engine.

"Yes!" Perkins screamed as he watched the foo fighter drop out of the sky. His exultation was short lived, though, as he realized he was dropping through 45,000 feet and both his engines were cold.

He immediately began the emergency procedures to restart.

■ ■ ■

On board the bouncer, the F-14 that had lost both engines and tried to stay in formation disappeared off the radar screen.

"Shit," Turcotte muttered. He hoped the pilot and navigator ejected before the plane went down.

"One foo fighter is going down!" Zandra reported.

They watched the display on the small computer screen, the data relayed to them from Cheyenne Mountain.

"The other is hit too!"

A voice came over the radio. "This is Lieutenant Commander Perkins. We have splashed two foo fighters and are heading home."

■ ■ ■

Perkins felt the thrust of the two Pratt & Whitney engines push him through the back of his seat and banked hard right. He could see the other F-14, engines on, pulling in beside him, the pilot holding his left hand thumbs-up so Perkins could see.

"That's one for the record books," Perkins said to Stanton.

"Damn good shooting, sir," she replied.

"Damn lucky," Perkins muttered.

■ ■ ■

"Let's go," Turcotte said. "We've got to get in there and get the ruby sphere."

The pilot immediately pressed forward on the controls and they were heading for the Rift Valley.

"The foo fighter that hit my headquarters in Antarctica is back at the foo fighter base," Zandra noted.

"That means they're all back there now, right?" Turcotte asked.

"Correct," Zandra said.

"Perfect."

Turcotte thought it most interesting that a foo fighter had targeted Scorpion Station. Obviously the Easter Island guardian knew something about STAAR and its base; more than he himself knew, Turcotte darkly thought.

■ ■ ■

"Ready?" Commander Downing asked.

Tennyson's hands were wrapped around a large red lever on the bottom floor of the *Greywolf*. "Ready." He had just removed two bolts that kept the lever locked in place.

Emory was strapped into his chair. "Ready."

"Release," Downing ordered.

Tennyson pulled the lever over. There was a grinding noise, then the sound of thousands of steel ball bearings rattling against metal. Underneath the *Greywolf* the submersible's ballast was sliding out of the portal Tennyson had just opened.

Tennyson clambered up into his seat and strapped in. Minus the ballast the *Greywolf* began to slowly rise, picking up speed as the seconds went by.

The two foo fighters, picking up no power emission from the submersible, remained where they were, now guarding empty ocean.

■ ■ ■

On the surface, forty miles to the east, Kevin Brodie was a Department of Defense civilian assigned to the crew of the *Yellowstone*. For the past twenty minutes he had been putting his laptop computer through its paces, furiously calculating, looking up current and depth data, rechecking, putting in figures as they were relayed to him from the Navy weapons specialist who was sitting at his side. Finally he looked up.

"I've got it."

The weapons man picked up a radio mike. "*Anzio,* here's the coordinates."

■ ■ ■

Forty miles from the *Yellowstone,* the USS *Anzio,* a *Ticonderoga*-class guided-missile cruiser, was waiting. As the weapons man gave the coordinates, the captain of the *Anzio* maneuvered his ship to the designated spot on the ocean's surface and came to a halt. The ocean for forty miles in all directions was clear of surface vessels.

On the rear deck, weapons experts worked over a BGM-109 Tomahawk cruise missile. They were bypassing the sophisticated homing and arming mechanisms built into the missile and replacing them with a simple depth-activated ignitor. In other words they were reducing a missile worth four million dollars to a depth charge.

The petty officer in charge called up to the bridge and informed the captain they were ready. Shaking his head, the captain ordered the nuclear warhead in the missile armed. The petty officer did so, then stood back as a crane lifted the Tomahawk up and over the side of the ship.

Slowly the missile was lowered to the water's surface. The cable holding the missile was released and it sank out of sight. The ship's four General Electric gas-turbine engines had been running at high speed while this was going on. At the captain's order the drive shafts were engaged, and the twin screws tore into the water.

The *Anzio* raced away to the east at maximum speed, while on the rear deck a SH-60 Sikorsky helicopter lifted off.

■ ■ ■

The *Greywolf* was rocketing to the surface now and it passed the missile on its way down at fifteen hundred meters depth. It had been Brodie's job to calculate the exact location of the foo fighter base from the LLS reading, add in the local currents, temperature inversions, depth, weight and size of the missile and its warhead, and mix all those effects together to find the point on the surface where it should be dropped so that, falling free, it would explode, hopefully, right on top of the foo fighter base.

■ ■ ■

The *Greywolf* broke surface and the entire submersible popped into the air before settling down.

"Let's move!" Downing yelled as he reached up and began unscrewing the hatch. Tennyson crowded in and helped him. They pushed the hatch out of the way. It tumbled free into the ocean, but Downing wasn't worried about that. He climbed up onto the top deck and squinted into the fierce sunlight. He heard the chopper before he saw it.

The SH-60 swung over the top of the submersible, lowering a cage. Downing grabbed on to the cage and held it steady as Tennyson and Emory climbed in, then he squeezed in beside them.

"I'll miss her," he said to Tennyson as they were lifted into the air, the chopper heading east after the *Anzio* even before the cage began to be reeled in.

"She was a good ship," Tennyson acknowledged as the *Greywolf* faded into the distance, a dark spot on a blue carpet.

They all flinched as the entire ocean surface erupted in a massive waterspout where the *Greywolf* had been.

■ ■ ■

Brodie's calculations were excellent. The Tomahawk passed through the depth the igniter was set for less than fifty meters from the foo fighter complex.

The nuclear explosion took out not only the two foo fighters that had shadowed the *Greywolf* and the base, but a half-mile section of the East Pacific Ridge.

■ ■ ■

On the other side of the world Captain Mike Turcotte gripped Colonel Spearson's weathered hand in his.

"Bloody good to see you, even if you do come flying in on one of those weird saucer things," Spearson said.

"We need to get to the cavern," Turcotte said as Duncan and Zandra followed him.

"Right this way."

■ ■ ■

At the same time, back in the Pacific, Kelly Reynolds's bouncer was settling down on the runway on Easter Island.

Chapter 38

⬛⬛⬛⬛⬛⬛⬛⬛⬛⬛⬛

"**Y**ou've neutralized the foo fighter fleet," Duncan said as they rode the cog railway down into the cavern. "But what about the Airlia ships that are coming?"

Turcotte felt tired, the sort of tired he had experienced before in combat and in Ranger School when he'd gone for months with a couple of hours' sleep a night and barely one meal a day to provide energy. He knew the danger of such tiredness: thoughts became muddled, decision-making impaired. He closed his eyes for a few seconds and cleared his head, then he went back to the question Duncan had asked. He turned and addressed the man in the seat behind them.

"Colonel Spearson, do you have SATCOM with Area 51?"

"I can route through to that location," Spearson said.

"There's some people there I need you to send a message to."

Spearson pulled out a small notepad from the

breast pocket of his camouflage smock. "Go ahead."

"All right," Turcotte began. "The message is to Kelly Reynolds and Major Quinn." He nodded toward Zandra. "I'm going to need you to pull your ST-8 authorization."

"You've got it," Zandra said.

"All right," Turcotte said. "Here's what I need."

■ ■ ■

A tunnel had been blasted and drilled through the side of Rano Kau to the chamber containing the guardian. Kelly Reynolds went down the tunnel in a mental fog, her brain and heart swirling with thoughts and emotions she was having a very hard time sorting out and controlling.

She'd heard of the success in wiping out the foo fighter base and seen the military personnel at the airfield on Easter Island celebrating even while they were evacuating the island. Fools, she thought. All they had done was spit in the face of those who could save the human race. And there were still the talon ships closing on Earth.

Think what they had done to Atlantis, she wanted to shout at the idiots. Didn't they realize the Airlia could do the same to New York or Moscow or any major city?

She reached the bottom and entered the chamber. There was no one around. The U.S. military was getting everyone off Easter Island, clearing it of all human life. Her clearance from Major Quinn had allowed her to pass the military police guards and the captain in charge had warned her that if she wasn't back up in thirty minutes they weren't coming down to get her and she'd be on her own. Bouncer 6 had its orders, too, and the pilot took off and headed back to Area 51, leaving her stranded on the island.

She knew why they were evacuating the island and she knew why the captain was nervous. They wanted to destroy the guardian. They wanted to destroy the machine that held the key to mankind's history and its future. Just as they wanted to destroy the Airlia.

Kelly paused as she entered the chamber. The golden pyramid was surrounded by a haze extending out a few inches. She'd also been told that the guardian was now in constant communication with the incoming fleet. She had no doubt that Aspasia now knew of the destruction of his foo fighters.

Kelly walked across the smoothly cut stone floor to the base of the pyramid. She put her hands out and touched the strangely textured metal. "Please listen to me," she whispered. "Please listen to me."

■ ■ ■

Turcotte looked down at the control panel. He pulled a crumpled piece of paper out of his pocket.

"What's that?" Zandra asked.

"The code for the sphere."

"Will it fall in the chasm and be destroyed?" Duncan asked in alarm.

Turcotte shook his head. "No. The destruct code was in the Temiltepec guardian. That's gone. This is the code to release it." He placed his hands over the panel. He touched a spot in the upper left corner and a glow suffused the surface, seeming to come from within, highlighting a series of interlocking hexagons, eight across by eight down, each hexagon containing a high rune symbol.

Looking at the paper, Turcotte began touching the panel, following the pattern of symbols as they had been dictated to him by Nabinger. There were eighteen in all.

When he touched the last one, there was a loud hissing noise, followed by the startled yell of the SAS guards. Turcotte looked up. The ruby sphere had been released from the three poles going to the far side and two of the ones on the near side. The one arm in the center of the near side was retracting, pulling the sphere toward Turcotte. Twenty feet from the end the arm started to rotate, bringing the sphere up into the air, then going down, until the sphere rested at the edge of the chasm.

"We need to get that up to the surface," Turcotte ordered.

Chapter 39

∎∎∎∎∎∎∎∎∎∎∎∎

Five hours from arrival. The six talons were no longer dancing among themselves. They had spread out, ten kilometers between craft as they approached Earth.

■ ■ ■

On the planet they neared, troubling news was beginning to seep out. Nothing official had been released, but there were rumors of attacks by foo fighters; of a nuclear weapon being detonated deep in the Pacific; that the Airlia might not indeed be coming in peace. The rumors were not enough to stem the flow of optimism that blanketed the world, but they were enough to worry those in power and those who had always questioned the coming contact. But what was there to do? was the consensus. The world would have to wait and see.

Inside the War Room of the Pentagon the President and Joint Chiefs were helpless spectators as the plan devised by Eisenhower was being enacted by STAAR. The mood, though, was getting more positive as each victory was won. Still, the main screen in the front of the room pictured the six talons as seen by the Hubble, and that deadened any euphoria as they knew the biggest battle was yet to come.

■ ■ ■

Mike Turcotte was in a rush. They had attached the sphere to the outside of the bouncer by the expedient manner of four sets of nylon cargo webbing. He'd immediately gotten back on board along with Duncan and the two STAAR personnel.

The bouncer was now racing northeast at over five thousand miles an hour. Turcotte had spent the last thirty minutes on the radio, confirming with Major Quinn that the instructions Colonel Spearson had forwarded were being followed and all would be ready when they arrived at Area 51.

He had been disturbed to hear that Kelly Reynolds wasn't there; that she had flown to Easter Island on a bouncer. He knew her and he knew what she was trying to do. He gave her credit for trying; the only problem was that if she didn't get her ass off that island in the next hour, she was going to be sitting on ground zero. He had to try to contact her.

■ ■ ■

"Firing TCM," Larry Kincaid said, although the only person in the room to hear him was Coridan. Larry pressed the enter key on the console in front of him and the message was transmitted toward Mars.

■ ■ ■

Turcotte watched Area 51 approach. This was where it had all started, and it seemed appropriate to him that this was where the ending would be implemented.

The bouncer did not land outside Hangar One; instead, at Turcotte's direction, the pilot flew around the side to Hangar Two. As they flew over Groom Mountain, Turcotte could see the gaping hole in the mountainside where the roof on Hangar Two had been destroyed.

The pilot maneuvered the bouncer down into the hangar, landing next to the side of the massive ship. Turcotte was the first one out of the hatch. Major Quinn was there waiting for him.

"Do you have everything?"

Quinn looked worried. "Yes."

"Where's the bouncer I asked for?" Turcotte asked, looking about.

"It's already loaded inside," Quinn said.

"Great."

"Is it modified like I requested?"

"I had to get the boosters from White Sands. Flown here special on a C-5 and—"

"Is it done?" Turcotte's voice was sharp.

"Yes. But I can't guarantee that—"

"The specials?"

Quinn swallowed hard. "They're loaded too. I don't know who you got to authorize that, but—"

"Load the ruby sphere into the cargo bay with the rest of the gear," Turcotte ordered. Quinn nodded. He started to walk away, then paused. He reached into his pocket and pulled out what looked like a TV remote. "You'll need this. It's labeled."

Turcotte took it and slid it into the breast pocket of his dirty camouflage fatigues. Quinn turned and walked away toward a waiting crew of Air Force men.

There was a surprised look on Zandra's face. "You're not putting the sphere in the engine where it belongs? What exactly do you have planned?" she demanded.

Turcotte turned and stared into her sunglasses while Duncan quietly watched. "I'm going to give Aspasia what he wants. He wants the mothership and he wants the ruby sphere. I'm taking them to him. That way he has no need to come here to Earth."

Zandra was shaking her head before he was done. "That's unacceptable. You have no guarantee that he'll take the mothership and leave Earth alone. In fact . . ." She paused.

"In fact what?" Turcotte demanded.

"I can't let you do that," Zandra said.

"How are you going to stop me?" Turcotte asked.

"I have the President's authorization and—"

"You have an authorization from a president who has been long dead," Turcotte cut her off. "It's worked quite well with all these idiots who salute and would rather follow orders than think, but it doesn't work with me."

Turcotte saw Oleisa, who had remained mute and in the background throughout their long journey, start to move. He smoothly drew his Browning High Power pistol. He didn't exactly point it at the two women, but he kept it hovering in their general direction, freezing them both in place. "I don't know who you people are. You may be who you say you are, but this is where your interference ends. I'm taking the mothership up and there's nothing you can do about it."

Oleisa jumped forward and Turcotte fired, double-tapping as he'd been trained. Both rounds hit the woman right between her eyes, shattering the ever-present sunglasses and knocking her back onto the cavern floor. But that gave Zandra time to draw a pistol. Turcotte knew it was too late as he shifted to the new target; he could see the muzzle of Zandra's gun, a massive black hole centered on his own forehead.

Then a small red dot appeared in the middle of Zandra's chest and she staggered back a step, the gun wavering, then coming back up. The sound of a pistol going off again and again reverberated through the cavern as Duncan kept firing, her bullets hitting Zandra.

The fingers went limp and the gun dropped out of Zandra's hand as she collapsed to the floor. Duncan stepped forward, her weapon at the ready as she nudged the body with the toe of her shoe.

"She's dead," Turcotte confirmed, seeing where several of the rounds had come out of Zandra's back.

"Who the hell were they?" Duncan asked, looking up from the two bodies as MPs ran up, weapons ready.

"Everything's all right!" Turcotte yelled to the MPs. He put a hand on Duncan's shoulder. He could feel her trembling. "I don't know who they were. That's something we're going to have to

find out. But right now our big problem is coming
from thataway." He pointed upward.

"How are you getting back, Mike?" Duncan
asked.

"I'm coming back on the bouncer in the hold,"
Turcotte said.

"But they don't work that far outside the
Earth's magnetic field," Duncan noted.

"I know that," Turcotte said. He turned her to
face him. "Trust me that I will make it back."

Duncan nodded. "I do."

"I have to go now," Turcotte said.

Duncan stood on tiptoe and kissed him. "Good
luck."

■ ■ ■

Inside the chamber Kelly Reynolds's pleadings
echoed off the stone walls. Then she paused as a
golden tendril coalesced above the top of the pyramid. It wavered in the air, then reached down
toward her.

Kelly remained perfectly still as the translucent
golden arm wrapped itself around her head. The
tortured look on her face disappeared and her
features relaxed, a smile even touching her lips.

■ ■ ■

The message Larry Kincaid had sent had finally
made it across the gap from Earth to *Surveyor*,
silently orbiting above the planet. The on-board
computer came to life. The simple commands
Kincaid had programmed were sorted through
and acted on. Maneuvering thrusters fired and
Surveyor's orbit changed. It moved on a course

that would bring it over Cydonia in less than an hour.

■ ■ ■

In the air and water surrounding Easter Island, Navy ships and planes circled, forming up, waiting for the final word. Smart bombs were being made dumb, their sophisticated electronic targeting turned off and the crews preparing flight paths that would allow them to drop their ordnance from a safe distance and explode on impact, all targeted toward Rano Kau. There was enough explosive being prepared that the admiral in charge of the fleet had no doubt that by the third wave of planes, the would have blasted down the chamber that held the guardian.

Chapter 40

■■■■■■■■■■■

Turcotte looked through the stack of pages attached to the clipboard that someone had put in the pilot's seat. He found what he was looking for: three sheets in the basic instructions for the mothership's magnetic atmospheric drive.

Majestic-12 had figured out how to fly the mothership, using its magnetic drive; they just hadn't known they were missing the fuel core for the interstellar drive. The instructions had been placed there by the mothership experts at Quinn's order. Like the bouncers the mothership's control system was the essence of simplicity. Turcotte sat down in a chair that was much too large for him and read the notes.

Satisfied he knew enough for the job ahead, he pressed his palm down on a certain part of the console.

■ ■ ■

"Oh, shit, not again," Duncan whispered as she felt her stomach flip. She turned and knelt, throwing up as mothership's magnetic drive engaged.

■ ■ ■

The mothership lifted off its cradle for the second time in a month. But Turcotte was taking it much farther than the four-foot hover Majestic had done.

His left hand was moving on another console, directing the ship up. A panoramic view of Groom Mountain appeared on the curved wall in front of him as he gained altitude.

■ ■ ■

Lisa Duncan stared at the massive ship silently climbing into the sky. All around Area 51 work ceased and people looked up as the ship cleared Groom Mountain and rose farther and farther. Duncan's entire focus was on the ship, her lips moving in a silent prayer as it faded to a small dot and then disappeared into the dark sky.

■ ■ ■

The ship was accelerating, but the only way Turcotte could tell was by the way the ground below fell away quicker and quicker. Soon the long airstrip at Area 51 was nothing but a very faint line scratched in the desert floor below. Soon even that faded into haze.

Turcotte could see the curvature of the Earth now on the display. It had been night when he lifted off, the last night before the dawn that would bring the Airlia. Turcotte knew he was out of the atmosphere when he could see the glow of the sun around the curve of the eastern horizon.

He didn't feel any different, and Turcotte had to assume the ship had some sort of artificial gravity built in. He continued away from the planet, until he could see the entire world on the front screen.

Then he slowed the ship and reoriented it away from Earth so he could look outward. The mothership came to a halt in a very high orbit above the planet.

Turcotte could see nothing but stars and the moon off to the right. He knew the talons were out there, but he wouldn't be able to see them until they were right on top of him and by then it would be too late. The last data he'd gotten from Quinn had indicated the talons were just under an hour away.

Turcotte turned to the SATCOM radio that he had had Quinn install. He had Quinn route him through to the Easter Island chamber, where a SATCOM radio had been left by the departing UNAOC scientists. "Kelly, this is Mike Turcotte."

He tried again. When he got no answer, he had a very good idea what was happening under Easter Island. "Kelly, this is Mike. Listen to me carefully. You have to tell Aspasia that we are sorry. That we made a mistake. That we've put the ruby sphere on board the mothership and I'm flying it up to give it to them in orbit. That we just want to be left alone. And then you need to leave the island right away, Kelly."

Turcotte repeated the message three times, then turned off the radio. He had much to do. Turcotte shut down the magnetic drive, then began the long walk from control room to the cargo bay holding the bouncer, the ruby sphere, and the "specials" he'd had Zandra order.

■ ■ ■

Coridan indicated for Kincaid to move and took his place at the computer link. Coridan typed in some commands and a code word, then transmitted them.

Coridan turned his sunglasses toward Kincaid. "I am done here. Good day."

With that he walked out of the control room.

■ ■ ■

Kelly Reynolds was now totally enveloped in a golden haze. Her eyes were closed and her face peaceful and relaxed for the first time in a very long time. She'd heard Turcotte's message echo off the walls of the chamber and she knew the guardian had heard, too, taking it out of her brain and sending it to Aspasia.

She felt happy that Turcotte was still alive and that he finally understood. There was hope after all.

■ ■ ■

The first wave approached Easter Island. Composed of F-14's and F-18's, they came in at high altitude and released their "dumb" bombs on a glide path that would have them land right on top of Rano Kau.

The admiral watched the bombs float through the air, heading directly for the volcano, when suddenly they began exploding in the air, two miles from the island. The admiral had seen the same thing a week ago when he'd attacked the island with Tomahawk cruise missiles at General Gullick's orders. He picked up the mike and called Area 51. "Your 'dumb' plan might have worked with foo fighters, but this thing is different. We aren't going to be able to crack this nut."

■ ■ ■

In the chamber Kelly Reynolds's eyes were still closed, but her head turned up as if she could see what was happening miles above her. A smile played across her lips.

■ ■ ■

The six talons changed course. They were headed for the mothership now and they were going even faster than they had been.

■ ■ ■

Turcotte hummed to himself as he walked through the massive cargo bay, checking everything. All was set. The ruby sphere was chained to one of the bays that had once held a bouncer. The specials—four nuclear warheads—were lined up on the floor near the bouncer that Quinn had loaded for him.

The bouncer looked like a kid had gone wild and mixed together his flying saucer model kit with that of a rocket ship. Four rocket boosters had been attached to the outside of the bouncer, pointing out from the bottom in perpendicular directions.

Turcotte planned on giving Aspasia back the ruby sphere and much more. He knelt down next to each warhead and entered the PAL code that armed each. Then he checked his watch.

He climbed on board the bouncer and got inside. He shut the hatch behind him and powered the craft up. He could see the outside clearly. Flipping open the lid on the remote, Turcotte read down the buttons. He pressed the one that read: DOORS.

The massive doors to the cargo bay swung open with a hiss of the air escaping into space. They swung wide until Turcotte could see the stars again. Turcotte was glad everything had been tied down as he felt the artificial gravity in the cargo bay disappear.

■ ■ ■

The engine cut out and *Surveyor* began the long fall down toward Cydonia. Inside the capsule the scientific devices rested in their containers. Also inside was a small three-foot-long-by-two-wide cylinder. It had been loaded into the capsule prior to launch the previous year by someone with an ST-8 clearance. NASA had fussed and fumed about it, but in the end had accepted the authority of the clearance and reduced the payload elsewhere to make room and to make weight.

Inside the cylinder the codes Coridan had punched in armed the nuclear warhead. It was set to go off on impact.

■ ■ ■

A talon flashed by the cargo-bay opening. Reconnaissance, Turcotte knew. The bouncer was oriented in the cradle so that the front end, which simply meant the end that Turcotte faced when sitting in the pilot's seat, was facing out. He looked down at the rough controls that had been installed to the right of the depression he was in. He hit the lever that released the arms holding the bouncer in the cradle. Then he pressed the button that fired the booster pointing to the rear for just a second.

The bouncer floated free, slowly edging out of the cargo bay into space.

Turcotte swallowed, seeing all six talons lined up, tips pointing in his direction. "It's all yours, assholes," he muttered. He pressed the button again and held it for a few more seconds, picking up speed, accelerating away from the mothership. One of the talons turned in his direction. The other five headed toward the cargo bay, edging in.

A glow appeared on the nose of the talon that was following Turcotte. A golden beam of light flashed out. It singed across the bottom of the bouncer, burning into the metal.

Turcotte slammed his fist down on a button and the right booster fired, just as another golden beam of light again sliced through space where he had been. He rocketed away and as he did so he hit the firing button on the remote.

■ ■ ■

Inside the cargo hold, suited Airlia figures had been coming out of the lead talon, heading toward the ruby sphere, when the four nuclear weapons went off in a blinding flash of light and heat.

The thermonuclear explosion took in the ruby sphere and added its power.

■ ■ ■

Turcotte cringed in his seat as a second sun came into being behind him, flooding space with its light. The shock wave hit, knocking him about as the bouncer tumbled.

■ ■ ■

In Central Park it was thirty minutes before dawn and the scheduled Airlia landing. The dignitaries and millions crowded around the park looked up in awe as a false daylight came in the form of a bright orb of light that suddenly appeared overhead, shining even brighter than the noonday sun.

Chapter 41
•••••••••••

Then there was the darkness of space again,
Turcotte desperately firing boosters, trying to
regain control. After a minute he had the bouncer
stopped. Turcotte turned in his seat. The mothership was still visible, a tribute to the engineering
capabilities of the Airlia, but there was a tremendous gash over half a mile long in the side where
the cargo bay had been. There was no sign of the
five talons that had been in the entrance to the
bay.

Turcotte froze. The sixth talon, the one that had
fired at him, was between him and the mothership, several kilometers away. Turcotte relaxed
when he saw that the ship was slowly tumbling
end over end, out of control.

"Now comes the fun part," he muttered to himself as he looked down at the Earth under his
feet. He hit the transmit button on the SATCOM
radio.

• • •

Deep inside Easter Island Kelly Reynolds had cried out in pain as the guardian picked up the destruction of the talon fleet. But the guardian still functioned; it still kept the shield guarding the island up, and it still kept her in its field, a prisoner in the war Earth thought it had just won.

■ ■ ■

"I've got hold of someone from JPL who should be able to figure out how to get you a trajectory into the atmosphere without burning up," Quinn said. He hit the patch linking Larry Kincaid to Turcotte.

■ ■ ■

Turcotte fired the various boosters as directed by Kincaid, who was tracking him from the JPL control room. Slowly the bouncer got closer and closer to Earth's atmosphere, until finally it was caught in the gravitational well and pulled down.

Turcotte put his hands on the control bar for the bouncer as the craft hit the edge of the atmosphere, skipped, and then began to descend. Now came the tricky part, hoping the magnetic engine kicked in before he hit the Earth's surface at terminal velocity.

The skin of the bouncer reflected heat as the ship screamed through the sky, the air getting thicker around it. Turcotte pulled back on the controls: nothing.

"Goddamn," he whispered.

"Do you have any control?" Kincaid called out over the radio.

"Negative."

"One hundred and sixty thousand feet and descending," Kincaid informed him. "You've got plenty of altitude to gain control."

Turcotte looked about. He was over North America. As near as he could tell somewhere over the southeast, heading west.

A minute later Kincaid wasn't so reassuring. "Fifty thousand feet and terminal velocity. Have you got anything?"

Turcotte moved the control stick. "Nothing. I think the ship took some damage from a hit."

A new voice came over the radio. "Get out of there!" Lisa Duncan yelled. "Use the emergency gear."

Turcotte reached over and grabbed the parachute that was strapped to the floor next to his seat. He threw it over his shoulder, fighting the buffets the uncontrolled craft was sustaining as it fell.

He quickly buckled the chute on, then grabbed the snap link and hooked it into the cable that was just behind his seat, running up the top hatch.

He grabbed the controls, once more trying to save the craft. Nothing. "I'm getting out of here," he yelled into the radio.

Turcotte pulled a red lever up. Explosive bolts fired, blowing the hatch off. Air swirled in. Turcotte pushed himself out of the pilot's seat. He slid along the cable and banged into the top near the hatch. He pulled himself through into the hatch.

Then he let go and fell out of the bouncer. The static line for the parachute quickly paid out and the chute blossomed above him as the bouncer disappeared below.

Turcotte gained control of his toggles and

looked down. He was above desert, somewhere in the southwest U.S. He descended, feeling the air on his skin and listening to the gentle sound of the wind. He played with the toggles, controlling his descent until he landed on a dune. The chute dragged him across the sand. He popped the shoulder releases and the chute floated away. Turcotte simply lay there, his back feeling the soft ground underneath.

Slowly Turcotte stood. Looking to the east he could see the sun rising, the edge just coming up over the horizon, sending rays of sunlight high over his head.

Reaching down, Turcotte picked up a handful of sand. "It's good to be home," he whispered.

Epilogue

A golden tendril was stretched out from the guardian computer under the surface of Mars and wrapped around the head of the Airlia who had awakened the first echelon and sent them off in their talon ships toward Earth.

The guardian informed her of the destruction of the fleet and the death of her comrades. The pupils in her red eyes narrowed as she processed this information.

She twitched as the guardian picked up a small anomaly near Mars. She had the surface sensors focus on it. Something was coming toward her location, less than thirty seconds out. There was no electromagnetic reading and she almost ignored it, but she paused. She was the only one left awake. She could afford to take no chances. She mentally gave the commands.

■ ■ ■

In the center of the solar field array a bolt of pure energy shot upward. It hit the incoming *Surveyor* probe dead on.

■ ■ ■

The Airlia saw the nuclear explosion take place three miles above her location. It had been close but not close enough.

The Airlia began giving commands. She would wake the others. Then there was much to do.

The first battle had been lost, but the war was far from over.